Also by
Melanie Scott

The Devil in Denim
Angel in Armani
Lawless in Leather
Playing Hard

Playing
Fast

Melanie Scott

St. Martin's Paperbacks

This is a work of fiction. All of the characters, organizations, and events portrayed in this novel are either products of the author's imagination or are used fictitiously.

PLAYING FAST

Copyright © 2016 by Melanie Scott.

All rights reserved.

For information address St. Martin's Press, 175 Fifth Avenue, New York, NY 10010.

ISBN: 978-1-250-07721-9

Our books may be purchased in bulk for promotional, educational, or business use. Please contact your local bookseller or the Macmillan Corporate and Premium Sales Department at 1-800-221-7945, ext. 5442, or by e-mail at MacmillanSpecialMarkets@macmillan.com.

Printed in the United States of America

St. Martin's Paperbacks edition / September 2016

St. Martin's Paperbacks are published by St. Martin's Press, 175 Fifth Avenue, New York, NY 10010.

10 9 8 7 6 5 4 3 2 1

For my Sophie Cat aka The Fuzzy Girl
who played fast but didn't get to stay long enough.

Acknowledgments

Every time I sit down to write acknowledgments, I still get amazed that I've written a book that's going to be out in the world. And I'm always very grateful to everyone who helps me get the book done. So once again, thank you to Eileen Rothschild for editing awesomeness and for all the hard work put in by the team at St. Martin's Press. A huge thank-you to Miriam Kriss, my fabulous agent. Endless thanks to all my writing pals for encouragement and tough love when I need it. Especially for this book, to Keri and Sarah for writing escapes and to Robyn for virgo-braining. Also apologies to the friends and family for being a writer-hermit, at times. You know I love you all. And last, but never least, to all the readers out there who love books and devour stories, I say THANK YOU!

Chapter One

Eva Harlowe had been many things at work. Happy, bored, sad, stressed, excited. Occasionally pissed off. She'd never before been 100 percent mortified.

She looked down at the security pass she'd just run through the laminator and resisted the urge to flee the building.

Finn Castro.

That was whose face stared back at her from the otherwise innocent piece of plastic.

Finn Castro. Baseball player. Tall, dark, and trouble. Not to mention six years younger than her.

But despite his age and the fact that he apparently had a penchant for bar fights and partying, and leaving aside the fact he was a baseball player—an occupation that was firmly on her do-not-date list—Finn Castro was the man that Eva had had an unreasonable, melting-underwear-level, unrelenting crush on for, oh, at least a year.

She blamed that on his stupidly handsome face.

Of course, there was nothing wrong with having a

crush. Countless women swooned over actors and singers and, yes, athletes every day. Having a celebrity crush was harmless. Safe. They could live in your head and cheer up your day and maybe, occasionally, when you were having one of those days, spice up your nighttime fantasies.

One hundred percent A-Okay.

Until, of course, you found out that the object of your crush was coming to work where you worked.

Then it was mortifying. Totally, excruciatingly, horrifyingly mortifying.

So she was mortified because, exactly six weeks ago, just after New Year's Day, the New York Saints had announced that they were sending Finn Castro to play a season on their Triple-A team, the Preachers.

Where Eva was the administrative manager. Which was a glorified title for "does anything that really needs to be done and keeps things from falling apart at an inconvenient moment." Including getting new players set up with all the administrative things they needed to be set up with and, usually, giving them a quick tour of the place before they were handed over to the coaching team.

Which meant that any minute now, Finn Castro was going to come waltzing through her office door and she was going to have to act like a normal adult woman around him.

She'd seriously considered calling in sick to avoid the whole thing. She never called in sick. Besides, avoiding him for one more day was only putting off the inevitable. The universe, it seemed, had decided that Eva was to be its source of entertainment this week.

The universe should pick on someone else.

She stared down at the picture and Finn's gorgeous face smiled back at her. A smug smile. Like he knew her secret.

He was *never* going to know her secret.

Thankfully no one at the Preachers did. She'd worked there for a long time. Close enough to fourteen years. She wasn't dumb enough to admit a crush on a ballplayer to anybody on the premises, let alone a player from their parent team. She never would have heard the end of it. Nope, she'd kept her secret to herself and instead pretended to share her best friend Jenna's infatuation with Tom Hiddleston.

And she'd tried to get over the Finn thing, as she had dubbed it.

Tried desperately. Ever since Don Mannings, the Preachers' manager, had made the announcement that Finn was coming to Saratoga Springs at a management meeting back in January.

She had deleted every photo off her home computer. She unsubscribed from the hotties of baseball blog she'd been guiltily following. Stopped scanning the sports pages for mentions of him. Then she'd gone on a mad hunt for another guy who might distract her brain. She'd watched every TV show and movie she could think of. She'd scrolled through Pinterest boards for hours. And yes, there'd been a few guys who'd caught her attention. Men with beautiful faces and bodies sculpted to perfection. Men who made her girl parts happier just looking at them. She'd thought her plan had been working.

Until the photographs had leaked.

The ones from the sponsorship deal that Finn had lost

when he'd gotten into a fight in a Brooklyn nightclub. A nightclub owned by Raina Easton who was married to Mal Coulter, who was one of the part owners of the Saints, what's more. Long Road Home, a company that made fancy fitness gadgets, had made polite public noises about wishing Finn well and then dropped him like a hot potato from being the face of their forthcoming ad campaign.

But somehow the pictures of Finn they'd taken for that campaign had leaked.

They were amazing. Finn being athletic and manly with a big black masculine Long Road Home fitness band clamped around his wrist, each shot showing off his well-honed body to perfection. Climbing rocks and sweat-drenched in gyms and riding a motorcycle. But it was the last shot that had gotten her. Finn standing thigh-deep in the ocean. Wearing a wet white T-shirt and dark jeans, a storm brewing behind him.

Moody black and white and gray. Except the eyes. Those they'd left enough color in to let you guess they were brilliant green. Predator eyes. Dangerous eyes to go with the dangerous body outlined in wet fabric. It was a magnificent photo. She'd taken enough photos in her lifetime to know that. It was brilliant. The perfect embodiment of the male animal, barely contained.

The picture had been everywhere. Impossible to avoid.

It had reignited her crush like a match put to gasoline.

The image was burned in her brain. Popped into her head at inconvenient moments. Made her pulse race and her body want.

Want things it could never have. Because she did not date baseball players. Particularly not *bad boy, only in town because it was a pit stop back to the major leagues, never going to stay* baseball players. She'd seen enough of those in her time at the team to know one when she saw one. Finn Castro was definitely one. Sent to the Preachers in disgrace. Sent to redeem himself.

She didn't need a Taylor Swift song to know trouble was walking in her door.

So she would be rational and adult and treat him exactly the same way she treated all the other men here. Off limits. Not an option. No crushes allowed.

It was the only sane thing to do. Even though she was planning on leaving the Preachers at the end of the season, there was no reason to go crazy.

Except, as the door to her small office opened and the man himself walked through, she realized that the picture had, it seemed, done little justice to the real thing. His green eyes seemed to pierce her, like a physical blow, and her pulse stuttered. There was a pink scar bisecting the corner of his right eyebrow—probably a remnant of his bar fight—that he hadn't had when the Long Road Home photos had been taken. But not even a scar could detract from the fact that the man was almost inhumanly sexy.

And that a whole world of trouble had just landed in her lap.

Finn Castro looked down at the face of the woman behind the desk and got the feeling he'd done something to piss her off. Dark-blue eyes studied him through narrow black-framed glasses, their expression distinctly cool. Not the first impression he'd been hoping to make. Or rather needed to make. He'd been told to report to Eva Harlowe at the Preachers' headquarters today. The first day of his exile, as he'd been trying not to think of it.

What it was, really, was the grown-up version of a time-out. Because he'd done some dumb shit last year. Dumb enough to give himself a wake-up call.

Dumb enough to make Alex Winters, Lucas Angelo, and Malachi Coulter, the owners of the New York Saints, decide that he wouldn't be playing for the Saints this season. That he needed to prove himself all over again. The thought made his jaw tighten. He'd spent most of his life trying to prove himself when it came to baseball. And here he was starting from the fucking beginning again.

But he was the one who'd fucked up, so he was the one who had to suck it up. Keep his head down, work hard, get back to the Saints.

Be on his best behavior and make a good impression.

But here he was, apparently screwing that up already. Or maybe he was just reading her wrong. He tried a smile. His smile usually worked on reluctant females. His looks were an asset. He knew that. So it would be dumb not to use them when he needed to. "Hi. I'm Finn Castro. Are you Eva?"

"Just like the sign on the door says," she replied, pushing back from her desk to stand. Her voice was slightly husky. But still cool.

Definitely unhappy about something. He studied her a moment. Dark-brown hair pulled back into a bun, black sweater buttoned over a crisp white shirt. Dark liner highlighting the eyes that weren't impressed with him. But despite the demure attire, he got the feeling she wasn't all that demure. Because the lips that were painted a very neutral shade were full and the body beneath the clothes curved like a racetrack. Not that he let himself study it in any detail. She was already unimpressed. Staring at her chest wasn't going to improve the situation.

A trio of thin silver chains of varying lengths looped around her neck, and thin small silver hoops hung from her ears. Except in her right ear, the loop wasn't alone. Next to the hoop was a small silver shape. At first he thought it was just a stud, but when she moved her head he realized it was actually a tiny skull.

Definitely not demure.

More like . . . intriguing.

But, nope. He wasn't here to be intrigued. Let alone be intrigued by the woman whom Maggie Winters— wife of Alex and currently chief operating officer of the Saints—had told him was the heart of the Preachers' operation. The one who knew how things got done. The woman who had the respect and the ear of the coaching team and management. Not to be messed with.

And now they'd been staring at each other just that little bit too long.

Damn.

"Well, they told me to come find you when I got here," he said, to cut off the silence and any potential to grow more intrigued.

"Nice to see you can follow instructions, Mr. Castro," she said. She bent and scooped something up off her desk, held it out to him. "This is your security pass. It gets you into the building, the training complex, and the parking lot."

He took the pass. It was clipped onto a white lanyard with the Preachers' logo stamped in black along its length. Preachers. Not the Saints. His jaw tightened again and he relaxed it with an effort.

Suck it up.

"Now," Eva continued as she passed him a plastic folder that had a matching logo on the front cover. "This folder has the map of the complex, your IT login, and your schedule for this week as well as the plans for the first week of spring training next week. I've emailed you a copy of everything. Your schedule will be emailed to you once a week, and it and most other information is always available on the team's internal website. We have all your paperwork from the Saints, so unless you need to update any of the details you gave them in relation to your banking arrangements or uniform sizes, that should be all set up."

Was he imagining things or had she just given him a quick once-over when she'd said "uniform"? He must have been imagining it. Her tone was definitely not enthusiastic. "Everything the Saints sent you should still be up to date," he said, aiming for *enthusiastic and in no way going to be trouble for you* in his tone. Her expression didn't shift at all.

"The only information we don't have is your address here in Saratoga," she continued. "Did you find an apartment or house yet? Or are you in a hotel for now?"

"I have an apartment." He'd rented a place not far from the Preachers' home field, Hennessee Park. His

Manhattan apartment was sublet for six months. Alex Winters had told him he'd be in Saratoga Springs for a year but he was determined to get back as soon as possible. So he didn't need anywhere flashy to live. Just somewhere close where he could crash. He wasn't here to party, after all.

Not that Saratoga Springs was much of a party town, at least not the kind of party there'd been in Manhattan. The place seemed full of spas and, well, horse racing. He didn't know jack about horse racing and couldn't see himself getting interested anytime soon. But the spa part might mean there were plenty of women around who might be looking for some discreet no-strings fun if he got really bored. He was going to keep his nose clean—he wasn't an idiot—but not even the Saints could expect him to be a monk, after all. Still, right now he needed to focus on the woman in front of him—who was definitely not a candidate for no-strings fun. Which was a pity, but hooking up with someone at the Preachers wasn't going to convince the Saints he was a whole new man. "It's close to Hennessee," he said, realizing they were staring at each other.

"Great," Eva said, not sounding at all like she meant it. "Once you log onto your email, send me your details and you'll be all set. Now I'll show you around and then deliver you to Coach."

Finn kept his head down for the first few days. He went to his training sessions. To the gym. To team meetings. Took long runs around Hennessee Park and the area near his new apartment, trying to learn his way around.

Spoke to his parents and his sister, Em, back in Chicago. Then he went home to his very boring apartment and slept. Focus, that was the key.

Head down, do the work and be so damned good at his job that the Saints would have to call him back. No distractions. No thinking about the interesting Eva Harlowe.

Play it smart.

No trouble. Not so much as a hint. It was already clear that he had some ground to make up with most of his new teammates. Who knew he'd been sent here in disgrace. Knew he'd blown it at the Saints. None of the Preachers' players had exactly welcomed him with open arms. It was only the two real rookies, fresh out of college, who had spoken to him much at all. They were all enthusiasm, convinced they were going to conquer the world of baseball, eager to hear about his time in the majors. They reminded him of his idiot younger self. Which was kind of painful. But it was a start. The rest of the guys he'd have to prove himself to.

Work for it.

So head down and definitely no flirting with Eva, who was clearly a central part of the Preachers' organization. Someone the players regarded as part of the family. He knew a little about how guys reacted when other guys tried to date their sisters, having a sister himself. Eva was off limits. He would just have to ignore the fact that she kept popping into his mind and that the few times he'd seen her during the week, his attention had zeroed in on her like she was a lifeline and he was drowning.

It was an excellent plan until he tried to log into his

email on Thursday morning and the computer declared
he didn't exist. Or rather his password didn't. Which
meant he was going to have to go see the very interesting Eva after all.

No flirting, he reminded himself as he headed toward Eva's office thirty minutes later. Nice. Friendly.
Cooperative—that was the key. She'd been all-business
when she'd given him a tour of the complex on Monday.
Nothing but the facts. No shift in her demeanor despite
his attempts to get her to relax. He hadn't figured out if
it was him or if she'd been having a bad day. Hopefully
the latter. Though she probably knew exactly how he'd
washed up on her shores, so to speak. Knew all about
his fall from grace at the Saints. She must have come
across plenty of other players who'd been demoted.
Maybe she gave them all the cold shoulder.

Smart woman.

He deserved the cold shoulder. It would remind him
that he was walking the line, to steal a phrase from
Johnny Cash.

He hadn't ended up in prison last year but he'd been
lucky to escape charges after that dumb bar fight. Luck-
ier still that the Saints hadn't just sacked him and had
instead sent him to a six-week program that wasn't
exactly rehab . . . the consensus being he wasn't an alcoholic . . . but had definitely been in *Dude, you need
to get a handle on things* territory. No booze, more
health food than he ever wanted to see again, and daily
sessions with both a sports psychologist and the regu-
lar kind.

It had given him some clarity. Shown him what needed
to change if he was going to be successful in MLB.

Now he just had to prove that he could do it.

So Eva Harlowe might just be a good test subject. If he could convince her he'd changed, maybe he might actually succeed at getting back to the Saints.

He knocked politely on her half-open door, waited for her to say, "Come in." When she did, he pushed the door open carefully.

Eva stood at one of the file cabinets behind her desk, rummaging through a drawer. Her dark hair was piled up and she'd stuck a pen through it at some point. She was smiling absently as she flicked through folders. It made him wonder what she was thinking about. The deep-blue sweater she wore with a black skirt highlighted some very nice curves. He pulled his eyes back to her face as she turned her head.

The cool look that quickly replaced her smile when she saw that it was him clarified something else. She hadn't been in a bad mood on Monday. It was him she had a problem with.

He couldn't really blame her. She had to know his history. How badly he'd screwed things up to end up here. In her place, he'd have a problem with him, too. Which meant that he was just going to have to work a bit harder to prove that her low expectations were wrong.

"Mr. Castro," she said as she pulled a file from the drawer. "What can I do for you this morning?"

"It seems that your IT system has decided I don't exist. I couldn't get into my emails this morning."

"Did you try resetting your password?"

"Yes. But I got an error message. Plus even if it worked, I can't log in to get the reset link."

She looked at him over the top of her glasses, expression suspicious. "No one else has mentioned having an issue."

He held up his hands. "I swear I didn't do anything to it. I logged in fine yesterday."

"I'll get the IT guys to reset the account. Was there anything in particular you wanted?"

"I wanted to check the schedule again. Coach said last night that there had been changes to the travel arrangements for Tuesday." Their first game of spring training. He rolled his shoulders, suddenly nervous. He'd done fine in the training sessions this week. No reason for that to be any different when he got onto the field next week.

"Well, you're in luck. I just printed out a few copies to post in the locker room." She walked to her desk, lifted a big expensive-looking camera that was sitting on a pile of printouts, and picked up a piece of paper. "Here."

He took the paper. "Nice camera." He had no idea whether it was nice or not. Or whether it was hers. The Saints had a staff photographer who traveled with the team. He had no idea whether the Preachers' budget ran to that sort of thing.

She hitched a shoulder. "It does the job."

He nodded at the camera. "Do you like photography?" He knew he should really just take the schedule and leave, but he couldn't quite bring himself to make that first move toward the door.

"I dabble. I take shots around here to post to our social media."

"I'll have to check them out."

She frowned slightly. "You didn't list any social media accounts on the profile information you gave us."

"I closed them all last year when . . ." Exactly how much did she know about what had happened to him last season? Probably all of it.

"When you got in that bar fight?" she said coolly.

Yup. She knew. "Yes." No point trying to bullshit his way through, or put any spin on it. "Haven't really missed them much. But if you want me to set something up again, I can."

She shook her head. "It's not team policy that you have to have them, it's up to you."

He shrugged. "Trying to keep things simple. Keep my head clear."

Her brows lifted, just a fraction. "Well, like I said, it's not team policy."

He smiled and just for a moment he thought she was going to smile back. But then she looked away, reaching out to adjust a bright-red photo frame on her desk. He knew he should leave, shouldn't get in her way. Not give her any reason to dislike him any more than she apparently already did. But his eyes followed the movement of her hand.

The photo was Eva and three younger women. All dark-haired except the youngest, who was sporting cropped platinum blond. All with the same deep-blue eyes as her.

"Sisters?" he asked.

For once she actually smiled as her gaze dropped to the photo. "Yes. Kate, Lizzie, and Audrey."

"Eva, Kate, Lizzie, and Audrey?" he asked. His mom

was an old Hollywood movie fan. "Tell me, is Kate short for Katharine?"

"Yes," she said. She shrugged. "My mom loved old movies."

"Katharine Hepburn, Audrey Hepburn. Elizabeth Taylor." He ticked the names off. "But wait, I assume you're Ava Gardner? Didn't she spell her name with an *A*?"

"My dad wasn't such a movie fan. He filled out the birth certificate and spelled it with an *E*. My mom almost strangled him when she saw it but the deed, so to speak, was done."

"So that's why you're *Ay-va* not *Ee-va*?" He looked from her to the photo again. Her mom had obviously been psychic. All four of her daughters were gorgeous. Though Eva had that something . . . more than mere prettiness.

"Yup. There you go, the great mystery of my name solved." She stroked a finger over the photo and then turned it slightly again so he couldn't see it clearly. "Now, is there something else I can do for you, Mr. Castro?"

Chapter Two

By the time Friday night rolled around, Eva figured she had earned her weekly dinner date with her best friend, Jenna Ross. The week before spring training was always busy, but this year it had been more exhausting than usual. Probably due to all the mental energy she was spending trying not to think about Finn.

Not thinking about Finn was practically a full-time job. Every time she thought she'd succeeded in not thinking about him for an extended period of time, she'd had to do something that involved reading his name on the team roster or, worse, seeing the man himself, doing drills on the field or walking from the parking lot to the training building. Every time it made her remember all over again the sheer rush of heat through her blood that had stunned her when he'd walked into her office.

Stupid crush.

Jenna took a bite of her cheeseburger, chewed, swallowed, and made an appreciative noise as she reached for her Mojito. "Man, I needed this."

Eva grinned and stole a French fry off Jenna's plate,

sipping her own Cointreau and tonic. "Tough week in yoga world?"

Her friend nodded and drank. Then put the glass down. "Sometimes helping people be bendy and relaxed isn't all it's cracked up to be." Her gray eyes twinkled as she stole one of Eva's chili fries. "How about you? Your boys all geared up for spring training? Any new talent I should know about?"

She was so not telling Jenna about Finn. She'd survived the week without embarrassing herself despite the fact that proximity to Finn had in no way cooled her crush. Quite the opposite, in fact. Still, she hadn't thrown herself at the man. Or given herself away in any way as far as she could tell. So she was calling that a win. But not one she could share with Jenna. "Nope. Just the usual."

Jenna's eyes narrowed. "Damn. Wait. No, that's not right. What about Mr. Hottie from those ads that leaked? He's here this season, isn't he?" She took another bite.

"Finn Castro?" Eva worked to keep her tone disinterested.

"That'sh him," Jenna said, mouth still half full.

"He's practically an infant."

"A smokin'-hot infant," Jenna said.

"But still an infant. He's only twenty-six." It was sad that she knew his age. Hell, she knew his birthday.

Jenna gave her a you're-crazy look. "Yeah, because thirty-two is soooo much older than twenty-six."

Time to cut off this line of questioning before she gave herself away. "It wouldn't matter if he was thirty. Or forty. I don't date guys on the team. You know that."

"You know, that rule made sense when you still had the girls at home. When you were stuck here. But now? They're gone and you're going to be gone in a while, too, right? Why shouldn't you have some fun?"

"I'm not opposed to fun," Eva said, trying to remember exactly when her last "fun" had taken place. A couple of months ago? That guy from the bar Jenna had dragged them to. The one who'd been so very very boring the morning after. And not half as hot as Finn. "But fun isn't worth screwing things up at the Preachers for. Who knows, I might want to come back." She wasn't going to tell Jenna that she hadn't actually sent in her reply to the offer of a place in Isaac Haines's exclusive photography school. She'd dreamed about it for years. Sending in a portfolio had been a mad whim, one she hadn't expected to pay off in a million years. Moving to go to school in New York was one thing. Across the country was another. Lizzie had done it but Lizzie had had the confidence of being a nineteen-year-old going to college. Not a thirty-two-year-old who'd never left home.

Jenna snorted. "Girl, you are going to go to California, take that photography course, and never look back. Except when you come to visit me, of course. You don't need a backup plan. Besides, this is the twenty-first century. You can sleep with whoever you want. No one at the Preachers will care even one little bit."

Eva wasn't so sure about that. There'd been office romances at the Preachers before. Some had gone smoothly but some had not. "I know. But I don't want drama." She'd worked very hard for years to limit the drama in her life. Losing her parents was all the drama she had needed. She wanted smooth sailing. Guys like Finn, even if he wasn't playing for the Preachers, weren't smooth sailing. More like *pull you under and drown you.* "Workplace romances can only end in tears. And I haven't definitely decided I'm going to take the course yet." She'd only gotten the acceptance letter two weeks ago. She had until the end of May to enroll.

"Of course you're going to do it. And Finn Castro would be worth a few tears," Jenna said, looking wistful.

"Well, then you send Lana a Dear Jane email and have Finn all to yourself. If you want to change teams." Eva grinned at Jenna. Lana Carroll, Jenna's girlfriend, was a doctor. She was also currently in Kenya doing a stint with Médecins Sans Frontières. Still, even thousands of miles away, there was zero chance of Jenna ditching Lana and chasing after a twenty-six-year-old baseball player no matter how cute he was. Which made Eva feel strangely relieved.

That made her nervous. Very nervous. She reached for her drink, gulped it, and tried to shake off the feeling. It didn't matter who Finn Castro dated. It was never going to be her. Never. He had to have glamorous women throwing themselves at him daily. He didn't need to date a thirty-two-year-old who'd barely left her hometown and was nowhere near glamorous. Even if she had a fit of insanity and decided to break her rules, there was no way Finn would be interested.

Which was by far the most depressing thought she'd had all week.

She drained the rest of her drink.

"Feeling okay there?" Jenna asked, looking at her strangely.

"Yup. Long week, that's all. Hey, did I tell you that Kate got another promotion?"

Jenna grinned. "Is she running that accounting firm yet?"

"No. But give her a few more years."

"Queen of the bean counters," Jenna said. "Not my idea of heaven but whatever makes her happy." She reached for her glass but froze mid-reach, eyes fixed on something behind Eva.

"What?" Eva asked idly. "Spotted an old girlfriend?" Jenna had plenty of those. And a few old boyfriends as well. She, unlike Eva, hadn't spent her twenties raising her baby sisters.

Jenna blinked then shook her head. "Nope. But man, are you sure about that not-dating-players thing because that man is freaking hot."

What man? Finn? Finn was here? She felt her face start to flame. Cool. She needed to stay cool. "Who?" she asked, pretending not to know what Jenna was talking about.

Jenna's gaze didn't move. Her expression was frankly appreciative. "Finn Castro. Hottie. Who we were just discussing a few minutes ago." Gray eyes moved back to Eva then narrowed. "You're trying to play it cool by pretending not to know who I meant."

"I'm not pretending anything. We were talking about Kate." She hoped she sounded convincing. But Jenna looked skeptical.

"Honey, your sister's promotion is awesome but it does not trump this man. Not in any universe where women—or men—having working hormones."

"He's not that good looking," Eva muttered.

"Had your glasses checked lately?" Jenna retorted. Then her expression turned delighted. "Ooh, I think he spotted you. He's coming over."

Eva almost dropped her drink. He was what? God. Was it too late to make a run for the ladies' room? What on earth was Finn doing here? Leary's wasn't a cool hangout. It was a former-diner-turned-restaurant. It still served diner food—it had just added cocktails and beer and some more exotic burgers to the offerings. It was close to where Eva lived and not far from Jenna's yoga studio, which was why they'd adopted it as a hangout years ago, once Eva's sisters had been old enough not to need supervision for a few hours on a Friday night. It wasn't the sort of place the guys from the team usually ate.

But there was no time to run. Because Finn was suddenly there. In front of her. Wearing a dark-gray henley and jeans and looking, as Jenna had so helpfully pointed out, smoking hot. As always. Her stomach fluttered and she tried to squash the sensation. Tried and failed.

"Eva," he said. "Hello."

She managed a smile, trying to ignore her body's ridiculous reaction to the guy. "Finn, hi."

Across from her, Jenna shook her head and then stuck out her hand. "I'm Jenna. Jenna Ross. Eva's best friend."

"Finn Castro," he said. His smile broadened and Eva looked down and reached for her drink. That smile was going to be the death of her.

"I know," Jenna said. "I saw your picture on the Preachers' website. Welcome to Saratoga Springs."

"Thanks," Finn said. "It seems like a nice town."

"Why don't you sit with us?" Jenna said. Eva kicked

her under the table but Jenna just grinned evilly at her. "You're new in town. You can't eat alone."

"I don't want to intrude," Finn said and for a second Eva was relieved. She opened her mouth to agree with him but Jenna beat her to the punch.

"No intrusion. You can buy us drinks," Jenna said. She scooted over in the booth, patting the seat beside her. "Sit. You need to try the chili burger, it's awesome."

"Finn's in training," Eva said. "He probably needs to get home."

Jenna snorted. "It's barely the start of spring training. And it's Friday. The first game isn't until Tuesday. Let the man eat a burger."

Eva gave up as Finn apparently decided that he was listening to Jenna, not to her, and slid into the booth. Which left Eva with nowhere to look but straight at him. Damn.

Was she blushing? Her face felt hot. All of her felt hot.

She needed another drink. She looked around for the waitress.

"So how did you find this place?" Jenna said to Finn. "Usually you baseball boys go hang out at all the hot spots downtown."

"I saw the sign when I was running. My apartment's just a few blocks from here," Finn said.

"Really?" Jenna smiled at him. "Eva lives just by here, too."

Finn's gaze shifted to Eva. "You do?"

"Yes," she said, trying not to blush. His eyes were a truly ridiculous shade of green. Distractingly green. And right now entirely focused on her. Which was even more distracting.

"Just a block or so back from the day care center,"
Jenna added helpfully. Eva wanted to kick her again but
she was worried that she might kick Finn instead. The
last thing she needed was the man thinking she was trying to play footsie with him under the table.

"I'm near St. Joseph's," Finn said.

He was? That was practically around the corner from
her. She'd deliberately gotten Sal, who helped her with
the admin side of things, to put his details into their system. She hadn't wanted to feed the crush by snooping.
Damn. She should have snooped after all. Then she
might have been ready for an unexpected encounter instead of sitting here wondering how she was going to
get through dinner with the man without making a total idiot of herself.

"Convenient," Jenna said, aiming another wicked
grin in Eva's direction. "You two should carpool or
something."

Oh hell no. God, she was going to make Jenna pay
for this. Cover her favorite yoga mat in glue or something. "Finn doesn't have to start as early as I do." Which
was both true and something to be thankful for.

She looked away again and finally managed to
catch their waitress's eye. The short blonde came over
and produced a menu for Finn while she took Eva's
drink order. Finn ordered the chili burger and coffee—
earning himself a smitten smile from the waitress in
the process—and Eva kicked herself. Did he not drink
now?

Damn. She felt like an idiot for ordering another
drink in front of him.

"Not drinking?" Jenna asked.

He shrugged. "Like Eva said, I'm in training."

Which didn't really answer Eva's question. That could mean he didn't drink during training or that he didn't drink much during training or that it was an excuse not to mention that he'd given up drinking altogether. Which, given his history, might be a smart move on his part.

"Do you live around here, too?" Finn asked Jenna.

"I'm a bit farther north," Jenna said. "But my yoga studio is a block west of here."

"Yoga?" Finn said, looking slightly surprised.

"Yes. Ever tried it?"

"I've done a bit," he said. "I did Bikram now and then back in New York. Good for taking care of the sore spots after a game. But it's hard to get to a class regularly with being on the road so much."

Finn Castro doing yoga. Eva tried not to picture him half naked and sweaty in a hot yoga class and failed. Her face was suddenly as heated as Jenna's Bikram studio.

"Well, you should come along. We have Bikram classes every day. And the less sweaty kind if that's more your thing," Jenna said. She fished a business card out from her purse and handed it to Finn. "Here. First class is on me."

"Thanks," Finn said. He tucked the card into his back pocket. "I'll make sure to try it."

"Great, I'll look out for you."

The waitress reappeared with Eva's drink and Finn's coffee. She sipped hers as she realized she couldn't leave all the conversational effort to Jenna without appearing weird. "How's your first week been?" she asked.

Finn hitched a shoulder. "Good. It's always strange at first, settling into a new team."

"Have you moved around a lot playing baseball?" Jenna asked.

"Not as much as some do. I grew up in Chicago, went away for college, then the Cubs picked me up for their Triple-A team in Des Moines. Then eventually back to Chicago with the Cubs, then to New York City with the Saints, now here. Lots of travel during the season, but that's hotels and airports. We're never really somewhere long enough to get to know the place."

She tried not to let the envy she felt show on her face. She'd been to New York City, of course, but she'd really spent her entire life in Saratoga Springs. There hadn't been money for long vacations in their finances. She'd taken the girls around New York State and to Pennsylvania. There'd even been a few weeks in Maine a couple of summers when the previous manager of the Preachers had let her use his house there. "Saratoga Springs doesn't take that long to get to know. It's kind of small."

Sometimes she wondered if she was bound to Saratoga for life. Lizzie and Kate had flown the coop for big cities; even Audrey had spent time in Boston for college and lived in San Francisco for two years. She'd come back home now to start her own little web design business, but she'd been able to leave first. Whereas Eva was still here. Though only until the end of the season if she decided to take the plunge and take Isaac's course. Then it would finally be her turn.

One side of Finn's mouth quirked up. "Maybe not, but

there are still some attractions." His expression was innocent, but there was something about the way he was
watching her that made her stomach tighten again. She
fussed with the last of her fries.

"Well, nowhere is as cool as Manhattan," Jenna said.
"Bet you can't wait to get back to the Saints."

This time Eva really did nearly kick her again. What
the hell was Jenna thinking? It was kind of rude to talk
about the fact that Finn had been demoted. She watched
Finn, saw the green eyes suddenly go determined. She
knew that look. The look of a baseball player who
wanted his shot again.

"Would I like to play in the majors again? Sure. But
right now I'm here. And my only goal is to play the best
damned baseball I can while I'm here."

Her breath caught at his words. Well, that was blunt
enough. He had no plans to stick around. All the more
reason she should stay away. "Good plan," she managed
and sent a *Change the subject, dumbass* look in Jenna's
direction. Talk about anything but baseball. Anything
but Finn Castro. Anything that might help her figure out
how to put him out of her mind. Jenna opened her mouth
to say something, but luckily the waitress arrived with
Finn's burger before the conversation could get any
odder. She took advantage of the distraction to slip away
to the ladies' room to get a grip.

Finn resisted the temptation to watch Eva walk across
the restaurant and instead focused on the excellent chili
burger sitting on his plate and the woman sitting beside

him. Eva's best friend had dark skin and gorgeous big gray eyes that were currently studying him curiously. He'd gotten used to women watching him over the years but this felt different. In fact, he got the feeling he was being judged in some competition he didn't know anything about. He took a bite of burger while he tried to decide if he was imagining things.

"So," Jenna said as she watched him eat. "Now that Eva's not here, how are you really getting on at the Preachers?"

He twisted toward her, surprised at the question. What was she fishing for? "Just what I said, settling in okay. I've got some ground to make up, I knew that coming in." He had to assume Jenna knew his story. It had been plastered in the press. Plus her best friend worked for his new team.

"Well, if you can get Eva on your side, that will help," Jenna said.

"Everyone at the Preachers loves her, that's clear," Finn said, warily. "She's been there a long time."

"Since she was eighteen."

"Interesting choice of career for an eighteen-year-old."

"Following in her dad's footsteps," Jenna said. "Not so odd, maybe."

Finn shrugged. Maggie Winters had been an owner's daughter, so he had gotten a taste of what someone born to eat, sleep, and breathe baseball was like. He didn't think Eva fit the same mold. And it was obvious that Jenna wasn't telling him the full story. "What do her sisters do?"

That earned him arched eyebrows. "You know about her sisters?"

"I know she has three," Finn said. "I saw the picture on her desk. The name thing is kind of cool."

Her expression turned approving. "Kate's an accountant in New York at one of the big firms—I can never remember which one—Audrey's just moved back here to Saratoga, she's a web designer, and Lizzie graduates from college this year. She's going to medical school next. She's in San Francisco."

"Smart girls."

"Eva's smart, too," Jenna said.

"Trust me, I have no doubts about that." Though it did beg the question of why she was the only one who'd never gone to college. Wasn't the oldest usually the trailblazer? Certainly Em had set the bar high in his family, getting straight A's all through high school and keeping her GPA perfect at college then having her pick of law schools. Amelia Graham, Em's best friend, who'd basically grown up as part of his family, had been a near-perfect student, too. "She didn't want to go to college?"

Those gray eyes shadowed a little. "I think if you want to know Eva's story, then you're going to have to get Eva to tell it to you."

He held up his hands. "Okay. Sorry. Wasn't trying to snoop."

"But you're curious, right?" She smiled at him. "That's good."

"Why? And who says I'm curious?"

Her smile went wider. "Let's just say Eva deserves a little curiosity."

Well now, that was interesting. Was Jenna saying Eva was interested in him?

Then she frowned. "But fair warning: If you mess with my friend and hurt her, I will hurt you."

He nodded. Message received. "I'm not here to cause trouble," he said and then wondered why she laughed.

Chapter Three

When Eva came back to the booth, Jenna and Finn were laughing like they were old friends. The spike of envy that stabbed her gut as she slid into the seat took her by surprise. "What's so funny?" She made herself smile as she asked the question, worried all over again that she'd give herself away. She'd given herself a pep talk in the bathroom about the stupidity of her crush. Apparently it hadn't done any good.

"Nothing," Jenna said but she looked a little too satisfied with herself. Eva didn't like that look. It was the look of Jenna Ross on a mission, and she had a horrible feeling that Jenna had decided her mission was to get Eva and Finn together.

Which was the last thing in the world Eva wanted. She wanted to fly under Finn's radar, stay out of his way. It was the only option until her hormones came to their senses and moved on to a new target. They had to do that eventually, surely? She couldn't go a whole season feeling sweaty and awkward every time she was in Finn's presence.

And she doubted she could successfully hide her inconvenient lustful thoughts about him from Jenna for very long, either. Jenna was no dummy. She knew all Eva's tells when it came to men. Friendship since kindergarten did that to a person. Not that there were many reasons that she, Jenna, and Finn should be in the same space at once very often, but Jenna liked baseball and often came along to Preachers games when they were playing at home. So it was likely she'd run into Finn again.

Jenna even let Eva drag her along to the odd away game when Eva went with the team. Which happened more often these days. When her sisters had been at home, it had been nearly impossible to travel to see the guys play on weekends, let alone weekdays. Too many dance classes and soccer matches and part-time jobs and all the other things that went with teenage girls to juggle.

Finn had finished his burger. "That was great." He pushed his plate away. "But I'm going to leave you two to finish your girls' night. We have a practice game tomorrow and I've intruded long enough."

"You're not intruding," Jenna said, but Finn slid out of the booth with an apologetic smile.

"Gotta get my beauty sleep," he said and nodded at Eva. "Thanks for the company. Maybe I'll see you tomorrow?"

At the game, he meant. Staff and family and friends of the teams were always invited to the practice game just before the spring training season officially started. She'd been planning on skipping it this year, but with Finn's eyes focused on her, it was hard to remember why.

She felt the word *absolutely* start to form on her tongue and bit it back with an effort. "I usually go." There. Neutral. Polite. Good job. Colleagues, that's all they were. Of course, she'd never had to try so hard to stop staring at a colleague's ass as he walked away from her before.

As Finn went through the restaurant door and disappeared from sight, Jenna let out an exaggerated sigh and passed Eva a napkin.

"What's this for?"

"Wiping the drool off your chin."

"There is no drool on my chin."

"It's metaphorical drool. Because you know, you have the flaming panties for that guy."

Eva tossed the napkin back at Jenna. "Do not start."

"Well, I could run after him and offer him the napkin. I'll bet you about a million dollars that he's suffering metaphorical drool as well."

"Don't be ridiculous. He is not. Is he?" The last two words popped out before she could stop them.

Jenna's expression turned triumphant. "Ha! You want to know. You *are* drooling!"

"Am not. Like I said, he's too young."

"Good grief. That argument would be dumb if you were ten years older than him. And you're only six. He's hot. He's nice. That's a very good combination. And you know, he didn't strike me as an infant."

"He might not be an infant, but he's not exactly a good guy. Good guys don't start bar fights and get demoted from the majors."

"He was drinking coffee tonight. Maybe he's reformed."

She didn't think bad boys reformed in just a few

months. "Whatever you're thinking, please just stop. Not going to happen. As in never. Give it up."

"Give what up?" Jenna said and batted her eyelashes exaggeratedly. "Me looking out for your best interests? I'll always do that."

"Finn Castro is not my best interests."

"You don't have to marry the dude. Just let him give you some screaming orgasms for a few months and then let him go."

"Not my style," Eva said, even as she tried not to think about screaming orgasms with Finn. If she thought about that then her underwear probably would go up in those flames Jenna had mentioned.

"But why the hell not?" Jenna said, looking exasperated. "I mean, I get it. You had to behave yourself while you had your sisters to worry about. But you did that. And now they're gone and you've spent so long thinking about Kate and Lizzie and Aud, I'm not sure you have any idea what your style really is. You deserve to find out. You deserve some fun. Who cares if he's not a longtime prospect? You're leaving anyway. A hot fling with a guy who looks like Finn sounds like a damned good send-off to me."

Eva opened her mouth to argue then stopped as she realized she didn't really know what her argument was. "Guys like that don't date girls like me," she managed after an awkward pause.

"That's lame," Jenna said. Then she grinned. "And that means you've thought about it."

"Shut up."

"Keep up with those snappy comebacks and you might just convince me."

"I hate you."

"No, you don't. And news flash, you don't hate Finn Castro, either."

"Nervous, Castro?"

Finn looked up after tugging his shoelace into place to meet the grin of Connor West, the Preachers' veteran pitcher. "About a practice game?" He waved a hand out at the field and shrugged. "Nope."

"Interesting that you've retied your shoes four times since you sat down then," Connor said. He twirled the bat in his right hand before tugging his cap farther down over his dark hair with his left. His gray eyes were amused.

"New shoes," Finn said with another shrug. He leaned forward on his bench, glancing toward the stands where Eva was sitting with a couple of the other office staff he recognized and three other women he didn't know. He'd seen her walk in and take up her spot a few minutes ago. That was when the nerves had hit. Nothing to do with the game, everything to do with the fact that he'd wanted her to come today.

Which was dumb on a whole new scale of dumb.

Connor craned his neck looking in the same direction. "Something in the stands you like?"

Finn snapped his gaze back. "Nope."

"Remind me to play poker with you one night soon. You're a terrible liar." Connor looked back at the stands. "Who's caught your eye? Eva?" He laughed. "Good luck with that. Greater men than you have tried and failed to win that heart."

They had? Who? There was no way he was going to ask that question. "I'm just here to play ball."

"Aren't we all?" Connor rolled his shoulders, stretching. "Doesn't mean you can't enjoy yourself in the process." His face went serious. "Though if you do decide to date one of the women who work here, the rule is treat them well. Or the guys will have something to say about it."

Finn nodded. "Got it. But like I said, here for baseball, not girls." He hesitated as Connor didn't look away. "Any guys in particular got a thing for Eva?"

"Not really my place to say. But you're new here and I know you have some ground to make up, so I'll just say that our esteemed team captain has a very soft spot for her."

Crap. That was just what he needed. Pissing off Greg Cutler, the Preachers' captain, wasn't going to help Finn win any friends here. He resisted the urge to look back at Eva. "But is it reciprocated?"

"She's never said yes to any of his invitations that I know about," Connor said. "Her decision in the end." He nodded. "Like I said, many have tried and failed."

Was now a good time to keep asking for more info? he wondered as the coach yelled for them to get onto the field.

"Tell you what," Connor said. "You get me out today and I'll buy you a beer tonight." The team was split in two for the practice game.

"You sure about that? Everyone tells me you're a better pitcher than you are a batter." He'd leave the part about him not currently drinking until later.

"I'm good enough to get past you. And you're buying if I do," Connor shot back, good-naturedly. He jerked his chin at the field. "I believe you losers are fielding."

"Well, then it won't be long before you're back here with time to think about where you're buying me that beer." Finn picked up his glove and jogged onto the field to take up his position at first base. When he reached the plate and settled into place he realized that Eva was sitting right in his line of vision.

For a moment he thought she was looking right at him, though the dark sunglasses she wore hid her eyes. The sensation of contact made something tighten low and hot in his gut. Damn. He looked away. If he kept watching her instead of getting his head in the game then Connor would be drinking for free later.

Eva glared out the window and tried not to feel cranky. It was spring. She wanted sunshine. Not rain. But the rain pounding down outside was evidence that the weather gods didn't much care what she wanted. On Sunday mornings she usually went for a long run, but the rain was heavy enough today that she would've just been soaked in a few minutes. She didn't mind getting a bit damp on a run, but sodden shoes and frozen fingers were not her idea of a good time. It had been a perfectly nice sunny day yesterday, but she'd spent it trying not to watch Finn every second of the practice game. By the time she'd gotten through an afternoon of dragging her eyes away from him whenever she caught herself watching again, she'd gone home cranky and in need of ice cream to fuel her denial. The memory of

Finn in the tight-fitting black-and-white Preachers' uniform required a lot of denial.

Ice cream, even the really expensive full-fat, full-sugar, full-everything kind she'd bought, hadn't worked. Neither had a bad movie and a glass of wine.

The crush was running to full throttle and, thanks to Jenna's little pep talk the night before, she'd kept having the ridiculous thought that maybe it didn't have to stay just a crush.

She was working hard to squish that thought. She'd worked hard through a broken night's sleep. It had been sheer force of will that had propelled her out of bed this morning determined to run it out of her system.

Only to discover the rain. The evil plan-thwarting rain.

So instead she'd set about cleaning the house, but by lunchtime she was still feeling restless and on edge. Every time she stopped moving, annoying thoughts of a certain baseball player she didn't want to think about intruded. She needed to burn him out of her brain. Or at least out of her body.

There was a treadmill down in her basement, one she'd had for years, but it was getting old and temperamental and being stuck down in the basement was just a reminder of the crappy weather. Of course, there was a great gym at Hennessee. One she was allowed to use whenever she wanted. She bit her lip, looked at the clock. The team had had practice this morning but it was nearly one now and they should all be long gone, given the weather. She could have the gym with its lovely not-on-their-last-legs treadmills all to herself. Could plug her iPod into the system and blast some girl-power pop and not care what anyone thought about her choice of music.

Either that or eat her weight in doughnuts. Which wasn't going to help. So the gym it was.

The rain was even worse by the time she made it to Hennessee, and her jog to the training building left her half soaked despite her umbrella. Still, the team had probably been using the gym that morning so the heating system would be on. She'd dry out fast enough on the treadmill.

When she stepped into the building, the lights were on. Damn. Was someone here? Oh well. She could put her headphones on and still use the treadmill even if someone else was in the gym. It might be empty anyway. One of the coaching staff might be in one of the other rooms. There were a couple of small offices and a meeting room with the video set up where they reviewed footage of games and other teams.

She headed down to the gym, pulling her earbuds out of her bag and tucking them into her ears. She had just started blasting Pink when she pushed open the door to the gym so at first the steady *thump thump* of someone running on a treadmill didn't register.

She dropped her bag on the nearest bench and stripped off her rain jacket. When she turned and saw Finn on one of the treadmills, she froze. He'd been arresting in his uniform, his long body all grace and power. But now he was simply jaw-droppingly sexy.

He wore shorts over compression tights, and his body was a true work of art. Muscles carved curves and planes designed to make a woman melt into a puddle along his arms and down his torso. The only thing breaking up the expanse of male beauty was the dark line of a stark black tattoo that ran up one side of his abdomen, curving around his ribs and snaking around to cross his back before it reappeared at his shoulder beneath his right collarbone then continue down his arm. The spiky lines intersected with curving loops of text that she couldn't read but suddenly desperately wanted to. The T-shirt he'd obviously stripped off was a crumple of navy cotton beside his machine.

For a second she considered turning right around and leaving—or maybe *fleeing* was the right word—but that would give her away. A woman who had no interest in the man wouldn't care that he was working out half naked. No, that woman would just walk over to one of the other treadmills and get on with her workout.

Finn had been running hard but he lifted his chin at her in a very male gesture of acknowledgment and hit the button to slow the machine down to a walking speed, yanking his own headphones from his ears.

She did the same. It would be rude not to.

"Hey, Eva," he said, sounding slightly out of breath. Which, really, just made his deep voice sound sexier. Unfair. How could he look so good? She liked to run but she was fairly certain she didn't look like a god fallen to earth when she was hot and sweaty and working hard. Nope, she was just a normal red-faced hot mess.

"Finn," she said. She waved at his treadmill. "Don't mind me, I don't want to interrupt your workout."

He nodded at that and smiled before replacing his headphones. His hand tapped the control panel and he eased effortlessly back into a faster pace.

Which left her with no option other than to get on with her own run. She stared at the row of treadmills. Would it be weird if she took the one on the far end of the line to his? Probably. After all there was no reason for her to be avoiding him, right?

Right. She walked over to the machine next to Finn's and climbed on. She started her warm-up, put her earbuds back in, and turned up the music on her phone in the vain hope it would distract her from Finn's nearness. It helped, particularly as she picked up the pace, but only a little. She could smell him. Fresh sweat—unlike the familiar too-many-guys-work-out-here smell of the gym—and whatever aftershave or deodorant or cologne he wore. Did guys wear cologne to work out? She had no idea. But something was scenting his skin, something warm and slightly spicy and dark.

Delicious. It made her want to bury her face in his neck and breathe him in. Taste him.

Gah.

She hit the speed button and made herself run. Felt her breath start to quicken and the warmth spread through her muscles as she fell into the rhythm of it. Her mind finally started to blank as she sank into the movement, keeping her eyes firmly fixed on the wall in front of her treadmill. There was a big flat-screen up there that the guys on the team usually had tuned to ESPN or a music channel, but Finn hadn't turned it on. She could see her reflection and his in the dark glass of the monitor so she dropped her gaze to the plain cream-painted wall. She hit thirty minutes. Finn hadn't slowed his pace. Sometimes she wanted to keep things short but today she needed the burn, Finn or no Finn. So she kept running.

At fifty minutes her thighs and calves started to protest but Finn was still moving smoothly beside her when she risked a glance in his direction. Arms pumping, face blank, bare chest rising and falling like a sculpted machine. His skin glistened with sweat but other than that, there was no sign that he was anywhere near done.

Damn.

Most of the guys on the team took their fitness seriously, but Finn was apparently taking it to a whole new level. He had to have been running for well over an hour now, and that after whatever training session the team had had this morning.

Definitely driven.

Working to get back to New York. To the Saints. To his real life.

So why not enjoy him while he's here?

The thought snuck in against her will, almost made her miss a step.

No. Just no. Endorphins were obviously making her loopy. She knew all the reasons he wasn't a good idea. So it didn't matter how inhumanly hot his body was and it didn't matter that he seemed, despite all rumors to the contrary, to be a nice guy—or at least was trying to be a nice guy. He wasn't for her.

The timer on her treadmill hit sixty minutes and she let herself slow. She wasn't a professional athlete like Finn, and while she sometimes ran for longer outdoors, an hour was long enough to have to stand beside Finn and pretend not to notice him.

She swigged water and wiped her face off as she walked to cool down. She'd pulled her hair back in a braid, but that didn't change the fact she was undeniably dripping. Well, if Finn couldn't handle a sweating woman then that was only more proof he wasn't right for her.

As she slowed the treadmill again and tugged out her earbuds, Finn finally brought the pace down on his, too, and reached for his towel, mopping his face before he turned his head toward her with a smile. On him sweaty looked good. He practically gleamed. Like he'd been spotlit.

"Good workout," he said, eyes focused on her face. His smile widened, as though he liked what he saw.

The expression made her stomach tighten. There was too much *I'm happy to see you* in his expression for her comfort. She didn't want him to like her. That would make pretending she didn't like him even more difficult. But she had no reason to be rude to him. "You too," she said, trying to ignore the flex of his abs as he continued to walk. His six-pack was more like an eight-pack.

"I've always liked to run," he said. "Clears my head. Gets me away from my problems for a while."

She understood that. That seeking of oblivion from the noise behind your eyes. There had been months after her parents died when she'd snuck down to the basement after the girls had all been asleep and climbed onto the treadmill to run as if her life depended on it. Run until she couldn't think. Until she was too exhausted to continue. Run to leave the grief and the fear behind for a time. So she could sleep for a few hours. Without that treadmill she might have given up before the first twelve months had passed.

Even with all the help she'd received, it had been overwhelming. She'd spent every minute worrying. Worrying that she would fail. That she'd screw up. That her sisters would be taken away from her. Even after she'd been granted guardianship, she worried. Worried that she was fucking them up in new ways, trying to be a parent when she was barely an adult. But Finn, from the few things he'd shared at dinner, had had a pretty happy childhood. So what demons drove his body into motion?

And there was exactly the sort of thought she shouldn't be thinking. Shouldn't be wondering about who he was and what made him tick. He was too young. Too temporary. She'd done temporary before, but always on her terms. Finn wasn't the sort of guy a woman could sleep with and then throw out of bed easily. He was too damned good looking. Too much exactly what her body wanted. Some part of her knew that if she let herself get a taste of him, it would be addictive. She didn't do addictive men. Didn't want crazy blazing love. That kind of love hurt too much if you lost it. She'd had her world blown to pieces once. She wasn't going to let it happen again. So she just nodded at him, brought her treadmill to a full halt, and then fled the gym before she forgot all her good intentions.

Chapter Four

Finn blew out a breath and jogged a little on the spot, trying to ride out the nerves curling his gut and the chill in the air. Erie, Pennsylvania, like Saratoga, was proving reluctant to produce any springlike weather. The afternoon was fine but cold, the wind still icy, and the dugout he was standing in was freezing. The Sea Wolves' players fanning out across the field didn't look any warmer than he felt, most of them bouncing on their toes or pacing a little as they settled into their positions.

This time last year he'd been in Florida, at the Saints' spring training. Soaking up the sunshine and hyped on the excitement of moving to New York. Full of stupid levels of optimism and the conviction that he was going to set the Saints on fire.

He shook his head, remembering just how arrogant he'd been. He didn't miss being an idiot but he wouldn't mind getting back some of that conviction in his own ability to get this done.

First game of spring training with the Preachers. First

chance to start winning his way back to the Saints. He really didn't want to screw it up.

Around him, his new teammates were going through their own little pregame rituals. Each dealing with before-the-game nerves in his own way. Connor, twirling his bat as usual, caught his eyes and smiled wryly.

"You'd think it would get easier over the years," he said.

Finn shrugged. Connor, true to his word, had taken Finn out to a bar after the Saturday practice game. He hadn't blinked when Finn had asked for soda, not beer. And Finn had enjoyed himself. It was good to hang out with someone from the team who seemed interested in being friendly rather than competitive. He tapped his own bat against his calf. "If you're not nervous, you don't want it enough."

Every freaking single coach he'd ever had had drummed some version of that sentiment into his head. Maybe he'd taken the lessons a little too much to heart. He'd had plenty of time to learn new ways of dealing with stress over the last few months. Some of them helped. Some of them didn't and when that happened, he tended to head to the gym or run. Which was why Eva had found him in the gym last Sunday.

Eva.

He shook his head. He needed to think about the game, not Eva Harlowe. Who had looked incredibly good in her gym gear, even if said gym gear was plain black exercise tights and a faded Wonder Woman T-shirt. She'd moved easily on the treadmill, the glow of the exercise warming her pale skin, face determined as she'd run for an hour. He'd been thinking dirty thoughts about what it might be like to peel her out of those gym clothes after just a few minutes, which had made him crank up his own treadmill a few notches to chase those thoughts away before his body reacted to them.

It had helped for a while. She'd left almost as soon as she'd stopped running, which had made it clear that she wasn't keen to hang around and talk to him. So he was just going to have to keep his thoughts of toned legs and pale curves and curls of dark hair falling to frame those very blue eyes to himself.

Which apparently his brain was all too keen to do whenever he'd woken up over the last few nights, pregame tension making his sleep worse than usual as it always did for the first few weeks of the season. After that the travel and the schedule were usually enough to make him fall asleep within minutes of crawling into bed each night. But now without the added assistance of the beer or three he might have drunk before, it took longer. During which time his brain taunted him with thoughts of Eva.

Eva who apparently was sitting out there, somewhere in the stands again today. So if he screwed up, she would get to see him screw up. Wasn't that just the icing on the cake?

He could really live without that happening.

So the only thing to do was not screw up.

Three hours later, Finn was relieved that he'd managed to do just that. He'd made a couple of runs, caught one long hit from his position in the outfield—he hadn't been given a stint at first base this game—and generally played decent ball. The Preachers had been a little shaky, still settling into working together—after all, that was the whole point of spring training—but they'd won the day by two runs over the Sea Wolves in the end.

All in all, not too shabby. Maybe Eva would be impressed.

Idiot. He doubted Eva would be impressed by anything he did. She really didn't seem to like him much. He showered and packed up his gear. They had another game tomorrow and then it was back to Saratoga on Thursday ahead of their Friday-night and Saturday-afternoon series.

Coach Mannings had already given his postgame analysis, so there was nothing left to do but head back to the hotel. As he pushed open the door, he wondered if Eva was staying at the same place as them or if she was heading back to Saratoga already.

Then he stopped dead. The last person he expected to see standing outside the locker room was Oliver Shields.

Oliver tipped his chin. "Castro. That was a nice game."

"Thanks. What are you doing here?" Finn asked, keeping his tone light, even as his gut tightened. He and Oliver weren't exactly best friends, though their relationship was starting to improve. Shields was dating Amelia Graham, who was practically Finn's sister. That situation hadn't been welcome news last year and he'd handled it badly. Disastrously, in fact. Since he'd come out of the not-rehab he'd been doing his best to mend fences with Amelia. He'd said something fairly unforgivable to her but she seemed willing to forget it. More than he deserved.

The fact that Oliver was here was more than he deserved, too.

"How's your hand?" he asked.

Oliver hitched a shoulder. "Better." He held up his right hand. The pink scars running across it stood out starkly against tanned skin. His expression was cool as he watched Finn's face.

Finn tried not to wince. Oliver had injured his hand in a car accident, driving Finn home from a Saints party. Because Finn had been drunk. Finn had escaped the accident with a concussion and bruises. Oliver's hand had been sliced open. The injury had cost Oliver his chance to play in the divisional series with the Saints last year. It remained to be seen if it would cost him more than that. First basemen needed their hands. "That's good," he managed, gut tightening

He and Oliver didn't have the easiest relationship yet. Finn had been a dick last year, so focused on trying to take Oliver's first-base spot that he had made himself see Oliver as nothing more than an obstacle, instead of a teammate. It said something about Oliver and how much he cared for Amelia that he was willing to talk to Finn at all, let alone travel out of his way to watch a Triple-A spring training game.

It made it a little easier to like the man. What wasn't so easy was the fact that when Finn looked at Oliver, he still felt the burn of jealousy that Oliver was playing for the Saints and Finn wasn't. Even though he knew damned well he had no one to blame for that fact but himself. What did that say about him?

"Is Amelia here, too?" he asked, craning his neck to look past Oliver. Amelia was currently working in Hong Kong; Oliver had been with her there last time they'd spoken. But maybe he was back for spring training with the Saints.

"No," Oliver said. "But she sent me."

Finn tried not to smile at that. Amelia sending Oliver to check up on him was a sign that she hadn't completely written him off. And Oliver coming was proof that the guy loved Amelia. Because he definitely didn't love Finn. In fact, Oliver had pretty much told Finn he had his head up his ass last year after Finn and Amelia had fought. Finn hadn't been able to argue the point; in fact, Oliver's speech had been one of the things that had jolted Finn enough to make him see that he needed to change something or else blow up his entire life. The whole situation was complicated and Finn wasn't sure that Oliver turning up right now was what he needed to help him untangle the mess he'd made. Amelia would've been easier. But Oliver . . . well, Oliver was part of the things Finn needed to atone for while he was here at the Preachers. "I see," he said.

"She had meetings in New York this week and I had an appointment with my surgeon," Oliver continued. "She flew back this morning."

"You got the all-clear to play?" Finn asked.

Oliver flexed the hand in question again, expression hard to read. "I got the *we're happy enough with your progress that you can start getting back into training*."

"So you're heading to Florida?"

To the Saints. The envy flared again and he clenched his jaw.

A nod. "I'm just going to train for the first week or so and then Dan will ease me back into the roster. At least that's the plan." Oliver frowned, stretching his fingers again before dropping his hand back to his side. "No way to know for sure how it's going to hold up until I try."

"It'll be good," Finn said. He didn't know what else to say. "Did Amelia and Em get a chance to catch up while she was here?"

Oliver shook his head. "Emma couldn't make it over from Chicago."

Damn. It was bad enough that he'd screwed up his own relationship with Amelia; he flat-out hated that he'd driven a wedge between Emma and Amelia, too. Pity that he had no idea how to fix it. "Maybe next time."

That earned him a shrug and a shrewd look from dark eyes. "You had a good game. I told Don Mannings you were wasted out there in the outfield. He should get you on first base."

"Pietro's been playing first base a long time," Finn said, trying not to show his surprise. Oliver had to know that if Finn did well at first base here, he'd be a better candidate for that position at the Saints if he made it back.

"Yeah, and he hasn't made it to the bigs. You're better than he is."

"Not looking to rock the boat first thing," Finn said. "I need to earn my stripes."

"Learned your lesson, did you?" Oliver said with a wry smile.

"Let's just say I'm trying to demonstrate team spirit."

"Well, that's one approach. Might not be the one that gets you back to the Saints, though."

"Who says I'm trying to get back to the Saints?"

"If you're not, I'm telling Amelia that you need to go get your head checked out again. I mean, the Preachers are a good team and there are good people here but this isn't the majors. You've got more to offer than this."

Once upon a time he'd have been nothing but happy at that assessment. But his recent flame-out was still too fresh in his mind for him to be comfortable with the praise. Especially when it came from Oliver. "Didn't work out so good last time."

"That's where learning your lesson comes into it. Speaking of good people, is Eva here tonight?"

"You know Eva?" Finn tried to keep the bristle out of his voice. Oliver had been quite the ladies' man before he'd hooked up with Amelia, and Finn didn't exactly like the idea of him hanging out with Eva. Which was dumb. Damn, he was really trying to move away from getting into situations where he did dumb things. But Oliver apparently didn't notice his tone because he just nodded, his smile genuinely pleased this time.

"Sure. Maggie helped them start the youth program down here years ago. She used to drag me down to help out when I was around. Eva's cool. Her dad was a good guy, too."

"You knew her dad?" He still hadn't asked anyone exactly what had happened to Eva's father. Part of that whole not-rocking-the-boat thing.

"I met him a few times. It was tough on the whole

team after the accident." Oliver frowned. "Can't imagine what it's like to lose both your parents like that. Or have to turn around and raise three sisters at eighteen."

She'd what? He tried not to let the surprise show on his face. Eva had raised her sisters? For how long? Back at the diner, Jenna had told him that Eva had been eighteen when she'd started at the Preachers. He'd thought it had been through choice. But now it seemed more like necessity. He realized Oliver was waiting for him to say something. "Yeah, she's a smart gal," he managed, mind whirring. Jesus. No wonder everyone here was protective of Eva.

Oliver cocked his head. "Pretty, too."

Finn frowned, feeling that instinctive bristle again. "Yes." He managed to sound casual. Just.

"So don't be an idiot," Oliver said. "If you're trying not to rock the boat here, don't even think about it."

"Who says I was thinking about it?"

"Haven't met many guys from the team who haven't at least contemplated the lovely Miss Harlowe. None of them have had any success," Oliver added. "She doesn't date guys from the team."

This was not news. But maybe Oliver was a safer source of information than Connor. "Who does she date?"

Oliver shook his head. "I'd say that's her business."

So much for getting any information out of Oliver. But Ollie was right. Who Eva chose to date was her business. So the person he needed to raise the topic with—if he decided to go there—was Eva.

But that wasn't a subject to discuss with Oliver, who'd only try to talk him out of it. Talk about the pot calling the kettle black. Oliver had no issue dating people associated with his team. He'd dated Maggie Winters, daughter of the Saints' former owner, when he was younger; now he was dating Amelia, who was practically Finn's sister.

But before Finn could think of an easy way to change the subject, Eva walked around the corner of the corridor, headed toward the locker room. She wore tight black jeans and a Preachers jacket, her hair slicked back in a ponytail, her lips painted deep pink. A camera bag and a big black purse hung from one shoulder.

A whole lot of *happy to see you* surged through his body. Damn. He schooled his face to casual. "Hey, Eva."

Oliver turned at his words, a grin spreading across his face. When Eva saw him, an answering smile bloomed. Finn's breath caught. He hadn't seen her smile like that before, flat-out happy. Delighted even. It turned her from arresting to something several leagues past gorgeous. And God, he wanted to make her smile like that. At him. And then kiss her as she smiled. Double damn. He couldn't see how that was going to happen. Eva certainly hadn't directed that sort of expression at him.

There'd been a couple of maybe-too-long looks—or maybe that was just in his head—but she wasn't directing smiles of delight in his direction.

"Ollie, I didn't know you were coming," she said. She gave Oliver a quick hug, then stretched up a little to kiss his cheek. This time the surge of jealousy that rushed him was a hot flood that shook him a little.

Deep breath, Castro. Oliver was deliriously in love with Amelia. There was nothing between him and Eva.

"Last-minute decision," Oliver said. "I'm headed down to Florida tomorrow but thought I'd come and make sure you were still running things properly here."

"Don't I always?" Eva said, still smiling. "Did your bosses send you to check up on the Preachers or Finn?"

Oliver laughed. "I'm sure you've got Finn under control by now. Just like everyone else at the Preachers."

For a moment, something passed over Eva's face that Finn couldn't quite decipher. Her cheeks were pink from the cool night anyway but he thought the color deepened slightly as she glanced at him and then away.

Interesting.

"I don't need to be under control," he said. "I'm not looking to cause trouble."

"Turned over a new leaf? Good," Oliver said with a grin. "See that you continue to do so. It would be sad if I had to come back down to rescue you because you got your butt kicked by Eva here."

Finn gave Ollie the eye-roll that comment deserved. He would have given him the finger but that wasn't the kind of thing likely to convince Eva that he was a good guy.

Eva didn't react to the silent exchange, her attention firmly on Oliver. "You should have told me you were coming. You could have come up to the box."

"I like sitting in the stands when I get a chance," Ollie said. "Doesn't happen that often."

"Don't you get mobbed?" Eva asked.

"Nah. Wore a Yankees cap, dark glasses. No one is expecting to see me here. Particularly not now when I've been out of the country."

"Yeah. Hong Kong. I heard about that. How's that

going? And your hand?" Eva asked. "If you're headed to Florida, do you have the all-clear to play?"

"Close enough," Oliver said. "Time will tell." He shrugged a shoulder. "I was just about to ask Finn here if he's gonna buy me a late steak. Care to join us?"

Finn tried not to look too hopeful with this suggestion. Eva wouldn't have said yes if he'd asked her to dinner, but Oliver might succeed. But damn it, she was shaking her head, the fine silver hoops in her ears dancing.

"Thank you, but no," she said. "I'm heading back to Saratoga. Just squeaked a seat on a late flight. Someone has to keep things running back home, so I can't stay for tomorrow's game." She smiled, her gaze moving to Finn for a moment. "Nice game tonight."

He tried to keep his smile to a normal size. "Thanks. We did all right."

She nodded. "Let's hope it continues." She stood on tiptoe to reach Oliver's cheek for another quick peck. "It's good to see you. Tell Maggie hi for me and I hope your hand works out okay." With a quick nod at Finn, she disappeared into the locker room.

Oliver watched her until the door closed and then focused on Finn again. "Pretty girl."

Finn shrugged. No good could come of letting Oliver know exactly how pretty he thought Eva was or how she'd captured far too much of his attention. "Yes. I'm not sure she likes me very much, though."

"Don't tell me the Castro charm is failing you?"

He kept his face deliberately casual. "I'm not trying to charm her. Like I said, not looking to make trouble. I'm here to play ball."

One of Oliver's brows lifted. "So she's got you pegged as the young hothead who's just looking for his ticket back to the bigs? Always knew she was smart." He studied Finn for a moment. "I guess she's seen plenty of guys like you in her time. A girl who's seen it all before and who won't be taken in by any bullshit. Might be just what you need."

"Oh yeah, hooking up with the girl that most of the team seems to think of as their sister. That's not going to cause any trouble at all. What part of 'not looking to cause trouble' did you not understand?" He thought of the picture on her desk. Her and her sisters. Sounded like they'd had enough trouble in their lives already. So maybe the best thing to do for Eva and for him would be to really try to forget about the way her face kept floating through his mind. Then he remembered that smile.

Yeah, that wasn't going to happen.

"They're heee-eerre," Carly singsonged, sticking her blond head around the door of Eva's office as she passed by around noon on Thursday. Carly worked for the coaching staff, so she was usually the first to know when the team arrived back.

Eva pretended not to hear. Pretended to ignore the little hitch in her pulse at the thought that Finn was back.

Why should she care?

Yeah, right, her body retorted, *you care*. If her office had a window that looked out on the parking lot instead of toward the park, she probably would've had to get up and look, just to see if she could catch a glimpse of Finn.

Stupid body.

It really didn't know what was good for it. It had spent far too much time since Tuesday's game thinking about Finn bloody Castro and the way his lean body had moved on the field. She'd spent way too much time with him front and center in her viewfinder. The camera loved him.

He'd looked just as good in person, freshly showered and wearing dark jeans and a dark-green henley standing outside the locker room afterward. He'd made Oliver Shields look ordinary—and that was quite a feat given that Oliver was six-foot-plus of dark-eyed, dark-haired, olive-skinned gorgeous.

But Oliver might as well have been Quasimodo as far as she was concerned. Her body had been firmly focused on just one man.

Finn.

She gave her body the finger in her mind and turned her attention back to the travel bookings she was checking.

But flight numbers and hotel reservations had lost their fascination. Instead her brain was, once more, full of images of Finn. She'd downloaded the photos she'd taken at the game once she'd gotten home—very early Wednesday morning. She'd been kind of horrified to realize exactly how many of the shots had been of Finn.

Finn looking damned good in tight-fitting black baseball pants.

He looked damned good wielding his bat or running or even just standing in the outfield.

Damn the man. He just looked damned good all the time.

She'd whittled the photos down to a few of her favorites that she could keep for the team archives and the website. But she hadn't been actually able to make herself delete the extras of Finn. She'd just moved them off the memory card and onto her hard drive on her home computer. Where they kept calling to her. She'd found herself at her desk, scrolling through them three times last night before she'd turned the damned computer off at the wall and practically fled down to her basement to hit the treadmill. Talk about humiliating. She really needed to delete them. She *would* delete them. Tonight.

One of her jobs today would be to put some of the shots up on the team's website. She'd edited her choices last night and even though sometimes she just sent them to the IT guys to put up on the site, for some reason this time she wanted to do it herself.

Nothing to do with looking at the ones of Finn again. Nope. Definitely not.

"Hey, Eva."

She jumped, and then blushed. She didn't need to look up to know it was Finn. She'd only known him a week or so but she was already very familiar with the sound of his voice.

One deep breath. Take one deep breath and stop acting like a crazy person, she told herself. She did just that. Summoned what little cool she possessed and looked up.

"Finn. Hi. How was the trip back?"

"Six hours on a bus with forty-odd guys," Finn quipped. "What's not to like?"

She'd spent some time on the team bus over the years.

It wasn't exactly the most luxurious way to travel. But Ben Kelly, the Preachers' CEO, preferred to keep their travel budget tight—particularly for spring training. Gave him more money to spend on players, he said. So the bus was it for any trip that wasn't going to take a whole day or interfere with the game schedule. The guys moaned about it from time to time but mostly they seemed to enjoy it.

"You must have done all right with the traffic. The schedule had you back a bit later this afternoon, didn't it?"

"Yeah. But now you get the delight of our company earlier. Just when you were probably enjoying the lack of testosterone here."

"It does make a nice change," she said. "Though actually, I've never minded working with lots of men. It was all girls at my house."

She saw his face go still. Crap. Her stomach sank. He knew. They all gave her that look when they first found out about her parents.

"Did you need something?" she asked, trying to change the conversation before he made the inevitable sympathetic noises. She appreciated the sentiment but even now, after fourteen years, having people tell her they were sorry for her loss just made her sad all over again. Grief was a bitch.

Fortunately Finn seemed to accept her change of conversational tack. "Actually, yes," he said. "I saw you had your camera with you at the game on Tuesday."

"Yes. I usually do." Was she imagining things or were his cheeks actually a little red beneath the olive tones of his skin?

"Well, it's like this," he said. "Did you take any photos of me?"

He sounded kind of embarrassed. Which was strangely adorable.

"Keeping a scrapbook?" she asked, unable to resist teasing him. If only to make him squirm a little. Finn off balance was a Finn who hopefully wouldn't try to flirt with her. With her body still shaking a few internal pom-poms just because he was standing in her office again, she definitely didn't need flirting.

"It's not for me," he said, sounding horrified. "It's for my mom. She has this thing where she has to have a picture of my first game of the season. So I thought if you had one, I could send her a good one instead of her finding some random one on the Internet."

"It's only the first game of spring training," she said.

"Trust me," he said ruefully. "That counts in her book. She now does the start of spring training *and* the first game of the season."

"All the way back to Little League?" He was definitely the kind of guy who'd played Little League. She could tell the players who'd been doing it all their lives versus those who'd discovered the game a bit later. She wasn't sure how but there was just something about the way they moved on a field. Some tiny change of posture when they stepped out onto the turf. They got taller. Looser. Grounded. Like the space between the lines of a baseball diamond was where they became whole.

She'd watched it happen to Finn at the game. Seen the quick wide smile that had crossed his face as he'd jogged out to take up his place in the outfield for the first inning.

"All the way back. In fact, I'm pretty sure she has a picture of the first time I picked up a baseball bat. It was a Christmas present. Some terrible plastic thing."

She tried not to picture a very young boy with big green eyes and dark curly hair wielding a plastic bat. Finn all sweet and innocent. Unlike the man standing before her now. Who was pretty far from innocent, and despite his protests about not looking for trouble, she didn't think people changed so fast. It was only a few months since his crash and burn at the Saints. He might be trying but that didn't mean he'd succeeded. There'd been tension between him and Oliver after the game. She'd seen it in their body language even though their words had been civil. And Oliver's "turning over a new leaf" comment had hardly been the subtlest of warnings to her that Finn wasn't Mr. All-American Nice Guy. She had to remember that there was some darkness beneath the oh-so-pretty exterior. Remind herself why it would be a very good idea to keep the pretty firmly at arm's length.

"I'm sure I must have a shot of you," she said, trying to sound like she didn't know very well that there were. Hoping her face didn't betray her. Because darkness or not, his pretty was hard to ignore. Damn. She was hopeless.

Finn's face brightened. "Great. Can we look now? Do you have them here?"

Her camera bag was sitting on the side of her desk. Hard to miss. So she could hardly deny it. "Yes." Might as well get it over with. If she sent him away while she looked, she was only going to have to talk to him again anyway when she found the pictures. She leaned over and grabbed the camera bag then froze. For him to be able to see the pictures on her monitor he was going to have to come around the desk and sit next to her. Way too close.

She ignored the renewed waving of pom-poms in her veins.

Suck it up, Harlowe. She pointed to the visitor's chair. "Bring that around here and you'll be able to see." She busied herself extracting the memory card and slotting it into the card reader to distract herself from the unsettling nearness of him as he brought the chair around and sat next to her. God. He smelled good.

She made herself keep looking at the monitor. A few clicks of the mouse brought up the photos. She clicked through fast. He needed to be out of her office as soon as possible.

"Hey, slow down." He leaned toward the monitor, his shoulder brushing hers. The contact sent a spark of sensation down her arm, nerves flaring and warming, but she kept her eyes on the screen.

"These are really good," Finn said.

"It's mostly the lens." The telephoto lens had been a present from the players for her birthday when she'd turned twenty-five. It was worth more than her car and was one of her most prized possessions. She took a breath but that was a mistake because all it did was deliver a lungful of pure delicious Finn smell to her nose. Her fingers flexed around the mouse. "Good glass helps a lot."

Finn shook his head. "No. You've got a feel for the game." He tapped the screen where she'd captured Jeff Sampson leaping full-stretch sideways to catch a ball.

"This tells a story. That's more than a lens." He glanced sideways at her. "You're good."

"Thanks." She couldn't help smiling. Damn it, why did he have to be so likable?

So you can put on your big-girl panties and ask him out already? She could almost hear Jenna's exasperated tone in her head. Trouble was, if Jenna was the devil on her shoulder making suggestions that were sure to end in disaster, then the angel who should have been making the sensible opposing arguments was awfully quiet.

Grrrr.

She clicked through the photos, more slowly now, pausing when Finn made admiring noises at a few of them, but moving through them steadily until she came to the cluster of three that she'd kept of Finn. One at bat, his bat cocked over his shoulder and his expression intent as he waited for the ball, one of him diving for home plate, and one of him, with a grin on his face, spotlighted against the green grass by one of the tower lights, just looking like a goddamned handsome piece of man having a great time playing ball.

He laughed when he saw the last one. "That one."

"You don't want the one where you made the run?"

"No. Mom will say she can't see my face in that one. She'll like the one with the lights. She'll show it to all her friends." He rolled his eyes but he was smiling.

"Mothers are like that," she said. "Proud of their kids."

"Yeah," he said. Then he looked at the picture on her desk. "You must be proud of your sisters."

She waited for him to ask the next question. The one

everyone asked. About her parents. But he didn't. Damn it. She didn't want to like him. But she did. Double damn it. She tried to think of all the reasons why she shouldn't but all she could hear in her head was her devilish side saying, *Say something. Ask him out. Or at least something civilized to let him know you don't hate him.*

She was suddenly completely incapable of speech.

"I should get out of your hair." Finn sounded vaguely reluctant. He stood slowly, eyes back on the photos on her monitor. "You'll email me that shot?"

"Sure," she said, unable to come up with anything else to say. Her mind was full of an image of her trying to make a move and Finn politely turning her down. Horrifying.

Horrifying was good. Horrifying would keep her from doing something stupid.

She swallowed, tried to think, tried to make her mouth form another sentence that might keep him here a little longer, but he was already halfway out the door. As he closed it behind him, she dropped her head onto the desk, wishing desperately that she were anywhere but here. And that she weren't such a total coward.

Chapter Five

Later that day, Finn headed back toward the gym. He was feeling fairly good after the game but it was still early in the season and he hadn't played a full game for months, let alone two days in a row. Between that and the bus ride—God, the travel was the crappiest bit of playing baseball—his body had a few sore spots despite the training session Coach had put them through and the massage the team's physical therapist had given him that afternoon.

He probably needed to swim or, even better, take Eva's friend up on her offer of a free yoga class, but it was raining outside and a slow run on the treadmill and some stretches seemed the easier option. Then he might be able to go home and sleep properly. The bed in his new apartment still felt odd. Not his. But he was used to sleeping in strange beds. He'd get used to this one.

He might even stop wishing that he wasn't the only one in it eventually.

Dumb.

Maybe he should do just the opposite. Go out and find

some woman who'd be happy to go home with a baseball player, even a screwup like him. But whoever she was, she wouldn't be Eva.

Eva who had smiled at him this afternoon and made his whole day.

And didn't that just suck? Everything he found out about her made him more certain that she wasn't an option. So apparently he was just going to have to learn to handle the stressful side of his career in a healthier way. No partying. No Eva.

Treadmills and cold showers all the way.

Didn't that just sound fun?

He snorted at the thought and turned the last corner to see Eva coming out of the gym, face flushed, her hair piled up on her head. She had a Preachers hoodie on but it only reached her butt, leaving those very nice long legs, clad once again in running tights, on display. It couldn't hurt to look, could it? Just one quick look? He let himself drink her in for a second then pulled his eyes back up to her face before she'd even realized he was there.

She paused when she saw him. "Shouldn't you be home by now? You have a game tomorrow."

"Soon," he said. He didn't need her knowing that he was once again running to keep his demons—and his hormones—at bay. "Good run?"

She shrugged, pushed a stray piece of hair off her face. "Not bad."

Ha. He knew a fellow addict when he saw one. He wondered what exactly was driving Eva to chase a running high these days.

"Thanks for the photo." It had turned up in his email shortly after he'd left her office. Eva was definitely efficient. He wondered if that was her version of feeling like life was under control. You probably had to learn to be efficient if you were bringing up three sisters. "I sent it on to my mom. I'm sure she'll love it."

"It's no problem," she said, giving him another smile. Still not the full-on delighted version she'd bestowed on Oliver, but it was better than nothing.

"You're really good," he said. "You should ditch these guys and take up photography."

She went still, smile vanishing. "This club has been here for me when I've needed it."

Damn. Had he hit a sore spot? "How old were you when you came to work here?"

"Eighteen. And three weeks. My parents' accident happened one week after my eighteenth birthday."

He winced. So young. Too young. "I heard about that. I'm sorry."

She hitched a shoulder, eyes wary. "It was a long time ago."

"Not sure time makes much of a difference with that sort of loss." He couldn't imagine losing his parents or anyone close to him. Didn't want to. "Eighteen's really young to go to work full-time." Let alone take on raising three sisters.

"I needed to work to have any chance of being granted guardianship."

"There wasn't anyone else to help?" He'd always had his family close by. Relatives by the bucketload on both sides.

Her chin lifted. "No one who could take all four of us. My mom's sister has five kids of her own and my dad was an only child. I didn't want to lose my sisters."

No. He could see that. See the choice that she'd made. She probably hadn't thought twice about it. Knew that Em probably would have done the same thing for him if the unthinkable had happened. But one kid brother wasn't the same as three younger sisters. Eva had done a brave thing. A brilliant thing.

But what dreams of her own had she given up in the process? He moved a step closer, wanting to touch her, to somehow ease the hurt she'd borne. Was bearing still. Dumb. She didn't want his help. She'd done just fine without him. Raised her sisters. But they had all left home now and she was still here. Through choice? Or from wanting safety? He understood wanting that. Wanting to lock down fear and uncertainty. He'd walked that path himself. But fear and uncertainty were part of the deal. You just had to learn to live with them and make your life despite them. "Your sisters are lucky to have you."

"I'm lucky to have them," she said simply.

The certainty in her voice shook him. For her, it was simple. The people she loved had needed her and she put them first without hesitation. Done what needed to be done. Hadn't thought about herself. She was one of the good ones. He wanted to know more about her. And to figure out how to be the kind of guy she might think was one of the good ones, too.

It was cold when Eva closed the door to the admin wing behind her on Monday evening. The wind curled around her, finding the gap between her neck and her scarf with an icy touch. Spring was being indecisive about arriving. They'd had a couple of mild days over the weekend but now it was back to wintry weather. The team was heading for Richmond in the morning. Virginia. It was supposed to be warmer there. She was going to play hooky and follow the team. Spring really needed to get its act together. She shivered, pulled the wool tighter around her throat, and made a beeline to the parking lot, glad she'd swapped her heels for tennis shoes. Her car was in its usual spot. The only other car left in the lot was a battered dark-green truck. Finn's truck, a few rows away from hers. It annoyed her that she knew which car was his.

Annoyed her that seeing it made her heart beat a little faster, because it meant that he was still around somewhere.

She'd spent the weekend playing yet another round of *Should I or shouldn't I?* in her head. She should have been focusing on making her choice about whether to enroll in Isaac Haines's course or play it safe and choose a school in New York. Instead she'd cleaned again, Skyped with Lizzie and Kate, gone to yoga with Jenna. She'd been supposed to catch up with Audrey on Sunday for brunch but Audrey had called to cancel, saying she was sick. She'd sounded bad on the phone but had refused Eva's offer to bring soup over and fuss. After all, Audrey had Steve to look after her now. In fact all her sisters had boyfriends.

It was only Eva who was single and therefore able to obsess about Finn freaking Castro.

She glared at the truck.

Why was he even still here? Getting in another late workout before the team headed off again tomorrow?

Damn, now she was thinking about him all muscley and sweaty and half naked again.

She really had to figure out how to kill this crush. Kill it until it was dead and then put a stake through its heart for good measure. Either that or just do something desperate like kissing him.

That prospect made her heart flat-out pound.

She shivered and unlocked the car.

No more thinking about Finn Castro. She pulled the car door open with a bit more force than was necessary and tossed her bag into the passenger seat.

The man should come with a health warning. She'd never had a guy get under her skin this way without even touching her.

She didn't want to think about what might happen if she let him touch her.

Mostly because she knew just how damned good it would be.

She'd dreamed it half a dozen times. Woken hot and sweaty and aching.

Cursing Alex Winters for sending Finn to the Preachers.

Cursing Finn.

Cursing herself.

And now here she was, thinking about him again.

Damn it. Her key jabbed into the ignition and she turned it, preparing to put some distance between her and any reminder of Finn. But instead of the Volvo's usually polite engine noise, she got two sputtering coughs and then nothing.

"Oh hell no," she said to the car. "You are *not* dying on me."

The car, apparently, didn't care what her opinion on the subject was. It remained stubbornly lacking in working engine sounds. Turning the key only produced a dull clicking noise.

"Fuck." She thumped the steering wheel in frustration. Stupid car. Sure, it was fifteen years old and had way too many miles on it, but did that give it any right to abandon her in her hour of need? She pulled out her phone and dialed AAA. Fought the urge to swear again when the dispatch guy told her it would be at least a thirty-minute wait. The car was freezing.

Turning on the heater switch produced just as much nothing as turning the key had. No heat. Not even a hint of something warmer than icy. Which made sense because the heater required the engine. Or the battery. Or something. She didn't know much about cars, other than how to check the oil and put air and gas in and find good cheap mechanics. She fought the urge to scream *fuck* again. Instead she pulled the keys from the ignition savagely.

Okay. New plan. Go back to the office for twenty-five minutes then come down and see if the AAA guy had arrived. Hopefully it was just a dead battery and she could be on her way again in no time. She climbed out of the car and slammed the door with another muttered curse.

"What did the poor car do to you?" Finn's voice came from behind her.

She jumped about a foot in the air. Then whirled, heart hammering at about four thousand beats per minute, jabbing her finger in his direction. "Do *not* sneak up on people at night in a parking lot."

He held up his hands. "Right. My bad. Sorry. But my question stands."

"It won't start. I think the battery died," she said without thinking, then kicked herself mentally. Fright had apparently knocked all the sense from her head. "It's okay, I already called AAA," she added hurriedly. The last thing she needed was Finn trying to be all gentlemanly and helping her out. Even if he did look edible standing there in a faded gray sweatshirt that stretched the remnants of CHICAGO in big blue letters across his chest and ancient jeans, his dark hair damp and curling slightly in the night air. He didn't look the slightest bit cold.

That was because he was young and male. She glared at him. "You don't need to wait."

"Yeah?" he said, folding his arms. "How long until AAA can get here?"

"Thirty minutes."

"Which means more like an hour. Okay. We can wait in my truck."

Get into his car with him. Oh no. Not going to happen. "I can wait inside."

"You can't see the parking lot from your office. What if you miss the AAA guy?"

"Fine. I'll stay in my car."

"You said the battery died. You'll freeze with no heat. My truck is the sensible option. Plenty of room and I have a full tank of gas so we can keep the engine running."

"You don't have—"

"There is no way I'm leaving you to wait here alone

at eight at night." His chin stuck out slightly, its perfectly carved angles declaring that no argument was going to be entered into.

She sighed. "Fine. You can wait with me." She rubbed her hands together. It was really cold. She was adding the weather gods to her list of things that were fucking with her.

"Good. And since I don't want to freeze out here—for one thing, Coach will kick my ass if I get sick—we'll sit in my truck."

"Fine," she repeated. It wasn't fine. Not even close. But she didn't see how she was going to get out of it. The options were awkwardly hanging out with him in her office and potentially missing the AAA guy—which would only extend the process or, worse, result in her having to let him drive her home—or sitting awkwardly with him in his car. With only a few feet between them. But heck, it was only for thirty minutes. It couldn't be that bad, could it? She could put up with anything for thirty minutes. Even if the thing was restraining her hormones in the presence of Finn Castro.

She'd been doing it for a couple of weeks already. She was a big girl. Not stupid enough to throw herself at a man with *bad idea* written all over him.

Finn was already walking toward his truck. She followed him, wishing horrible things on whoever had designed her Volvo and was obviously the cause of this mess. He held the passenger door for her and she shot him a look as she climbed in.

"Seriously?"

"Manners maketh the man," he said with an evil grin.

She pulled the door shut with a little more force than was necessary and then made sure she slid as far toward it as she could while he walked around the car to his side. Put as much space between them as possible. That would be the smart thing to do.

Finn put the keys in the ignition and the engine purred to life. A few seconds later heat started pouring out of the vents, and she tried not to moan in pleasure. She held her hands up to the vent for a minute until her fingers warmed and then she sank back in the seat, happy to be out of the cold.

For about five seconds until her brain, no longer distracted by being half frozen, registered the fact that Finn Castro was sitting about a foot away from her. The whole goddamned car smelled like him. She didn't know what cologne he wore but it was a good one. Something warm and dark. Sexy. But he could probably have doused himself in anything and still smelled good.

She wanted to breathe it in deeper. But that would be weird. Instead she tried to think of something to talk about before being here with him in the dark and the intimacy of such a small space short-circuited her brain and her common sense altogether. She shifted on the seat a little. Baseball. That was what he was here for, right? It was the one subject that never seemed to get old around her, even though there were times when, despite her love for the Preachers, she thought she might scream if she had to talk about baseball for one more second. Baseball was safe.

"Ready for the game tomorrow?" It sounded inane. But inane was better than insane.

He turned a little in his seat, so that he was facing her. It made the gap between them slightly smaller, and she felt her grip on sane slide a little farther toward the edge. She shifted again, looked at him briefly, then away again.

"It should be a good one. I've never been to Richmond before."

"It's nice," she offered. God. She sounded like an idiot.

"So I hear. Guess I'll have a few chances to find out this year."

"Are you still in the outfield?"

He nodded. "Don said he's going to give me a swing at first base sometime soon. But I guess I'm still the new guy. Gotta earn my place."

"Keep your head down and work hard and you'll get what you want?"

His head tilted, eyes looking suddenly darker. "I generally believe in going after what I want, yes. When it's a good idea."

Her heart stuttered a little. Was he still talking about baseball? "Is first base not a good idea?" Then realized that there was a whole other way that sentence could be interpreted. A fact that, judging by the grin stretching across Finn's face, wasn't lost on him.

"First base is always a good idea," he said. "In fact, I'm fond of all the bases." His voice was a little deeper.

She felt her cheeks go hot. Please, God, let him not flirt with her here. "You know what I mean." Time to get the conversation back to safer ground.

"Hey, can't blame a guy for taking a swing if you send a ball like that over the plate."

God. He was definitely flirting.

"I was talking about baseball," she said firmly. Which would probably be more believable if she weren't blushing. Pale skin was the worst.

He studied her a moment, then shook his head. "You should never play poker."

"Excuse me?"

His smile was delighted. "I've been reading you wrong, Eva Harlowe. All this time I thought you didn't like me. But now I'm thinking perhaps the opposite is true."

Busted. *Crap.* She should get out of the car. Leave. Before she did something stupid. Oh but he made her want to be stupid. Made her want to slide across the bench seat and admit the truth. See if he tasted as good as he smelled and looked. Ease the ache and the itch that filled her every time she heard his voice. Oh, she wanted to.

Would it really be such a bad idea? To just give in and let go and find out what she'd been missing?

But she wouldn't. She curled her hands into fists as though she could hold on to reason and logic. "I think you need to think again." She managed the cool tone she wanted. But she couldn't manage to meet his eyes while she said it.

"Oh, I've thought plenty. Every time I see you, I think all kinds of things. But I thought I was alone in that particular dilemma. But I'm not. Am I?"

"I don't know what you're talking about."

"Liar." He laughed softly.

Her chin came up. She met his eyes. "I'm not a liar."

"Then admit it."

"Admit what?"

"That there's something here." He gestured between them, his fingers almost brushing her arm.

She shivered. He laughed again. "Your body isn't such a good liar."

"My body isn't in charge."

"Oh really? Care to bet?"

"What are you talking about?"

"A wager. If you win, we never have to talk about this again. If that's what you want."

"It's what I want." Those might be the least convincing four words she'd ever spoken. If she really didn't want to talk about this . . . to see where it might lead . . . then she'd be out of this truck and heading for her office already. But her resistance was fast vanishing. She couldn't look away from Finn. Couldn't move away from him. "What do I have to do to win?"

"Come over here and kiss me. Then tell me there's nothing here."

God, he was a cocky bastard. She didn't know how he was so sure of himself. After all, he'd embarrassed himself publicly and then lost his place at the Saints. Outcast in Saratoga Springs. He'd had the rug yanked under him and yet he still seemed to have a solid footing. She'd had her rug yanked out from under her fourteen years ago, and some days she still wasn't sure she'd ever find solid ground again. Her loss was bigger and she'd been younger but still. She wanted to know how he did it. What kept him standing, even if he was faking it. Wanted to know if maybe, just maybe, he could help her feel the same way.

But mostly she wanted to know what it would be like to kiss him.

And with him sitting there looking at her like that and smelling so damned good, she really had no idea anymore what her objections had been. He was the one suggesting this madness. So there went the problem of thinking he'd laugh at her if she made a move. There'd been other excuses in her head as well but they had apparently vanished.

She leaned a little closer. Just a little. Finn sat still, looking relaxed. But his eyes were steady on hers, the invitation clear.

One little kiss. It might just get him out her head. Maybe he would be a terrible kisser. Then she'd be cured.

"One kiss and that's the end of it?"

He nodded. "If that's what you want."

"Pretty sure of yourself, aren't you?"

"No," he said. "I think you're a tough nut to crack, Eva. But that doesn't change the fact that I want to kiss you. That I've been wanting to kiss you for a while now."

"You have?" She heard her voice go breathy and weird. She was used to the fact that she thought about him. But somehow she hadn't thought about the reverse. About the fact that maybe he thought about her, too. That he might want her. The thought fogged her brain.

He nodded. "Yes."

There should be a response to that. Something a

sensible adult would say. But the sensible adult part of her was melting away with her objections. Turning to steam, perhaps. Something heated and insubstantial that was no help at all in maintaining any resistance to him. "Oh."

That made him smile again. Which was good. That smile was good. The man had good lips. Lips she really *really* wanted to get closer to.

"So is it a deal?" Finn said.

"Okay." Two syllables. That was an improvement. She waited, not sure what happened next. Finn, on the other hand, seemed to know what to do. He slid closer on the seat—God bless bench seats—and suddenly his hands were cupping her face, and he leaned in and kissed her.

Deep down, she'd known it was unlikely that the kiss would be bad. What she hadn't banked on was just how good it would be. It was as if someone had given the man a manual on precisely how to kiss her. His mouth on hers felt both strange and familiar. Hot and sweet and just insistent enough to make her wrap her arms around his neck and pull him a little nearer, heedless of the awkward angle.

Finn's hands dropped to her waist and caught her closer as he deepened this kiss. Her mouth opened and his tongue met hers. The taste of him hit her like a shot of whiskey, taking her over, until she was dizzy. So good. So damned good all she could do was let herself give in. Fall into the kiss. Let him take her over.

Finn's hands clutched her harder but didn't move. Didn't stray. Didn't touch the parts of her starting to ache and want as he kissed her. Instead he just kissed her. Kissed her like a teenager making out in a car for the first time. Hot and hungry.

Though he kissed far better than any teenage boy she'd kissed ever had.

Kissed her like she was the only thing in the world.

Made the world disappear, in fact, with each move of his mouth on hers, each little touch of his hands, restless at her waist. There was only her and Finn and the kiss.

Until a set of headlights lit up the car like a searchlight.

The unexpected beam made her freeze, brain lust-fogged and slow. Who was coming to the parking lot at this time of—oh crap. "It's the AAA guy," she managed to say.

Finn blinked at her. He looked just as mind-wiped as she felt, his breath coming fast. "What?"

She pulled away, realized all the windows were completely fogged up. God. They really were acting like teenagers. "The AAA guy. For my car. I have to go." She reached for the door handle.

He put his hand on her arm. "Wait."

"I need my car fixed," she said. It was true but it was also an out. A way to get clear so she could figure out how she felt about what had just happened. Her body was making it clear that it was really happy about it— or rather really annoyed that it wasn't still happening— but she needed her brain to step up to the plate now.

"We need to talk about this." Finn said.

"Not now. Tomorrow."

"I'm on the plane to Richmond tomorrow."

"Then when you get back." She pulled her arm free.

Finn shook his head. "No. That's too long. You'll think yourself into this being weird if we wait that long." He nodded toward her car. "I could follow you home."

Oh no. That wasn't going to happen. If Finn set foot in her house tonight then she was pretty sure that they'd end up sleeping together. Which would be freaking fantastic based on the kisses but she really wasn't ready for what came after. "No. Not tonight."

"Breakfast then," he said, the no-argument tone back in his voice. "I'll bring something to your place."

"We could go out."

"Not sure that this is the sort of conversation you want to have in public."

Outside the car, the AAA guy leaned on his horn and she jumped again. "Okay. Breakfast."

That earned her a grin that made her wonder why the hell she was getting out of the car. "Good. Now, one last thing."

"What?"

"You'd better tell me your address."

Chapter Six

He really hated AAA, Finn decided as he stared at Eva's front door at seven o'clock the next morning. If the AAA guy hadn't turned up when he had, then maybe Finn would already be inside Eva's house, instead of standing out here, hoping like hell she hadn't made up her mind overnight to kick him to the curb. He hitched the bag that held bagels and yogurt and all the other things he'd grabbed at the market and tightened his grip on the cardboard tray holding the two coffees. He'd gone for black. Eva seemed liked a black-coffee kind of gal. Even if he was wrong about that, then hopefully she'd have milk or whatever she liked to add in her house.

Quit stalling.

Nothing for it. He swallowed against a mouth gone dry. God. He really hoped she hadn't come to her senses overnight. Kissing her had been amazing. More than amazing. He'd wanted to pull her closer and closer, had wanted to pull her clothes off and find out if the rest of her tasted as good as her mouth. He'd been hard as a rock and it had taken a large chunk of his willpower to keep things to just kissing. Kissing that had been amazing but not enough. At least he'd managed to keep enough of a grip on things not to go any farther and scare her off in the process.

He'd known she'd was as into it as he had been. Until that damned horn had blown and she'd bolted from the car like he was a serial killer.

Shit.

He lifted the bag holding the food and reached toward the doorbell. Eva's house was bigger than he'd expected. A family house rather than a place he'd expect one woman to live in alone.

Then he realized it just might be her family house. One her parents had left her.

She'd definitely have the home-ground advantage here.

So he'd just have to be on his game. Remind her how it had been back there in his truck before the world had intruded.

He leaned on the doorbell and the door swung open so fast he wondered if she'd been standing on the other side, knowing he was there and just waiting for him to ring the bell.

She was dressed for work, hair pulled back, makeup in place. She had a dark-gray dress on—one of those sleek-fitting office things women wore—and a deep-pink cardigan over it. She looked far more pulled together than he felt. Until he noticed that her feet were stuck into blue slippers that had googly eyes at the toes.

"Cookie Monster slippers?" he said. "Good choice."

"What?" She looked down at her feet then blushed. "Crap. I forgot."

"Hey, I like Cookie Monster. I am pro-cookie in general. Can I come in?" He lifted the bag of food. "Breakfast as promised."

Her expression went unreadable and for a moment he thought she was going to say no. Then she stepped back and waved him in.

So that was good. Kind of like making it to first base. Safe. Temporarily.

He followed her through the house, not noticing much about it other than the walls were all pale and there were lots of pictures hung on them. Photos mostly.

Had Eva taken them?

Time enough to figure that out after they'd talked.

The kitchen was big, oak cabinets lining the walls. More framed photos crowded the parts of the walls not covered in cabinets. He dumped the food on the counter, held out the tray of coffee. "They're both black, I didn't know what you liked."

"Black is good," she said and took one. "I have milk, if you want it. And sugar."

"No, I'm good." He put the other coffee down and unpacked the bag. The table, which matched the cabinets and looked well used, had plates and a couple of bowls and silverware set out. "I brought bagels and stuff. Yogurt. Granola."

"Sounds good."

She didn't move toward the table. In fact, she looked like she was deciding whether or not to flee the room.

"Hey," he said, moving closer. "You're not supposed to be freaking out. It's just breakfast."

"Is it?"

Two short words shouldn't be able to shatter his good

intentions. But they did. He moved closer. "I thought breakfast was what we agreed to. Unless there's something else you wanted?"

Her eyes darkened, the blue turning to drowning midnight as her pupils flared. "I—"

"God, Eva." He couldn't think straight, not with her standing there, looking at him like she wanted to eat him up. "I swear I didn't come here to do this."

"Do what?"

"This." He pulled her close, put his mouth on hers, and kissed her again. Felt her mouth open to him and fought to not go too crazy when she slid her tongue against his and kissed him back.

And once again kissing her meant losing his mind. She was delicious. Drugging. Hot and soft and warm against him.

This time there was no awkward angle, no car seat to get between them, and he pulled her into him, hand hard at her back so he could feel her against his cock, which was wide-awake and ready for something more than breakfast.

But no, that would be crazy. He'd come here to eat, to talk. Not to do this.

He should stop.

But he didn't want to.

Eva's hand sliding down to yank his T-shirt up and sliding smoothly across his belly seemed to suggest that she didn't want him to stop, either.

He wanted to touch her skin, too. But her clothes didn't give him many options to get to her. Not without trying to undress her completely. He pulled his face back and buried his lips in the curve of her neck so he could breathe her in. When his teeth scraped gently across the muscle there he felt her shiver and clutch at him and he went a little crazier.

Lifted her and smiled when her legs wrapped around his waist without hesitation. He raised his head, managed to spot a sofa through the open door at the far side of the kitchen. Flat surface. Good idea.

He carried Eva out of the room and down onto the couch, rolling on top of her, pressing his hips down into hers.

The pleased moan that escaped her made him do it all over again.

God. He wanted her. Wanted to take her right here on the couch but some small speck of sanity remained. Too fast and she'd have the perfect excuse to run. He pulled back. Ran his hand down her hip, over the nubby fabric of the dress until he hit flesh at her thigh.

No stockings. There was a God.

A God who'd made Eva perfectly. His fingers slid up her thigh, tingling from the contact with warm, soft skin. She shivered but she didn't protest. In fact, she did the opposite. Arched up to him, shifted her legs farther apart.

So he kept going. Let his fingers hit lace and silk and slip under them. Kissed her while he touched, while his fingers slid into heat and slide and soft. Kissed while she moved against him and urged him on.

Kissed her while she suddenly clamped around him and came, eyes going wide and shocked as she called his name.

* * *

When Eva opened her eyes, Finn was staring down out her, looking almost as surprised by what had just happened as she was.

"Hey," he said, lifting his weight off her. His hand was on her leg now. Good. She maybe had some hope of being able to think if his hand was only touching her leg.

"Hey," she said back. One-syllable words. Those were easy. Unlike what had just happened. That was . . . fantastic. And fantastically complicated. Still breathing hard, she sat up and he moved back, to the free end of the sofa.

"Are you okay?" he asked.

That was a hell of a question. Her body was more than okay, the ripples of the aftershock of the orgasm still moving through her. But the fact that she'd just had an orgasm thanks to Finn was a bit of a . . . well, *mindfuck* was the term Jenna would use. It seemed as good as any. "Yes," she said cautiously.

He looked relieved. "Okay. I swear, that's not what I had in mind when I invited myself around for breakfast."

She managed a smile. "You know, some girls would get insulted at the implication you didn't want to get into their pants."

"I didn't say *didn't want to*. Just that I had no intention of acting on that particular impulse." He smiled, the expression tentative. "At least, not today."

"Cocky," she murmured.

"Hopeful," he countered.

If he was cocky, he'd just proved that his faith in his abilities was well founded. The man had moves. Maybe he was six years younger than her but apparently he'd learned a lot in his twenty-six years. She wasn't sure she'd ever come that fast for a guy before. The thought—and the memory of how she'd just clung to him and let him have his way—made her face heat.

Damn.

"Well, I will say it beats granola for breakfast," she managed.

Finn laughed. "Good to know. But that brings us back to what happens next?"

"Next?"

"With us—this." He gestured between them like he had in his truck last night. "I think we've gone a bit beyond that silly bet last night."

Yup. It would definitely be hard for her to claim that she didn't like him now. "Seems as though we did."

"So as far as I can tell the question is, are you looking to go any farther?"

The easy thing to do—the smart thing—would be to lie. To say no. To send him on his way before this got out of control.

But there was no version of her that was going to say that right now. Still, that didn't mean she needed to leap into crazy without some ground rules. "I like you," she said.

"Why do I feel like there's a *but* coming?"

"Because there is. I like you. You like me. It's obvious that we have some chemistry going but honestly we don't make sense."

"I don't understand."

"Look at us on paper. I'm older than you. You're hot. You're going to be rich and famous. You're going to be leaving." She wasn't going to bring up the fact that she was leaving, too. He didn't need to know that. Not yet. It was enough that he understood this would be temporary. That way, no harm, no foul. She could walk away unscathed and start the next chapter of her life.

"I'm here now."

"Yes." She nodded. "So what I think we should do is enjoy it while you're here. But when you go it's over."

He blinked. "You want an expiration date?"

"I want uncomplicated. You should want uncomplicated, too."

"Why?"

"You said you didn't want any trouble." And she wanted to believe he'd been telling the truth about that. To know that there was a good guy beneath the issues he'd had last year. Otherwise this was a really bad idea.

"I want you," he said, voice turning stubborn.

"You don't know me. I don't know you. This could burn out in a week." She doubted it. He wasn't a crush now, a secret thing that existed only in her imagination. Not now that she'd kissed the flesh-and-blood version. Not now that she'd had his hands on her body. But that was a problem she'd have to deal with later. Right now, when she couldn't yet walk away, all she could do was try to minimize the inevitable damage.

"And if it doesn't?"

She steeled herself. "Then we have until the end of the season. That's the deal, Finn. Take it or leave it."

Finn ran a hand through his dark hair, looking at her as if she were crazy. Then he nodded. "Fine. Maybe you're right. Maybe this is doomed to burn out or I'm too young or you're too old or whatever crazy story you have going on in your head. But you can't pretend you don't want me now and I'm sure as hell not going to pretend that I don't want you. So great, you think you can walk away at the end of the season, I'm fine with that. But I have two conditions."

"Conditions?" What the hell? Though she'd just set down some rules, so she didn't have much ground to stand on if he wanted rules of his own. As long as they weren't crazy.

"Yes." He leaned in closer, put his hand behind her head, kissed her hard. Then pulled back again. "One, no other guys but me."

She couldn't imagine juggling two guys at once. Couldn't imagine why anyone would want to if one of those guys was Finn. "That's fine with me. Same goes for you. What's the other one?"

"No sneaking around. We do this out in the open."

"What?"

He stepped back. "You heard me. I'm not going to be your secret midnight booty call. If we do this, then people need to know about it."

"Why?" She didn't know exactly how she'd thought this would work but she hadn't expected Finn to take a hard line on outing them to the team.

"Sneaking around never works. Someone always finds out and gets pissed off. We might as well deal with the pissed-off part up front. Then it's done. Secrets are just complicated." He stopped, studied her a moment. "Is there someone in particular likely to get pissed off?"

"Not that I can think of." She'd never dated one of the Preachers. Didn't mean she was oblivious to the fact that there'd been a few who'd carried a torch over the years. But that was their problem, not hers. She'd never encouraged any of them.

Finn's head tilted, green eyes turning a little darker. "Heard a rumor that Greg asked you out a time or two."

"Did you also hear that I said no?"

He looked smug. "Yes. But that doesn't mean he's not going to be annoyed."

Greg was a good guy. But not her type. It had been over a year since he'd last asked her out. She hadn't thought about it for at least that long. Damn. What had Finn heard? Was Greg still interested in her? Surely not. "Isn't that an argument for not telling everyone? At least not straightaway? He is the captain, after all. I thought you were Mister Team Player."

"I am. So I'm not going to lie to my teammates. If this is going to be a problem for any of them, then best to get it out in the open and dealt with straight off."

"So, what, you want to march in there today and tell everyone that we're dating?"

"Not necessarily but I don't want to hide it. I want to be able to take you out. To tell people the truth if they ask."

The thought of everyone at the Preachers knowing made her cringe a little. She'd spent a long time keeping her private life—what little of it there was—private. She didn't want to be the center of attention. It felt like everything was going too fast. They'd kissed for the first time last night and now he wanted to tell the world? She hadn't even told anyone at the Preachers that she was planning on leaving at the end of the season yet and she'd been planning that for two years. "I need some time to think."

"I'm not back from Richmond until Thursday."

"I know," she said.

"Is that long enough?"

This time the answer wasn't so easy to come by.

At nine p.m., Eva's phone buzzed. She was sitting at her desk, flicking through photos on her computer. She'd planned to watch a movie but when she'd gone to curl up on her sofa, she'd been overtaken by memories of Finn's hands on her that morning and had fled to the desk instead.

She picked up the phone, expecting it to be one of her sisters, only to see Finn's name at the top of the message. He'd put his number in her phone before he'd left. But she hadn't really expected him to call so soon.

Blue, the message said.

Is that code?

You said we didn't know each other. Thought maybe we could change that while I was on the road.

By sending each other colors?

Think of it like Jeopardy! *I'll send you an answer. You have to guess the question. If you do, then you get to send the next one.*

Shouldn't you be out bonding with the team?

Who says I'm not?

Please tell me you're not sitting in a bar texting?

She had visions of one of the guys grabbing Finn's phone and discovering who he was talking to.

No, we had dinner earlier. Coach read us the riot act because we lost so we're all back in our rooms early.

No party like a Preachers party.

Something like that. So, you want to keep me from watching bad TV?

She should probably say no. Until she knew what she wanted, whether she was going to say yes to his conditions, it would be kinder to keep her distance. But who could resist finding out more about Finn?

Okay, she sent.

Great. So, blue.

Favorite color?

Nope. :D

Do I get another guess?

Hmmm.

Hmmm isn't an answer.

Seeing as you're new at this, I'll take it easy on you for now. Two guesses. Though maybe I'll take bribes for extra guesses.

Bribes?

One kiss per question.

She laughed at that and then typed, *Keep on dreaming.*

You're the one begging for extra guesses.

Color of your first car.

!!! We have a winner. Didn't think you'd get that. Your turn.

What did she want him to know? Maybe it was better to keep it safe for now.

Hot dogs.

Easy. Favorite ballpark food.

Right.

Daniel Craig.

Favorite James Bond?

Yes! Do you like action movies?

Sometimes. Depends on how hot the lead is. Daniel Craig meets the criteria :D.

So you like blonds?

Would you dye your hair if I say yes?

Hell, no. Been there, done that.

You dyed your hair blond?

High school girlfriend talked me into it. Bad idea. Not so much blond as neon orange. My mom almost fainted. Then she marched me to the hairdresser to have it dyed back. But not before my sister took a picture and managed to send it to most of the kids in school. You can stop laughing now.

Not laughing. She typed with unsteady fingers, glad he couldn't hear her giggles.

Liar.

Remind me to work out how to bribe your sister to send me that picture.

Trust me, teen me was not impressive.

Now who's lying? He was too gorgeous to have been a gawky teen. Scrawny maybe, or lanky perhaps, given he had been playing ball since he was tiny. But she'd bet a lot of money that he'd been a good-looking kid. The kind of guy who'd had his pick of the popular girls.

Still was. Which made her wonder again what exactly he was doing spending his night texting with her.

Tell you what. I'll show you mine if you show me yours, came the next message.

Unless her memory was failing, she'd already shown him hers this morning.

No deal. Next answer.

It's your turn.

She'd lost track.

Why don't you just ask me something?

That makes it too easy. Unless you're going to tell me your secrets.

Not sure I have many secrets to tell. Doubtful that he'd ask her about going to photography school. Other than that, she wasn't that mysterious.

Everyone has secrets, Eva.

Not sure I want to commit mine to writing.

Can I call you?

She hesitated. She wanted to talk to him. To hear his voice. But that was scary in itself.

It's getting late. You have another game tomorrow.

It's not even 9:30.

You need your beauty sleep.

Says who?

Aren't you planning on sweeping me off my feet with your dazzling good looks?

I thought I already had :)

Don't rest on your laurels, Castro.

You want to be dazzled?

She was already dazzled, that was the problem.

Maybe. But tonight, what I mostly want is sleep. Good night, Finn.

Good night. Have some interesting dreams. You can tell me about them tomorrow.

Worry about winning the game.

And then you'll tell me? Deal.

He was ridiculous. And charming. She shook her head at the phone. *Good night, Finn.*

'Night. TTY tomorrow.

Her phone didn't buzz again and she didn't know whether she was relieved or annoyed that he hadn't kept trying. She put the phone down, then shoved it into a desk drawer so she wouldn't be tempted to text him again. Charming or not, sexy as hell or not, she had to decide if she was willing to agree to what he wanted. To complicating her life just when she wanted it to be uncomplicated, to stay how it was until she was ready to change. She wasn't sure Finn realized what might happen at the Preachers if they went public. She'd never dated anyone from the team. It was going to cause friction. And then, at some point, she was going to have to confess she was also leaving. It all seemed too hard, mind-blowing orgasms or not. Maybe it would be easier to just say no.

Chapter Seven

"Haven't you worn out your thumbs yet?" Connor asked as he dropped into the seat beside Finn in the small airport lounge and put a travel mug of coffee on the table between them. Finn shook his head and slid the phone into the pocket of his team jacket.

"Just checking out the results from this week's games." He'd actually been checking for a text from Eva but that was information that no one else needed to know yet. She hadn't sent anything last night after telling him she was having dinner with her sister. The lack of communication had him wishing they'd been flying back straight after the game instead of this morning. He wanted to see her before she did something dumb like talking herself out of giving them a go.

"How are the Saints doing?"

"You don't know?"

Connor leaned back in the chair, rubbing at his right shoulder. "Not much chance I'm going back to the majors. So nope. I don't start my morning checking the results from spring training."

Finn wasn't sure what to say to that, which made Connor roll his eyes. "Kid, there is more to life than baseball."

"So people keep telling me," Finn said. "Not sure I believe 'em yet."

"Give it another ten years, see how you feel. The appeal of mornings that don't start with ice packs and physical therapy will grow on you." Connor rolled his shoulder again and grimaced.

"Shoulder bothering you?"

"It always bothers me. Pro tip, try not to blow out your rotator cuff."

"Wasn't planning to."

"None of us plans to," Connor said. He reached for the coffee. "That's the bit that sucks about sports. Too many things you have no control over that can take you out of the game."

He didn't want to think about things that might take him out of the game. He'd already brushed too close to that at the Saints. If they hadn't given him this second chance, he could be out of baseball now. "Did you get out of the wrong side of the bed this morning, old man?" This conversation was too serious for eight a.m.

"Sorry, am I keeping you from your adoring Facebook fans or something?"

"No. I'm good. Are you?"

Connor grinned. "Sure. My shoulder isn't a tragedy, Finn. It recovered enough to let me play Triple-A. So for now, that's the plan."

"You thought about what comes after?"

"From time to time. We old guys do that. Not sure. Staying put in one place for a while sounds good."

"Find a gal, settle down?" Connor, unlike most of the other older guys, wasn't married.

"Something like that. Speaking of gals, how's it going with Eva? Made your move yet?"

Okay, this was a topic that he definitely wasn't going to talk about. Not when he didn't know if there was anything to talk about. "No comment."

"No comment? What's the matter, did she kick you to the curb already? Damn, Castro. Thought you had more game than that." Connor slurped more coffee, smirking.

"No comment," Finn repeated.

"Maybe she wants more than a pretty face," Connor said.

Maybe she did. Finn had no idea what Eva wanted, why she was so adamant they could only be temporary. But he was going to find out.

Eva was on the phone when Carly breezed past and delivered the "team's back" news before she kept going on to wherever she was going.

Finn's back.

That was what Eva heard. Finn was back and she was going to have to tell him no. It was too hard. Too crazy. She'd spent half the night wrestling with her decision.

He was a good guy. He kissed like a devil. But he wasn't the right choice when all she wanted was temporary. Hell, if he was still wrestling with whatever had driven him into disaster last season, maybe he just wasn't the right choice for anyone. So he wasn't the one for her.

That was her decision.

So why did she feel so reluctant to face him and tell him that?

She managed to keep track of the phone conversation, supplying the details that the person on the other end was asking for on autopilot.

The team's trip to Richmond had gone okay. One loss. One win. They'd won by more than they'd lost, so that was good, too. The team was coming together. Don Mannings never liked losing but he would be happy with that performance for early spring training against a team like Richmond. They had more money than the Preachers, though the fact that the Saints had turned their finances around and were starting to do a lot better was starting to trickle down to the Preachers.

Where it was needed, but the feeder team was never going to get the kind of cash the main team did.

So the Preachers had to work to build their team, make smart choices, and find the hidden gems. While dealing with taking the guys that the Saints saddled them with as well. Guys who were recovering from an injury or, like Finn, needed some time out to get their heads on straight before they could come back to the majors.

Exiles looking for a way home.

And while she'd told Finn that she only wanted something temporary, she already suspected that he'd be hard to let go of if she let him in.

Another reason not to start.

She had to focus on what she wanted. Getting out of here herself. California. Two years learning from Isaac Haines. Finally the chance to do what she wanted to do, not what she had to do. A fresh start and a clean break.

Nothing to pull her back to Saratoga until she was ready to come.

She wrapped up the phone call and reached for her notebook to see what was next on her to-do list. There was never a shortage of stuff to keep her busy and she usually just put her head down and powered through, but today her head wasn't in the game. She started doodling on the margins of her notebook as she stared at the list. The words might as well have been written in ancient Greek or something.

"Eva."

Finn. The sound of his voice was like a shock. She'd hoped he'd stay away, that they could talk later. Apparently he had different plans. She looked up, steeling herself for the sight of him. It didn't help. He hadn't miraculously become hideous in the two nights he'd been away. Her pulse bumped just looking at him. Damn it.

He smiled at her, green eyes warm, as he slid his duffel bag down off his shoulder and dropped it as his feet. "Miss me?"

Yes. No. Argh. "How was the trip?"

"That's avoiding my question."

"This isn't exactly the place to discuss that." She tried to see if there was anyone else in the hallway beyond him. Things were always busier when the players were at home.

Finn looked around. "No one else here. No time like the present. I missed you."

"Finn—"

He sighed. "I knew it."

"Knew what?"

"You've tangled this all up in your head while I've been away. Convinced yourself it's all too hard or some crap like that."

Her heart began to pound. He was skirting too close to the mark for her comfort. He got under her skin too easily. Dangerous. "Got me all figured out, have you?"

"No, but I'd like to."

"I don't think that's a good idea."

"Why? Because you're scared of what people will think? Worrying about what others think or if they approve is a quick path to driving yourself crazy. Trust me, I know that road."

"Do you?"

"Yeah. There was a lot of crap in my head last year. For the last few years, really. Didn't end so well. So better to quit worrying and go after what you want."

"I told you what I wanted."

"Yup. And I told you that you could have it."

"On your terms."

"On both our terms."

She shook her head, trying to remember all her well-thought-out arguments while the scent of him fogged her brain. "I don't think it's a good idea."

"You thought it was a good idea the other morning."

That brought her to her feet. "That's sex."

"I'm in favor of sex. And that's the thing we're working with, right? We want each other. You want to keep it simple. So it's simple. You can have a lot more of what you want if you're willing to stand up and let everyone know that you want it."

He was so goddamned sure of himself. "And if I don't want to do that?"

"Never picked you for a coward. What you did with your sisters, that's brave. Not many people would have taken that on."

"Isn't it up to me to choose what I get to be brave about?"

"Sure. But make sure you know why you're doing it."

"Oh? You think you know why I'm turning you down?"

He scrubbed a hand over his chin. He hadn't shaved that morning, and the stubble looked good. "I can tell you what it looks like to me. Looks like you're stuck."

"Excuse me?"

He waved an arm, gesturing at the office. "Stuck. Here. I get it. You had to dig in and get the job done to raise your sisters, but unless I'm mistaken your sisters are grown now. You're done. So why are you holding on so tight to this place? You could do anything you wanted."

"Maybe I like it here? You ever think about that? This is my home. Some of us don't want to spend our lives gadding about the country, soaking up the spotlight."

"Maybe that's true. But some people are scared to find out if they can be good enough to have the spotlight focused on them. So they don't try. They hide."

"Declining to have a . . . fling . . . with you is not exactly hiding."

His brows lifted. "Really? Because that's what it looks like to me."

She felt her jaw tighten. "That's because you don't like not getting your own way."

"Maybe that's true. But Eva, I know someone who's

avoiding when I see one. I know exactly how that feels. I've never seen somebody so ready to burn her life down. And trust me, when that happens, it's not going to be pretty. Unless you change something now."

His eyes bored into hers and she felt like he could see right through her. Like every secret frustration she'd ever felt was his to know. Which was weirdly exhilarating. But also infuriating.

But she wasn't going to let him goad her. Let him win whatever weird game he'd turned this into in his head. She'd made her choice. He needed to back the hell off and accept it. She planted her hands on the desk, leaned forward. "Finn. Go to hell," she said, then pivoted nearly on her heel and walked away.

She heard his muttered "Fine." Heard heavy footsteps head toward the door. Felt a crack of pain through the anger that had been fueling her.

Goddamn it. She pulled open one of the file cabinet drawers and slammed it shut, wishing she could shut Finn away just as easily.

"So you and Finn are getting along then?" Don Mannings's voice came from behind her.

Crap. She spun around, heart sinking. Heat flared in her face as she met Don's pale blue eyes. "How much of that did you hear?"

He shrugged, ran a hand through his short salt-and-pepper cut. "Enough."

"We're not—"

"Eva, I've known you a long time. I know you don't

tangle with the players." He nodded toward the chair in front of her desk. "Do you mind?"

She did but she couldn't exactly tell Don to take a hike. For one thing, he'd been nothing but kind to her the entire time she'd worked at the Preachers. He and his wife, Helen, had done their best to help her and her sisters out.

"Of course not." She pressed her hand to her cheeks, as if that could kill the blush. Unlikely. She waited for Don to sit before she took her place behind the desk. "Did you need something?"

He shook his head. "No. Just wanted to make sure everything was okay."

"It's fine. Nothing to worry about."

He leaned back in his chair, expression skeptical. "Mind if I make an observation?"

"No-o." She resisted the urge to squirm.

He grinned. "Knew you were too polite to tell me to butt out."

Sadly that was true. She tapped her fingers nervously on her mouse. "Am I?"

"Too late now," he said.

This was going to be awkward. Might as well get it over with. "Say what you want to say."

"Well, it's like this. You've worked here a long time. And like I said, I know you don't tangle with players. I've seen enough of them preen and strut and flex their muscles and try to charm you over the years."

"I don't think mixing work and play is a good idea."

"That's not a terrible rule. But you know it's not an actual rule here?"

"Yes." There'd been quite a few romances between office staff and players while she'd worked here. A couple had turned serious. But most had ended. Which was one of the reasons she'd stuck to her rule.

"Good. No one would care if you wanted to date Finn. Well, the guys might give Finn a hard time but that's Finn's problem. No one's gonna give you any trouble about it."

"Finn's not the guy for me."

"You sure? Because in all those years, with all those players doing their little dances in front of you, he's the first one I've seen catch your attention."

"He got my attention because he's annoying."

"For suggesting that maybe there's more to the world than this team? Hardly a capital crime. He's not even the first one to say it to you. But he's the first one I've seen get you worked up. So maybe he's worth another look."

She shook her head. "He's too young."

"Nope. Helen's five years older than me. Doesn't make a difference if he's the right one."

"He's not the right one."

"How do you know if you never give him a chance?"

"Because I can read. And there was plenty to read about Finn last year."

Don grinned. "Paying attention even back then, were you?"

Her cheeks flared again. She ignored it. "No. But I checked him out when he moved here. He's trouble."

"He had his head up his butt last year, sure. But he seems determined to turn over a new leaf to me. Not so much as a sniff of attitude since he arrived. He's put his name down to volunteer for the Little League program. Even asked to be considered for the girls' teams because he said he knew they sometimes had a harder time getting volunteers. He's talented. He works hard. Maybe he's learned from his mistakes."

Eva tried to wrench her mind away from the frankly adorable image of Finn surrounded by adoring eight-year-old girls. Some of the players she'd known had viewed any participation in the Little League program— which a couple of the local schools ran but the Preachers sponsored—as a form of torture. Maybe Don was right and Finn was changing but that didn't mean she should throw caution to the wind.

"If he's talented, then he's only temporary," she said. "He'll move on."

"And what, exactly, would be stopping you moving on with him? If it worked out?"

What? She figured no one at the Preachers had any idea she was thinking about leaving. "You trying to get rid of me, Don?"

"Nope. But maybe you need to think about things. I heard what Finn said. About your sisters. He's right. You did the work. You raised 'em right. Now they're gone. Maybe it's time to start working on getting the life you might have had if your folks hadn't died. I remember you back then. You were a handful. Excited to be off to college. To leave. You weren't scared then."

God, could everyone see right through her today? "Maybe. But I'm not that kid anymore."

"You're not the woman raising three sisters, either."

"I don't regret my decision."

"Of course not. You did a great thing. Made us all

proud to watch you do it. But you've finished that now. When things end, you have to figure out what comes next. Try some stuff out. See what sticks."

"I'm in my thirties. I can't make the same mistakes an eighteen-year-old would make."

"Sure you can. But you're smarter than an eighteen-year-old, so you won't make any really dumb choices. You'll still make some mistakes, though. We all do. Not to steal a saying from your dad or anything, but nobody ever got through life being right the whole time."

That made her smile. It was exactly what her dad would say. He'd never shied away from taking a shot at something. She didn't know if he'd approve of a guy like Finn, though.

As if he'd read her mind, Don grinned at her. "Your folks would want you to be happy, you know. And I think your dad would've liked Finn."

"That's playing dirty," she said, managing a smile. It was nice to think that might be true. But liking Finn and wanting him to date his daughter would've been two entirely different things to her dad.

"Probably. True though." Don stood, moved toward the door. "Your dad loved this team. But he wouldn't want you here if it's not what you really want. So figure out what you want. If that includes Finn Castro, then the world isn't going to end."

"You hitting the showers?" Connor asked Finn the following Friday afternoon after their weight session.

Finn put the barbell he was holding back in the rack and blinked back the sweat stinging his eyes. He grabbed his towel to wipe his face. A shower would be good but he wasn't ready to stop just yet. Stopping meant thinking. And thinking meant thinking about Eva. And how he hadn't spoken to her in a week.

Since that stupid fight in her office.

Which had apparently accomplished one thing for sure and that was making up her mind that she was saying a big fat no to Finn.

Dumb.

It had been dumb to turn up there like that. To push the situation, push her into a corner.

A smart guy might have taken her to dinner, charmed her for a while, made her remember what she liked about him before pushing his luck.

Apparently he was still just as dumb as he'd been last year.

He scowled at the weight rack. "I'm going for a run." The weather had finally improved and it wasn't dark yet. A run might tire him out enough to let him sleep tonight.

Connor lifted his eyebrows. "Want some company?"

"Think you can keep up, old man?"

"I've been running longer than you've been alive, Castro. You want to do stadium or complex?"

Finn didn't have to think about that. Running inside the park itself provided some shelter from the wind—which was still cold despite the warmer day—but the admin building faced the park. Eva's office faced the park. The last thing he wanted was to think about her sitting up there behind that way too neat desk of hers ignoring him. "Complex." There was a track that wound its way around the various buildings and perimeter of

Hennessee. Mostly Coach Mannings made them run that route when he was feeling vindictive and wanted them to do distance.

"Fine by me," Connor said. "Meet you outside in five?"

Finn nodded and headed for the locker room.

Ten minutes later he was following Connor through the first part of the loop, ignoring the tiredness in his legs from the weight session and trying to find the rhythm of the run. The motion that would wipe his mind and let him just move.

As they rounded the back of the gym building, the path widened and Connor slowed a little, letting Finn catch up to him.

"How many loops?" Connor asked.

"Three?" Finn said.

Connor grinned. "Something bugging you?"

"No."

"Okay then. Let's pick it up." He lengthened his stride and Finn focused on keeping pace. Three loops of the complex path were six miles. They'd had training sessions all morning and then the weights that afternoon. Six miles was not exactly a short run after that. In fact, it was probably dumb when they had a game the following afternoon. Connor took the lead after a couple of minutes. He was taller than Finn and apparently being eight years older hadn't put a dent in his fitness. The guy was in great shape.

Hopefully he'd be as fit when he was pushing thirty-five.

But Connor being older didn't mean that Finn was happy to let the guy beat him. He kicked it up a notch or two and overtook Connor at the next turn, grinning when Connor gave him the finger as he passed.

They continued to run, swapping the lead, indulging in a little good-natured taunting as they moved. Finn was actually smiling as Connor started to slow the pace about halfway through their last circuit.

Connor was becoming a friend. Which meant Finn was maybe starting to fit in. He'd been missing Sam and Paul and Leeroy, the guys he'd hung with most back at the Saints. Starting over in a whole new place for the second year in a row had been harder than he'd expected. So it was a relief to feel like maybe the hardest part was over.

Now if only he could figure out Eva.

"You want to talk about it yet?" Connor said from beside him. He was breathing steadily, looking like he could run a few more miles if that was what it took.

Finn kicked it up a notch. "Talk about what?"

"You've been walking around like someone stole your dog for the last week. You're playing great, so it's not that. So it's something else. Something I'm guessing might start with an *E*."

"Not that much to talk about."

Connor snorted. "Well, I guess that's better than 'no comment.' She put you back in your place?"

"Not exactly." Finn eyed the path ahead of them. It narrowed. If he sped up then he could ditch Connor and stop this damned conversation.

"Then what?" Connor kept up as Finn put on a burst of speed.

"We had a disagreement."

"And you're giving up?"

"Not sure pushing is going to do much good."

"Giving up never helped much, either," Connor said.

"Relationship advice from the guy who's still single in his mid-thirties."

"Dude, I'm not your agony aunt. You wanna screw up, go right ahead. But lose the woe-is-me if you do. No one to blame but yourself."

"With wisdom like that, I can see why you're still single."

Connor shrugged as they rounded the last bend in the path. "Single now doesn't mean I always was. Or always will be. And when I find the next gal who I spend as much time mooning over as you do over Eva, then you can bet I'm not going to let her slip through my fingers without a fight."

Chapter Eight

Eva woke on Saturday morning, feeling cranky. Jenna had canceled their Friday-night dinner due to an emergency in the yoga studio with a leaking shower, and that had left her with nothing but time on her hands to think about things.

Things meaning Finn.

Her discussion with Don had been a challenge. What did she want?

Other than the obvious.

Finn. Who hadn't called since their argument in her office.

Of course, she hadn't been able to pick up the phone and call him, either.

Damn the man.

The Preachers had a game today in Maryland, but she hadn't accepted the invitation to take the bus with the team. So now Finn wouldn't be back until Sunday night. Leaving her with too much time to think.

Thinking was exhausting.

She needed a girls' night. She grabbed her phone and

called Jenna to see if the plumbing disaster had been handled. Turned out it had and Jenna was free. So that was one girl. But a proper girls' night required at least three. So she dialed another.

"Hey, sis," she said when Audrey answered the phone. "You want to come out with Jenna and me tonight? Grab some food, go listen to some music or something?"

"Steve's coming home tonight," Audrey said.

"Yeah but not until late, right? That's what you said the other day?" Audrey's boyfriend Steve Anders worked for some sort of tech company. They were based in Seattle but Steve, like a lot of the staff, worked remotely. Apart from the weeklong trips to Washington State every month.

"Yup," Audrey said. "But you know, my stomach's still wonky after that bug I had. So I'm not really up for a big dinner and booze."

"You don't have to drink."

"So I get to sit around and be the killjoy? Sorry, sis, but nope. I'm gonna stay put and be here when my guy gets home."

She sounded so happy at the thought of Steve coming home that Eva felt a pang of envy. "Everything's good between you two then?"

Audrey giggled. "Yes. I mean, I don't like him being away so often but otherwise it's great."

"Good," Eva said, trying to rein in her mama-bear instinct to push for more details. Audrey and Steve had met at a conference less than a year ago and had decided to move in together after just a couple of months. All very fast. But they were happy, she told herself. So she had nothing to worry about. Steve seemed like a good guy, a bit too hipster geek for Eva's tastes but he seemed to love her sister and that was the most important thing. "But once you're feeling better, we're going out, okay? It's been too long since we caught up. We used to talk more when you were in Seattle."

"I know. It's just been so busy since we got back. I'm getting lots of clients but that means lots of long hours."

"Nice problem to have," Eva said. "But you gotta have a life."

"Hello, pot, have you met kettle?" Audrey said. "You're the one who's all work and no play. You know, that team's called the Preachers but that doesn't mean you have to be a nun."

Eva sighed. "I'm not a nun, Aud." She bit her lip, wondering if she should say anything about Finn. She'd gotten into the habit of keeping the guys she'd dated or hooked up with out of her sisters' way during the early years. It was a habit that was hard to break apparently. But then again it wasn't like there was anything to tell. So it was better not to get Audrey's hopes up.

"Good. Then go find some hot guy when you go out tonight. Just think, if you find someone, we can double-date."

"Do people even do that?"

"Well, couples hang out with couples," Audrey said. "You know, all adult and shit."

Eva laughed. "When did we get so old?"

"Speak for yourself, I've still got a two at the start of my age. Speaking of which, Lizzie's birthday is next month. I'm wondering what to get her . . . got any ideas?"

Eva hooked onto the change of topic gratefully and

by the time she put down the phone nearly an hour later she and Audrey had plotted on the phone about cool things to send in a birthday care package to Lizzie— Eva had offered to fly her home for a birthday weekend but Lizzie had claimed she had too much work to do to miss a weekend. She'd already been accepted to medical school at Berkeley but she was determined to keep up her perfect GPA to the end.

Which Eva could hardly fault her for. Still, it was hard having her out there in California and only seeing her a few times a year.

That would change if Eva decided to do Isaac's class, of course. But then she'd only see Kate and Audrey a few times.

Why did the country have to be so damned big?

Sometimes she missed the days when they'd been at home together. The house was too big for just her. The four of them had inherited it jointly when their parents had died. The life insurance had paid off the last small part of the mortgage and left enough for Eva to put away to cover most of the costs of college for Kate and Audrey and Lizzie. It hadn't made sense to move then; they'd needed the space with four of them.

Since Lizzie had moved out to go to college, Eva had been trying to save money to go toward photography school and upgrading her cameras, so it made no sense to try to convince the girls to sell up when the real estate market was still recovering from the global financial crisis. So she rattled around here, living with memories.

A thousand thousand of them. A lifetime's worth. The photos she'd filled the walls with reflected those.

Pictures of her parents and from the years after they'd died. The four Harlowe gals together time after time; shot after shot of her sisters doing what each of them loved to do. She walked over to the wall in the hallway, looking at the images. There was a section with the shots of each of them at their senior proms with their dates. There were more shots of the girls with various guys after that but none of Eva with a guy after that last prom photo.

She touched it, thinking. Robbie Scarletti. High school sweetheart. He'd been great straight after her parents died. Helped her as much as an eighteen-year-old boy could be expected to know how to help his girlfriend through the death of her parents. But he'd been off to Harvard and once he'd left the inevitable had happened and they'd drifted apart, Eva drowning in her new responsibilities and Robbie fading away into fraternities and study and a life she couldn't imagine at all.

Fourteen years. Damn. Was that really the last time she'd had a relationship with a guy that had lasted more than a few weeks or nights?

It seemed crazy. Like she'd blinked and a decade and a bit had passed.

The obvious question was whether or not she was going to blink and let another year or two or ten slip past and still be stuck here in an empty house?

Or did she want to let herself move from behind the camera, from the mother-hen role worrying about everyone else, and change?

She pulled back from the photo, suddenly knowing that she had to at least start. Maybe Finn Castro wasn't

Mr. Right but he was definitely the right guy to get her out of the rut she was in.

All she had to do was let the world know she was turning over a new leaf.

Eva was sure she felt the exact moment the team bus rolled through the gates to Hennessee Park. Like there'd been a clap of thunder or a lightning strike. But no, the sky remained cloud-scudded blue outside her window.

It was only her that felt a change in the atmosphere.

She knew the Preachers' routine well. When they got home on a Sunday morning, Don tended to save the postgame analysis until Monday morning and send everyone home to spend time with their families.

On those days, like today, players shot off the bus, saw their gear stowed, grabbed their luggage, and got out of the park before Don had a chance to change his mind. The coaching staff didn't hang around, either. Thirty minutes tops and the parking lot would be empty except for her Volvo. And maybe Finn's truck. If he'd noticed the note she'd tucked beneath his wipers this morning.

The one that just said *Wait*.

Thirty minutes had never crawled by so slowly. The extra five she decided she needed, in case anyone was lingering, took an eternity.

But eventually they passed and she made herself walk, on legs that felt distinctly wobbly, down to the parking lot.

Finn stood in the sunshine, the light practically spot-lighting him, leaning against the door of his truck; he was reading something on his phone. She took a moment to take him in, blinking a little as always, as the force of his beauty hit her all over again.

God.

When he looked up and their eyes met, her nerve almost failed. But somehow she kept walking.

"Eva," he said, a little warily as she reached him. "I assume this is from you?" He held up the note.

She nodded.

"I'm here. Do you have something to say?"

He wasn't going to let her off easily, that was clear. She was going to have to say it.

"I wanted to tell you I changed my mind. That I'm in. If you still are, I mean."

"No sneaking around?"

"No sneaking around. But no promises beyond this season, either. That's my condition."

Silence stretched. God, was he going to tell her no? Had she left it too late? But then he smiled and the sunshine had nothing on that smile. "I always like coming home to good news."

"In that case, why don't you let me drive you home and we can discuss the good news in more detail?"

One dark eyebrow lifted over a very green eye. "Discuss?"

She nodded. Talking. There'd be talking eventually. But right now, now that she'd agreed to this madness, she was suddenly very eager to get to the part that didn't involve much talking at all. "Something like that."

He smiled. "Well, in that case, what are we standing around here for?"

* * *

They didn't speak on the short drive over. She was too busy trying to remember how to drive to talk and it seemed Finn didn't need to say any more now that he had the answer he wanted.

She pulled the Volvo into the drive of her place, not his, not bothering with the garage. Then she led him toward her house, up the porch still painted the same sunny yellow that her mother had chosen all those years ago and through the blue front door. She ignored the light switch; she wasn't sure she was ready for light any brighter than what was coming through the windows in the room beyond the front hall. The dim entry still offered some small illusion of protection, of not having to think too hard about what she was about to do.

The trembling in her skin had become a heavy beat in her heart, a pulse she felt at her throat and between her legs. She dropped her purse in the direction of the hall table and heard Finn close the door behind them. Heard the click of the dead bolt and then he was behind her. Not quite touching her. Close enough that she could feel his heat. Could smell him. Could hear the breathing that was somewhat steadier than hers but not entirely smooth.

"Eva," he murmured. Then his hand ran down the length of her hair before he gathered it up and tipped it forward over her left shoulder, leaving the right side of her neck bare.

The house was cool but the goose bumps that sprang to life on her skin had nothing to do with the temperature.

Finn ran a finger along the curve of her neck from ear to shoulder then started back again, just a fraction lower. When he hit a spot that made her shiver and suck in her breath, he said, "There." Then he lowered his mouth to the spot, sucking gently. The heady sensation that soared through her, both too much and yet not enough just from that one point of contact, made her breath catch and she made a noise that was half gasp, half moan, and tilted her head farther to give him easier access.

The sensation was both familiar and shockingly new. The memory of him doing this or something like this in her kitchen mirrored with the reality of his mouth on her skin, sent heat like a wave through her.

She'd been wrong about him, she realized with the last shreds of clarity as his mouth continued to tease her skin. Wrong to think she shouldn't do this. He was trouble, yes, and he was younger than her, yes, but for this, this need and blind chemistry between them, a little trouble would be worth it.

Even a lot of trouble.

He wasn't Mr. Right but he was the perfect Mr. Wrong.

One she wanted desperately.

One she was going to let do whatever he wanted to her as long as it meant she got to do it with him.

Just one season, she thought desperately, trying to cling to common sense. That was the deal. Just one season. She could have this for just a while and then she would be done.

As he found another spot that made her shudder, she thought that maybe one season was optimistic. She wasn't sure she could survive just one night with him if this was going to burn so fierce between them.

"Finn," she said softly, not knowing if it was question or encouragement, and he made a murmured response and splayed his fingers across her stomach, pulling her tightly back against him while he continued to kiss her neck. Until she tipped her head back and snaked a hand up to pull his mouth down to kiss him again.

She wanted those kisses. She could fall into those kisses, not thinking, not doubting, just being. Sanctuary and danger all in one. Maybe that summed up Finn himself.

Finn who had taken her by surprise and hell only knew where he was going to lead her before he vanished from her life again. She only knew that right now she was willing to walk that path. Go with him, as long as she got this. Got him.

She twisted in his arms so they were face-to-face and took the kiss deeper.

His hands slid down to her ass, fingers guiding her closer still to him, so there was no doubt that he was as turned on as she was. His cock was hard and unyielding against her where they pressed together and she couldn't help pushing into him until she felt him against her right where she ached. The throb of pleasure spread out from between her legs, flooding her body. Finn groaned against her mouth, pressed into her, then pulled his mouth free of hers.

"Bedroom?" he said, which was the best idea anyone had had all day as far as she was concerned. She had to pull herself back together enough to think but managed to say, "End of the hall. Stairs. Left."

Finn lifted her—God, she loved how strong he was, she wasn't small and yet he picked her up as easily as he might have wrapped his fingers around a bat—and she put her legs around his waist and he walked, still kissing her, through the house and up the stairs until they reached the doorway to her room. She hadn't closed it that morning in her rush to leave, which made life easier, and soon they were inside. She hadn't fully opened the curtains, so the room was mostly dark; what light there was, mellow and golden.

Finn let her down and when she found her feet, he started to slide clothing from her body. First her jacket; then he went to work on the buttons of her shirt. That slowed him down a little, as he seemed determined to kiss each inch of flesh as he bared it.

Eventually, she pushed him away, slid her arms free, and let the shirt drop to the floor. She bent to deal with her boots; when she straightened, Finn had ditched his blazer and had his hands on the back of his shirt. He tugged it free while she watched, his eyes fastened on hers.

She'd seen him without his shirt before.

Knew the layers of muscle and skin he was revealing. But apparently seeing him shirtless in the gym was different from seeing him half naked in her bedroom knowing that she was about to see the rest of him as well. She wanted to taste all that skin. Learn the lines of his tattoo and the words that marked his body.

Her breath left in a rush and she backed up a few steps, until the mattress bumped the backs of her thighs. But Finn didn't give her time to catch her breath. He closed the distance between them with two quick strides and kissed her again. She put her hands on his chest, feeling the flex of muscle beneath skin that felt burning hot.

The heat of healthy, hungry male.

His hands dropped to her waistband and flicked open the button of her jeans; the hiss of her zipper followed. One hand slid inside, down to her panties, to slide against her with deadly aim, making her moan again before it withdrew and he yanked her jeans down. She stepped out of them and decided that two could play at that game.

Button. Zip. Then her hand was pressed against the length of him, fingers curling as she slid them up and down over the smooth cotton of his underwear.

This time it was him groaning her name. She smiled up at him.

"You wanna fight dirty, huh?" he said.

"Yes, please."

It was enough of an invitation, it seemed. He stepped back then scooped her up and dropped her on the bed. By the time she'd stopped laughing, he was beside her, having somehow lost the rest of his clothes in the intervening seconds.

Finn Castro naked in bed with her. She had a few seconds to take him in, to admire the body that was a work of art, before he put that body to work driving her crazy.

His mouth worked a path across her skin that she was half convinced must be glowing with pleasure in its wake. Hot tongue against the lace of her bra created a friction that made her nipples ache—and then he'd pulled the lace free and tasted her, teeth and lips teasing her until she cried out.

Then he continued, moving down. Licking, pressing

his teeth to sensitive spots she hadn't known she possessed. Like someone had handed him a map of all the places on her body guaranteed to make her melt.

When he reached her underwear and tugged it away, all she could do in reply was widen her legs and let him do whatever the hell he wanted. His tongue dragged across her clit slowly once, and she thought she heard him chuckle as she pressed hungrily into him; and then he went to work. Fingers joined his tongue, one then two sliding easily against the wetness of her, filling her as she moved against him, needing more. He was relentless, fierce, and she wanted it to last forever, to float in pleasure, but he didn't let her. Instead he pushed her higher, made it better, made her into a panting, aching, spiraling mass of need until finally she reached the edge and came hard against his tongue.

That didn't stop him, either. While the shock of it pulsed through her, he moved back up her body, hands soothing and igniting again at the same time. He rolled away for a second then came back, condom in hand. She barely had time to take in the sight of him rolling it over his cock before he was over her, settling between her thighs.

He slid against her once, twice, setting all the nerves that were still buzzing into an ache that was almost too much before he positioned himself at her entrance, hard and wide.

"Okay?" he said and she nodded and lifted her head to kiss him as he slid into her with one sure thrust.

God. The stretch of him filling her felt amazing, almost too good, her flesh sensitized and arching. She closed her eyes, the sensation overwhelming. Finn above her. Inside her. Hard and steady as a rock. Unmoving. Inescapable. Filling her world.

"No," he said fiercely as she tried to move beneath him, tipping her head back while she arched to draw him closer. "No. No turning away, Eva. No closing your eyes. Maybe you're going to change your mind again but if you do, if you're going to kick me out in the morning, then so be it. But you're not going to forget me."

He flexed against her, sank deeper then withdrew again, so controlled, so slow that she felt every fraction of an inch of the movement. Felt the connection between them, saw the heat and need and undeniable determination in his eyes. Eyes that looked more black than green in the darkness they shared, the slips of moonlight that stole past the edges of her blinds enough to show her his face, to make it impossible for her to hide.

So she gave up the fight. Fastened her eyes on his and wrapped her legs tighter around his waist. Watched him as he moved inside her and around her. Watched and gave in to the sensations, the unrelenting pleasure and need as she moved with him. Watched as his eyes went darker and more focused until it seemed like all she could see was his face as she came with his name on her lips.

Chapter Nine

The next week passed in a blur. There wasn't really any chance for Finn to push his no-sneaking-around rule because they pretty much spent every spare moment that they were both in Saratoga and not at work in bed.

Eva didn't really know how he had the energy to still play baseball but apparently great sex only improved his game because Finn hit two home runs in a game and then helped Connor pitch a no-hitter with some truly brilliant first-base work in the next-to-last game of spring training.

The man had skills both on and off the field.

Skills she was only too happy to explore as often as possible.

On Friday morning, she collapsed back on her pillow boneless and content after Finn had woken her at six a.m. for a bout of morning sex that beat any alarm she'd ever had.

She lay there, trying to catch her breath and fighting

off the urge to go back to sleep while, beside her, Finn started to climb out of bed.

This was the part she hated. The part when he left. She pulled the quilt closer and rolled to her side to watch him gather his clothes into a pile.

"Your schedule sucks," she said.

"Well, my boss is your boss, so you know who to complain to." He grinned down at her. "Bad form to be late for the last game of spring training. At least it's a home game. So I'm all yours tonight."

"This is true." That was a thought to give any woman a happy.

Finn straightened. "So tomorrow is the family day."

"I'm aware. After all, I organize it."

"Seems like a good time to go public."

She sat up, her happy mood dissolving, replaced by nerves. "Really?"

"Yes. What, did you think I'd forgotten about it?"

"No." Yes. Or at least she'd been hoping he had.

"You're not backing out on me, are you?"

"No. A deal's a deal. I just thought that maybe you'd tell a few people at a time. Some of the guys on the team."

"Doesn't seem like the right time, just before our last game. The only one I've told is Connor."

"Connor West? Are you and he friends now?"

Finn nodded. "He's cool. We seem to get along so far."

Huh. Once upon a time Connor West had been a bad boy like Finn. Though the last few years he seemed to have steadied. Maybe like called to like or something. Though Connor, who was tall and solid muscle— shoulders-wide-enough-to-block-out-the-sun kind of solid, with close enough to blond-brown hair and sky-blue eyes—was a different kind of guy from Finn, who was tall and leanly carved muscle, more quicksilver with his dark hair and wild green eyes.

"Well enough to tell him your secrets."

"He kind of knew I liked you," Finn said, frowning slightly. The movement made his scar wrinkle. It was beginning to fade, less prominent than it had been when he'd arrived in Saratoga but still there. A reminder that Finn wasn't Mr. Perfect and that she should keep a grip and stick to the plan.

He started pulling on his clothes. "Connor guessed we'd worked things out when I started being cheerful. But he hasn't told anyone. Or if he has, none of them have said anything to me. I figure at least a few of them would have wanted to make a crack or two if they knew, so I think we're good." He paused in the middle of buttoning his shirt. "Are you telling me you haven't told anyone at all?"

She shook her head.

"Not even Jenna? Or one of your sisters?"

"Definitely not one of my sisters," she said.

"Why not?"

"Because they'll get all excited and want to bond with you. I don't want them getting too attached."

The smile wiped off his face. "Because of your end-of-season rule."

She lifted her chin. "Yes."

"You're going to have to tell them something."

"I'll tell them I'm dating someone soon."

"What's the big deal? They must have met other guys you've dated."

She couldn't meet his eyes.

"You mean they haven't?" He sounded shocked. "Why not?"

"Because when I was raising them, it didn't seem appropriate. It's not like there were many guys knocking down the door to take on a girl my age who had three baby sisters to take care of. And once they were old enough, well, they'd all moved away."

"So you're telling me they're going to go ape-shit when they find out their big sister is finally dating?" He looked daunted rather than surprised.

"Something like that. But don't worry, it's not likely you'll meet them. Well, other than Audrey. She moved back to Saratoga a few months ago but her business is kind of crazy right now."

"Audrey. The web designer, right?"

"That's her." Finn had kept up the nightly texting sessions whenever he was on the road, and slowly they'd been finding out all kinds of things about each other. She knew his sister Em was a lawyer in Chicago and that Oliver Shields's girlfriend, Amelia, was kind of a de facto sister as well. His family had kind of taken her in during a tough time in her life or something. There was more to the story but she hadn't pressed so far. "You'll like her. She's a baseball fan."

"Which team?"

"The only team anyone raised in this house had any chance of supporting was the Saints. My dad brainwashed us all very young." Just as well; it would be awkward to work for the Preachers and root for another MLB team.

"Mal Coulter's wife, Raina, is a Yankees fan, actually.

Well, as long as they're not playing the Saints these days."

"I never heard that," Eva said.

"It's not the kind of thing she advertises." Finn shook his head with a smile.

"You don't have to worry about Audrey. She's a Saints fan. Steve likes the Mariners, though."

"Steve?"

"Her boyfriend. He's a tech guy. Programmer."

"Okay. But we're straying from the subject here, Eva. We were talking about tomorrow. The party. And you coming with me as my date."

"I think that would be you coming with me as my date. After all, I've been here a lot longer than you have."

"I really don't care who gets first billing. Just that we go together."

She wrapped the quilt tighter around herself. She'd known this moment was coming, but it still made her nervous. Despite Don's opinion, she knew the news that she was dating Finn was going to cause some waves at the Preachers. Finn was likely to bear the worst of it—though that didn't seem fair. But that was the deal she'd made and the one she was going to stick to.

"You really want to do it this way?"

"Ripping off the Band-Aid in one go is always better in the long run," he said.

"Sadist," she muttered but she nodded. "Okay then. Tomorrow it is."

In the end they had to agree to meet up at the family day. Eva, being one of the organizers, had to go in early to make sure everything got set up. The family day consisted of baseball for kid teams, parent-and-kid teams, and a staff-versus-players game. Plus half a dozen other forms of entertainment for people who didn't want to play or watch baseball, and BBQ with all the trimmings for several hundred people. She was at Hennessee at seven a.m.

Finn would have volunteered to help but the first part of family day for the team was sitting through several hours of post-spring-training analysis and the announcement of everyone's starting positions in the roster. He was hoping he might have done well enough to have a shot at first base. The Preachers' first-string first baseman was Pietro Renner, who'd played for both the Mets and the Saints in his time. But Pietro had been around for a long time and hadn't really been in great form over spring training. Which was the way it went sometimes. You couldn't be at the top forever.

Finn didn't intend to waste his best years here at the Preachers. His best shot at getting back to the Saints was to get that first-base spot here and bring his A game once he did. Dazzle everyone. If he could keep his batting up the way it had been the last few weeks, that couldn't hurt, either. He'd never been a specialist batter, but anything to make him a better value to the Saints couldn't hurt.

He found a seat next to Connor for the team meeting, with Michael Stuart on the other side of them. Michael was one of Connor's buddies from way back. Finn didn't like him quite as much as Connor but he was friendly enough and a damned fine catcher.

He found himself tapping his foot restlessly through the first part of the meeting—until Connor told him to chill. Then he forced himself to lean back and act like it was all cool to him.

Finally Don wound down his wrap-up of the season and beckoned for one of the assistant coaches to bring over a piece of paper. The magic list.

"Don't forget to breathe, kid," Connor said as Don began to read. Finn gave Connor the finger without taking his eyes off Don.

Thankfully he didn't have to wait very long. Don started with the fielding positions and when he got to first base, he looked around the room a moment then said, "First base. Castro."

Connor thumped him on the back and Finn tried to maintain his calm, limiting himself to a smile of satisfaction. There were a few mutters around them but there'd been a few mutters for each of the announced positions.

So there. First goal of the day achieved. Now he just had to get through the part where the guys all found out he was seeing Eva.

That was going to be interesting.

"You do realize that you just pinned that piece of paper upside down?" Jenna said, laughing.

"What?" Eva said, then frowned at the paper. Jenna was right, she had. God. Where was her brain?

Back in her bedroom with Finn.

Finn who any minute now would be coming out of

the team meeting with all the other players and would be coming to find her so they could show the world that they were together.

Her stomach twisted and she stabbed the thumbtack back into the notice board after she'd turned the roster the right way up with a little too much force.

"Hmm, someone needs coffee," Jenna said. Eva turned from the notice board and managed to smile.

Coffee wasn't going to help. Whiskey might be better. But people would probably notice if she got wasted at family day, so she was stuck with more innocent ways to soothe her nerves.

"Not coffee," she said, summoning a smile for Jenna. "Doughnuts."

Jenna shrugged. "I am on board with that plan." She bounced on her bright-blue Converses, looking far too wide-awake and enthusiastic for nine in the morning. In bright-red skinny jeans and a blue sweatshirt emblazoned with a Superman symbol, dark skin glowing with health, she looked ready to take on the world. Eva, on the other hand, kind of wanted to run away from it.

It was going to be fine, she told herself firmly. Even if the guys on the team took the news badly, they all had to be on their best behavior today. Ben and Don wouldn't put up with anyone causing trouble at family day. They worked hard to make the families feel involved with the team, to make them feel like the support they gave the players was valued and the sacrifices appreciated. The fact that the Preachers weren't just all baseball all the time was part of the reason Eva had stayed here so long. The feeling of being part of a family again had been nearly impossible to resist from the beginning. It was still hard to resist.

Maybe that was why she still hadn't decided which photography school she wanted to go to.

"The doughnut truck is over by the batting cages," she said to Jenna and tucked her arm through her friend's. The walk over took a while as they stopped to say hello to everyone they knew.

By the time they got there, Eva spotted Greg Cutler talking to Jed Sommers, one of the assistant coaches, in the doughnut queue.

Which meant the team meeting was over.

And that Finn had to be somewhere in the crowd.

Looking for her.

She bit her lip, looking at Greg. Of all the guys on the team, he was the one who was maybe going to be hurt when he found out.

"I've changed my mind," she said, coming to a stop. "I don't think I want doughnuts."

Jenna shook her head, hair bouncing in the breeze. "We always want doughnuts. I'm hungry." She tugged on Eva's arm, and took a step toward the truck, but Eva stayed put. Jenna turned to look back at her. "What's wrong, you're being weird." She peered at Eva then back at the truck. "Did Greg ask you out again? Are you trying to avoid him?"

Eva shook her head. "I'm just not hungry."

Jenna folded her arms. "Nope. That's not it. What's going on?"

Before she could answer, she heard Finn's voice behind her, calling "Eva!" Then he was there with them, tall and hot in the daylight. He looked at her a moment, a question in his eyes, then when she didn't say anything he leaned in and kissed her quick.

"Hey," he said as beside her Jenna said, "Oh. My. God. You two are together?" in a voice loud enough to carry across half the complex. Heads turned all around them.

Well, that did it. No keeping it quiet any longer.

Finn kissed her again and then pulled back, laughing. "Hey, Jenna."

Jenna grinned. "Hey yourself." Then she turned her gaze on Eva, pulling a face of mock outrage. "For this flagrant violation of the best-friend code, you are buying the doughnuts. All the doughnuts. How could you not tell me?"

"It only happened recently. I haven't seen you."

"There's this technology called a phone," Jenna said. "I knew it! I knew you two would be good together." She did a little boogie on the spot and beyond her, Eva saw Greg turn toward them, his attention caught by the movement. He wasn't the only one. But he was the one Eva was most concerned with right now. She saw him when he spotted them. Saw him start to smile and then saw him go still as he saw Finn, who'd looped his arm across her shoulders. Felt Greg's eyes meet hers and then watched as his expression went flat before he turned on his heel and walked away.

Damn.

She couldn't help the twinge of guilt. Even though she'd never encouraged Greg, he was a nice guy and she didn't want to hurt him.

"You have to tell me all about it," Jenna said, still bouncing.

"Not that much to tell," Eva said, trying to minimize the impact, but before she could think what to say next, Don Mannings's wife, Helen had appeared through the crowd.

Helen had a Preachers cap pulled down over her fading red hair and a take-out cup in the other. She looked delighted when she saw Eva.

"Sweetie, it's been too long," Helen said. Then she looked up at Finn. "Finn. I see you're settling in."

Of course Helen knew Finn. She always took the new players under her wing, having them over for dinner and making sure they met everyone at all the team functions.

"Yes, ma'am," Finn said and Helen laughed.

Damn, he charmed everybody.

Well, maybe that would be the saving grace. Maybe he'd charmed all the guys on the team as well and no one would get upset.

Then she remembered Greg's face. Or maybe not.

"Eva, you'll have to come for dinner soon," Helen said. "It's obviously been too long since we caught up." The last was said with a head tilt at Finn. "In fact, I think both of you should come. Maybe next week?"

"Maybe," Eva said faintly. Finn's arm tightened on her shoulders, a squeeze of reassurance.

It was okay, she told herself. It was Finn. And Finn was good for her.

So everything would be okay.

But before she'd convinced herself entirely, Don found his way to his wife's side. He lifted a brow at Eva, the side of his mouth quirking as he took in Finn's arm around her. She managed not to blush, which was a step in the right direction. "Hi, Don," she said. "Having fun?"

He nodded. "Good turnout. You've done well. You always do well." He smiled at her, then his expression turned more serious. "Finn, I was wondering if I could have a word with you for a minute."

Eva felt Finn stiffen, his arm drawing tighter around her. She slipped her arm around his waist, turned to look at him, but his expression was calm.

"Sure," Finn said. "Anything wrong?"

Don shook his head. "Walk with me a minute."

Her gut twisted. That hadn't exactly been an answer to Finn's question.

Helen, looking from her husband to Finn, also looked a little tense. "Eva and I will stay here and catch up. You two go on and talk shop."

Eva wanted to protest, to go with Finn. Which was crazy. One, because she had no place involving herself in player–coach business, and two, because she had no idea if Finn would want her to interfere. So she had to content herself with squeezing Finn's waist quickly before he let go of her and followed Don back down toward the training complex, where there was less of a crowd.

"Any idea what this is about?" she asked Helen. "Is it something about his position on the team?" Finn had played well all through training. There was no way Don was dropping him, was there? No. Finn wouldn't have looked so happy when he'd first found her if that had been the case.

Helen shook her head. "No. It's not about the team."

"But you know what it's about?" Eva knew damned well that Don told his wife most of his decisions before he told anyone else. She looked back to where Don and Finn were standing. Finn's face was grim and his arms were folded against his chest.

"What's going on?" she said to Helen, still watching the guys. Whatever was happening Finn didn't like it. Question was, how would he handle it?

"The schools turned down Finn for Little League," Helen said.

Eva swiveled back to her. "Are you kidding me? They turned down a former MLB player?" The Little League teams were usually begging for players with experience to get involved.

Helen looked resigned. "They'd heard about what happened last year. Said they couldn't be sure he would be a 'good influence.' Said he needed to prove he'd changed before they'd let him work with the kids."

"That's—" Eva cut off her protest. Fact was, she didn't think she knew Finn well enough to argue. Sure, he'd been behaving himself since he'd arrived here, but that didn't mean he'd changed for good. Maybe that bar fight was purely the product of too much alcohol and young guys blowing off steam—but young guys who turned to hitting people to blow off steam weren't the kind of guys you wanted teaching little kids. God.

She turned anxious eyes back on Finn, wondering if he'd make a scene. Don put a hand on Finn's shoulder but Finn shrugged it off. Then turned on his heel and walked a few feet farther toward the gym building. Every line of his body read *pissed off* and Eva held her breath. But Finn didn't explode. Instead, he just stood for a minute, head down, hands clenched by his sides. She couldn't see his face.

Part of her wanted to go and comfort him, but she really needed to know how he'd handle this without any help from her. Don walked back up to where she and Helen stood and put his arm around his wife.

"Is he okay?" Helen asked.

"He's disappointed," Don said.

That seemed to be putting it a little mildly. Tension was still radiating from Finn.

"I told him they'd be willing to take another look at their decision in a couple of months. If he hasn't been in any trouble by then, he'll be able to start helping out."

That seemed like a sensible approach, from the school's perspective. She doubted Finn saw it that way, just now. She bit her lip, watching him, until, after another minute or so, his hands relaxed, his head came up, and he turned back toward them. His eyes found hers and she finally let herself move, heading for him as he came toward her, a smile she wasn't entirely convinced was real pasted on his face. When they reached each other, she couldn't help it, she pulled his head down and kissed him soundly, which earned some catcalls from the crowd.

"It'll be okay," she said as she let him go and they stood just looking at each other for a moment. "It's all going to be okay." She hoped it was true. But she wasn't entirely sure if she was trying to convince herself or Finn.

Monday morning, Finn walked into the locker room at Hennessee, not knowing what he might be in for. The guys had been somewhat cool at the family day—there'd been a bit of ribbing about Eva—but the presence of kids and wives and girlfriends and all the staff had kept things civil. He hadn't kidded himself that that would be the end of it.

Today, with nothing between him and any potential fallout, would be the real test.

But hell, he could take it. He'd been a rookie at college and at various teams. He'd been in a frat. He'd put up with, and survived, various degrees of hazing his entire sporting life. He could handle any of the guys who decided they might have an ax to grind over Eva.

The main issue was whether he could keep it to just words or whether they would be dumb enough to take it further.

Don Mannings wouldn't put up with that kind of shit. And Finn couldn't afford a black mark. The Little League thing had been a reminder that he had a lot of ground to make up. He'd had the weekend to try to ease the sting of that decision but it still made him feel ashamed. Hell, Little League had been his life when he'd been a kid. He'd loved it. But now he was someone that other people didn't trust to create that for their kids.

God. He'd never expected proving himself all over again to come with quite so much pain. But Eva was on his side. At least, he thought she was. They'd spent the entire weekend together. And it had been good. So. He wasn't going to let anyone bait him into a fight. He might have screwed up last year but he wasn't going to make the same mistake twice.

He'd arrived early, meaning to get in, get changed, and get out on the field with as little hassle as possible.

But when he moved past the first row of lockers and benches to the second where his locker was, he found Greg Cutler, sitting there.

Waiting for him, it seemed, judging by the way Greg loomed to his feet at the sight of Finn.

"Greg," Finn said, dumping his bag on the bench. Hopefully if he stayed calm, Greg would, too.

"You got some nerve, Castro," Greg said, stepping so close that only about two feet separated them. He was a big guy, and every inch of him was tense.

So much for keeping things civil. Finn eyed Greg steadily. There were two ways to go with this. Finn could drag it out, pretend he didn't know what the problem was, or he could get things over and done with. Option two seemed like the most straightforward. "Eva's a big girl, man, she's made her choice," he said, keeping his voice free of any hint of gloating or satisfaction that he'd been the one she chose.

"Eva doesn't date players."

"I guess she changed her policy," Finn said. He held up his hands, trying to break the tension. "Look, I'm sorry. I didn't know you had a thing for her until it was too late."

"Fuck you, Castro." Greg moved in closer. Finn held his ground. If he let Greg back him up against the lockers, the only way out of the situation would be to go through the guy. That would get messy.

"This doesn't have to be a thing. Like I said, Eva's made a choice. I'm sorry if that's not the way you wanted things to be between you, but in the end that's her decision, not yours. So why not man up and bow out gracefully?" He let a little edge of *I'm not backing down* creep into his voice. Hell, Greg had been at the club for years. If he hadn't won Eva over by now, surely he had brains enough to recognize that it was probably never going to happen.

"Eva's not one of your little star fuckers, Castro."

Finn took a step forward on instinct. Then he stopped himself. "I'm well aware of that. I'm not an idiot."

Greg's jaw worked, as though he was considering debating that point. With his fist.

"I care about Eva," Finn said. "I'm not looking to hurt her."

"You—"

"Hey, Greg." Connor's voice came from the end of the row of lockers. "Why don't you and I take a walk?" Finn stayed where he was, not taking his eyes off Greg. He hadn't heard Connor come in, but for a big guy Connor was a stealthy fucker. A stealthy fucker who was apparently backing him up today. Good.

Greg didn't look away from Finn. "Butt out, West."

"Sorry, man, no can do. Or have you forgotten the part where it's my mission to stop my friends from acting like dicks?" Connor moved down the row then calmly stepped between Finn and Greg. Finn moved back a pace, interested to see if the tactic would work. Connor was slightly taller than Finn but he had a couple of inches on Greg and he was built more solidly than either of them. Maybe that fact would sink through Greg's hard head and deliver the message that starting something wasn't such a good idea. He heard the locker room door open again. Christ, a few more guys joining in the party; that was all they needed.

"C'mon, Greg," Connor said. "You need to back off.

Like Finn said, it's Eva's choice. Time to move on. It sucks but there it is. No one can win 'em all."

To Finn's surprise, Greg looked down. Stepped back.

Connor moved forward, put a hand on Greg's shoulder. "Come on. We're going to be late. You know Coach hates that on the first day." He managed to steer Greg toward the end of the row of lockers, and Finn breathed a sigh of relief as Pietro walked into sight as well. Behind him there was a babble of voices as even more players started to come through the door. He didn't think Greg would try anything with such a big audience. Not with Connor clearly not on his side.

So, trouble avoided for now. Though the look that Greg shot him, dark eyes full of anger, before he vanished from view told him that maybe this wasn't the end of it.

He avoided Greg as much as possible for the rest of the day, keeping a low profile. But the following day it was back on the bus for the first game of the season. Everyone had staked claims on their favorite seats during spring training. As luck would have it, his was only two rows back from Greg's. Great. He glanced behind him, but if he tried to take over one of the seats farther down the bus, that would cause an argument, too. Perfect. Instead he pulled his earbuds out of his jacket pocket, shoved them in, and leaned back in his seat.

Best idea was probably just to sleep the rest of the trip. He pulled his cap down over his eyes and leaned against the window, intending to do just that. But before he could actually doze off, Connor dropped into the seat next to him. Finn straightened. "Dude, get your own seat."

Connor glanced up at Greg. "Thought you might like some company."

The muscles along Finn's jaw clenched. "I don't need a babysitter. I'm not the one looking for a fight."

"Good to hear. You're not the only one on the bus, though."

"Greg's not going to start something with Coach right here."

"Just think of me as extra insurance."

Finn rolled his eyes. "Anyone ever tell you you're a drama queen?"

"Not often, no." Connor looked amused. "But I'm not going to let this get out of hand. I'm going to sit here and make it clear that I'm fine with you and Eva. That will take the wind out of some of the guys who might be thinking it will win points with Greg if they play a little game of *Fuck with Castro*. I've been here longer than he has. That counts for something. We need to focus on the game, not your damned love life."

"Amen to that," Finn said and, figuring it was still the smartest plan, Connor or no Connor, leaned back against the window for take two of his attempted nap.

Chapter Ten

The trip went fairly smoothly. Sure, there'd been the small matter of his gear bag mysteriously getting soaking wet between the bus and the locker room, but he'd packed his favorite glove and a spare uniform in his personal luggage in case someone pulled something, so it hadn't slowed him down. Connor and, to his surprise, Pietro had made a point of hanging out with him, and all in all, apart from a constantly scowling Greg and the odd mutter from a couple of the guys, they'd pulled together and won the game. So he was feeling good until he climbed off the bus at Hennessee, walked across the lot to his truck, and discovered he had a flat tire.

Coincidence, he told himself as he threw his luggage in the back of the cab and then dug out the jack. He believed it for about five minutes until Greg drove past him in his bright-orange Jeep and honked his horn. When Finn looked up, Greg just grinned, gave him the finger, and then tore off.

Dick.

He bit down on the urge to chase after Greg's dick car and tell him exactly how much of a dick he was being. That wasn't going to help. Or get his tire fixed.

The jack slid into place and he got the truck off the ground. When the tire was up he checked for damage. Nothing obvious to the eye. No neat slash that would prove that Greg the dick had knifed his tire. A dick but not completely stupid apparently. He'd used the good old release-the-pressure-from-the-valve method. Or gotten someone else to do it.

Well, at least that meant Finn wasn't out the price of a new tire. Just his time and effort to change to the spare and then go and get this one pumped up. An hour or so out of his day and maybe it was enough for Greg the dick to have gotten it out of his system.

Just as he'd finished wrestling the dead tire off and the spare on, Eva arrived, looking edible in a short red skirt and a black sweater, long black boots hiding her calves but drawing his gaze to her legs nevertheless.

"Hey," she said. "You taking up mechanics now?"

The tail end of his annoyance with Greg evaporated in the face of her smile. She was worth putting up with some shit for. "Functional fitness," he said as he lifted the tire into the back of the truck. "Haven't you heard? It's all the rage." He was probably covered in dirt and grease, but Eva's expression suggested she didn't mind. He'd shed his jacket to save his clothes from the worst of the mess. The white T-shirt he'd worn beneath was probably now doomed to be a rag. It had a massive black smear across the front.

"It seems to be working for you," she said. She leaned down, kissed him carefully. When he went to pull her closer, she darted back out of reach. "You are not smearing me with all that crap."

"Didn't you miss me?"

"Yes, but not enough to get engine and road gunk on a cashmere sweater." She grinned at him, eyes laughing over the tops of her glasses. "A girl has to have standards. But if you're good, I'll make it up to you later." She watched for a minute as he tightened the wheel nuts on the spare. "You run over a nail or something?"

"Or something," he agreed, tightening the nuts on the wheel.

Her smile disappeared. "Are the guys messing with you?"

"No more than usual," he said. "Don't worry about it."

Her arms folded across her chest. "Don't worry about it?"

"I can handle it. It's guy stuff."

She rolled her eyes. "Seriously? The guys are giving you grief because of me and I'm meant to just stay out of it?"

She didn't look happy about the idea. In her position, he wouldn't be happy, either. But he needed to convince her. "Yup. You jumping in won't help. As much as I appreciate the offer. And this is not meant to cast any aspersions on your ability to handle anything," he added quickly as her expression darkened. "Just team shit. We'll figure it out."

"Men are stupid," she said, eyes narrowed in irritation. "It's lucky for you all that you have parts we find useful."

"Can't argue with that. But hey, I'm happy to offer up any part of me you want to find useful later on."

"Where do you think you're going?" Finn said, sleepily as Eva started to roll toward the edge of the bed. His arm snaked around her waist, trying to pull her back toward him.

She tugged at his fingers. It was kind of like trying to move an iron bar cemented in place. Crap. She really needed to start working on her upper-body strength. Having a boyfriend who was built like a machine was great until she had to try to resist him in any physical way. In which case he always won.

Annoying.

The only places she could keep up with him were running and in bed. And she half suspected that the running part was him being nice and sticking to her pace rather than going at a speed that would suit him.

"I'm going to yoga. I promised Jenna."

"Yoga sucks," he muttered.

"You said you liked yoga," she pointed out, pushing at his arm. "Besides, this is your fault. I've canceled two Friday dinners in a row. Jenna is my best friend. I can't ignore her forever just because you like sex a lot."

"You like sex a lot, too," he said with a grin. "I remember last night."

She did, too. She wasn't sure she had enough strength for a yoga class after the moves Finn had put her through. But Jenna wasn't going to accept that as an excuse. "Well, this morning I like yoga."

"I can think of much more fun ways to prove you're bendy," Finn said.

"Stop it." She finally wriggled free and slid out of reach. Finn rolled onto his back. The sheet only covered his crotch, leaving the rest of him bare to her gaze. God. Talk about temptation in human form. She almost lost her resolve. "You could come, too. Might do you good after all those games this week. After all, I need you to be bendy, too."

He grinned. "I'm plenty bendy. I think we proved that last night in the living room."

"Shut up." She tossed a pillow at him. There would be no thinking about what he'd done to her last night on her sofa. If she did think about it, she'd just crawl right back into bed and let him do it again. And then Jenna would probably sack her as best friend. "You can stay here then. But you'll miss out on my yoga outfit. Did I mention it's hot yoga? Which means I can't really wear much at all." His eyes went dark and she laughed. "Got your attention, did I?"

"You have had my attention since I first saw you," he said. "But seeing you in tiny yoga clothes has a certain appeal." He waggled his eyebrows. "As long as I get to take them off you afterward."

"Deal. Better still, you can help me shower off all that sweat."

She grinned as the sheet started to show evidence that Finn liked that idea a lot. "But first you'd better take a cold shower if you don't want everyone in class to know how much you're enjoying the idea."

* * *

Forty-five minutes later, Eva wiped sweat from her eyes as she came out of her pose and decided, as she did at this point in every class, that she hated hot yoga. Today she might hate it even more as all the girls, and a couple of the guys, seemed to be spending a lot of time watching Finn instead of focusing on asanas. Apparently, that was what she got for dating a guy who looked like him. She was just going to have to get used to it.

At the front of the class, Jenna stepped into the next pose and raised her eyebrows when Eva caught her eye, tilting her head toward Finn. Who was proving that he was, indeed, very bendy. And very distracting shirtless and wearing only running shorts over bike shorts. As Eva watched, the girl on the mat next to Finn's turned her head to sneak a glance at him at just the wrong moment, lost her balance, and toppled over.

Eva bit her lip to keep from laughing. No sympathy for those who were obviously hot for someone else's guy. Finn, being nicer than her, leaned over and helped the poor girl get to her feet. She went a deeper shade of scarlet—the color clearly from more than just the workout—and refused to meet his eyes. Finn straightened and then moved back into his spot and into the next pose, which meant Eva could enjoy the flex of his back muscles while she did the same. Her thoughts were nowhere near the *Clear the mind, free the body* thoughts she should be having in yoga class. No, they were more like, *Drag sweaty boyfriend back to house and do immoral things to him in shower.* Her eyes crossed slightly as she thought about it and she felt herself wobble. Damn.

She dragged her thoughts away from Finn, trying to focus on Jenna's voice and the pull of her muscles moving and stretching instead. She didn't want to be the next one to end up on the floor in front of the entire class. Jenna would never let her hear the end of it.

But Jenna's voice didn't kill the buzz of needy anticipation that was making her damp skin tingle. In desperation, she tried to think of something entirely boring. Like the training schedule spreadsheet she'd been filling in yesterday, trying to set up something to make it easier to see where each player was supposed to be at any given time. What with individual coaching, small-group training sessions, team sessions, physical therapy and massage, and meetings with specialist coaches, things could get ridiculously hectic. Maybe she could go through each player's daily entries from memory.

It worked until she got to Greg's. Thinking of Greg only reminded her of Finn. Of trouble. Finn hadn't mentioned any more incidents with Greg and, even though she had her feelers out on the club's grapevine, she hadn't heard about any from anyone else. But she knew that the players could be very close-lipped when it came to internal team politics. If something was still going on, then they definitely wouldn't want her to find out.

It was telling that Greg, who usually came by her office or found her at lunch once a week or so, hadn't sought her out at all since the incident with Finn's tires. She'd known he'd had a crush on her but she'd thought she'd made her position clear to him. Apparently he'd still been holding out some hope. Not her fault but it was hard not to feel some degree of guilt. Not to mention frustration that someone she'd thought was a friend had now decided he couldn't talk to her anymore.

But all she could do for now was hope that it would blow over.

"I'm just going to check something on your computer," Finn said a few weeks later. "My phone's dead, and I left the charger at my place."

"Sure," Eva said. She turned back to the vegetables she was chopping for her pasta sauce.

She chopped for a minute or so, humming to herself, happy that Finn was here. The team had gotten back from Ohio just a few hours ago. They'd won but she cared less about that than the fact that Finn was going to be in her bed tonight.

She'd been lonely last night. Hadn't slept well at all without the warmth of him beside her.

She froze suddenly, remembering what she'd done to occupy herself when she'd given up on sleeping. She'd been finally filling out the paperwork for her acceptance of the offer to take Isaac Haines's class. Which was now lying on her desk, along with the brochure and the other bits and pieces about LA she'd printed out. Her desk. Where her computer was.

Where Finn was.

Crap. Maybe he wouldn't notice. Men didn't notice the details, did they? A pile of paper would be just a pile of paper. Still, maybe she should just go in and distract him. She put the knife down, turned, and saw Finn standing in the doorway. He held a bunch of very familiar-looking papers in his hand.

"Got something to tell me?" he said, voice very neutral. Way too polite, in fact.

Double crap. She walked over, held her hand out. "It's not polite to snoop."

He lifted the application up out of reach. "I didn't snoop. This was lying right there on your desk. What's going on, Eva? You're going to photography school? Where?"

So he hadn't read too much of the information. "Los Angeles," she said.

"California," he said slowly. "Huh. When were you going to tell me?" He thrust the papers at her and she took them. Folded them carefully and placed them in one of the drawers in the old oak dresser while she tried to work out what she wanted to say. She'd been up front with Finn. Just for the season. Which didn't explain why she hadn't been up front with him about going away weeks ago. Other than not wanting to spoil the fun she was having with him. More than fun. But she didn't want to think about that too hard.

"This isn't about you," she said, turning back to Finn.

His expression turned dark. "Nice. I'm just the guy you've been sleeping with for weeks. You could have told me, Eva."

"I haven't told anyone," she said. "Only Jenna." She stayed where she was by the dresser.

"You and your damned secrets. Why wouldn't you tell me?"

"Because you and I have a deal."

"Only until the end of the season?" He laughed. "Are you seriously telling me that you think you'll be able to walk away from this in a few more months? Christ, Eva, we spend every spare second together already. We're not exactly casual. I practically live here."

She shook her head, even though she couldn't deny what he was saying. "That wasn't the deal."

"The deal sucks. We need a new deal."

"No." Even as she said it, she couldn't help the little jolt of happiness that his words brought. But she squelched it as fast as possible. She was not going to let herself fall for Finn Castro.

"Why?"

"Because I'm leaving," she said. "Finally."

"Finally?" he echoed.

"Yes." She threw up her hands, anger starting to burn in her gut. "In case you haven't noticed, Saratoga Springs is a pretty small town. And I've been stuck here all my life."

"Raising your sisters, you mean."

"Yes. I know everyone thinks I'm freaking Saint Eva or something for staying here and doing that but trust me, it hasn't been all sunshine and rainbows and stupidly glossy movie montages. Teenage girls suck sometimes. Put three of them together—four if you count me—and there was hardly a moment when there wasn't drama of some kind going on. But I stayed. I didn't have a choice. But now I do. So I'm going to do what I want now."

"What do your sisters think about that?"

"I haven't told them yet."

"Why not?"

"Because I haven't. Partly because it's not their

decision to make. And partly because I'm allowed to keep some things to myself until I'm good and ready to share them, you know."

"Is that a crack about me not wanting to sneak around?"

"Sure. Because everything is about you apparently." She stared up at him, not entirely sure why she was so freaking angry. Other than she was.

"That's hardly fair."

"Suck it up, pretty boy, life isn't always fair."

His eyes narrowed. " 'Pretty boy'?"

"If the shoe fits."

"You know," he said. "This is exactly why I didn't want to sneak around. Secrets lead to this sort of shit."

"What's the matter? Not used to women standing up to you? Sorry, wrong girl if you think you're going to get your own way all the time."

"Trust me, I'm under no delusions about that."

"So why are you still here?"

"Because you're you. And you're hot when you're mad."

She was? For a moment she lost her train of thought. "Do not attempt to distract me with sex. Or charm me."

"I doubt I could charm you right now."

"Damned straight."

"I'm definitely open to the other thing, though."

"Men! Do you ever think about anything else?"

"Sometimes. Sometimes we think about baseball."

"Bite me."

"Is that an invitation?" He stepped closer and wrapped a hand around her wrist. Not hard enough to hurt but hard enough that it was clear she was going to have to ask if she wanted out.

She stood her ground. Stared up at him. "No."

"You sure about that?"

"Why would I want to have sex with you in the middle of an argument?"

"Because it's more fun? And this argument is dumb."

"You started it," she pointed out. "With your snooping."

"No, you started it when you didn't tell me you were leaving."

"I told you we were temporary. Close enough."

"Not really."

His fingers were too warm on her skin, his eyes very green up this close. Stupidly green. A green she wanted to fall into. No. Wait. The hell she did. They were fighting.

"Well, like I said, you're dating the wrong woman if you want someone uncomplicated."

"So we're dating? I thought we were just temporary. Is it dating when it's just temporary?"

She didn't know if he was trying to provoke her or just didn't know when to let well enough alone. Either way, she was tempted to kick him. She reined her temper back with an effort. If she calmed down, maybe he would and this stupid fight would be over. "I don't know. Does it need an exact term?"

"Maybe."

"Why?"

"Because if we're dating then we probably have to finish this argument."

That sounded about as much fun as sticking her hand in a fire. "And if we're not?"

He tugged her closer. "Then I vote we just skip to the fucking makeup sex already."

"Of course you do, you're a guy." She pulled back but his hand went flat on her back, pressing her into him. He was hard against her and he pushed his hips forward, sending a throb of angry lust through her.

"You like that I'm a guy." He did it again and she had to bite her lip not to moan.

"Right now, it's the only thing I like about you," she muttered when she caught her breath again.

Finn shrugged and his hand dropped to her ass, fingers digging in as he pulled her closer still. "Good enough for me," he said and then he kissed her.

Or something close to kissing. Lips met, and tongues and teeth. Nothing friendly about it. Only need and frustration and wanting.

His kiss drove her backward until her ass was resting against the dresser. Finn lifted her slightly so she was sitting on it. Just. He pulled one of her legs around him and she didn't need the encouragement to do the same with the other one.

Damn him. She wanted him. Even though she was still pissed at him. It was freaking annoying and she bit at his lip, nipping harder than she intended.

Finn just laughed at her. "Two can play at that game, you know."

He yanked her T-shirt up and tugged her bra down before she knew what was happening. Then his mouth closed over her nipple and sucked. Hard. Her head dropped back as pleasure shot through her, and this time she lost the fight against moaning. Teeth followed. Nipping and tugging and alternating his lips with his tongue in a rhythm that drove her completely insane.

She gripped the edge of the dresser and leaned back as far as she could so he had better access. His fingers found her zipper, yanked it down, and he shoved his hand into her panties as he sucked at her breasts again.

"Oh. God."

"Finn," he muttered, then his thumb brushed her clit, sending another shocking throb through her. "Say my name, Eva."

She pressed her lips together, fighting the urge to do exactly that. She couldn't stop herself arching into the pressure of his hand, though, or stop her legs from falling apart, her toes coming off the ground. Finn held her hip and it was the only solid point in the universe. The only part of her that wasn't coming apart at the seams.

His thumb moved, pressed, then lifted. "Say my name."

"Don't stop." She wanted him touching her.

"I'm all yours," he said. "All you have to do is ask."

"Fuck," she muttered.

"That too." His fingers moved. Just slightly. Just enough to register on the swollen flesh of her clit. Enough to torment but not satisfy.

"Say my name and I'll make you come," he said. "As many times as you want."

God. Why was she fighting it? Fighting him. She couldn't even remember anymore what they'd been arguing about. She just knew she wanted what he offered. Wanted the moment where they were together and everything else went away. He repeated the feather-light motion.

"Eva," he said softly. "Just say it."

"You suck," she muttered.

"If you ask me nicely, I will. Is that what you want? My mouth on you? My tongue where my hand is? Want me to make you come that way?"

God, his words shattered her. No one had ever talked to her this way during sex. Where had he even learned how? And why was it so fucking hot? To hear him say it. To offer himself to her like that. He kept talking, telling her exactly what he would do to her.

She twisted, trying not to think about him doing exactly as he said, but it was impossible. Impossible when his fingers were still right there and her nipples throbbed from his mouth and she could smell him hot and so damned close. Could taste him on her tongue. All she could do was give in.

"Say it," he said one last time.

"Finn," she practically screamed and then she stopped thinking as he did exactly what he'd promised.

Chapter Eleven

She woke up in bed with no recollection of getting there. Finn lay beside her, sprawled out facedown, fast asleep. Light spilled into the bedroom from the hallway. Apparently once they'd gotten here, neither of them had bothered with little details like turning off the lights.

She rolled toward Finn and felt her muscles protest the movement. God. She didn't remember coming to bed but she remembered before. Remembered the dresser and then the couch and finally the shower. Had she fallen asleep in the shower? She was certainly naked. She lifted the sheet. So was Finn.

She dropped the sheet again before his ass could sidetrack her. God. That body. What he could do with that body. All sorts of wicked delightful things. And some slightly less delightful ones. Like stopping arguments.

Damn the man. He was dangerous.

She lay there watching him sleep for a few minutes, watching the rise and fall of his chest. Here. Solid. Real.

Finn.

She wanted to snuggle up against him, feel his arm around her, pulling her close.

Being close to him felt right.

Her hand tightened around the sheet. No. No yearning allowed. Her parents had been here and solid and real, too. Then they'd been gone in an instant and there'd only been grief and pain. Just as real and solid. Still here. She wasn't going to risk that again.

Even if part of her wished she could.

Finn's head turned toward her and she caught the gleam of his eye then the flash of teeth as he smiled at her.

"How long have you been awake?" he asked, sounding nowhere near awake himself.

"Not long."

"Obviously I didn't wear you out enough."

"Seeing as I don't actually remember coming to bed, I don't think that's the problem."

He grinned. "Yeah, you kind of nodded off in the bathroom. Right after I wrapped you up in your towel. Cute. We'll have to work on your stamina."

"We had sex three times! I think my stamina is just fine."

"I don't know," he growled and snaked an arm out from under the sheet.

She slapped his hand away. "Oh no, you don't. Not unless you want me out of action for the next few days." Her girl parts were feeling the workout. Good sore but sore nonetheless.

"Definitely not," he said. Then he rolled up on his elbow. "So what are we going to do now that we're awake?"

She peered past him. "It's late. We could go back to sleep."

"Or we could finish our discussion. About you going to California."

"That's not up for discussion. I'm going."

"You haven't sent in the paperwork yet."

"No. Because the money for the tuition is in a term deposit that matures next week."

He sighed. "Okay. I get it, you need to do your thing."

"Yes. I do." She did. "That's why I said only until the end of the season."

"I know. And I agreed."

"Yes." She hesitated. But had to ask. "You know, if you want out, I understand. Cut our losses."

He sat up slowly. "Is that what you want?"

"I don't want to hurt you."

"I'm a big boy. I can take it."

"Really? Because I'm not going to change my mind about this, Finn. I've waited a long time for my turn."

"I understand. I don't like it but I understand." One side of his mouth quirked. "Is it wrong for me to hope California falls into the ocean before then?"

She laughed. "Yes. Because you have to focus on your career. You're too good to be stuck here in Saratoga. You need to get back to the Saints. Show the world what you can do."

His expression turned shuttered. "I guess. Though I kind of like it here."

"That's just sex addling your brain. You're made to play baseball."

"Maybe my body is. After last year, I'm less sure about my brain."

"Really?" She reached over to her bedside table, picked up her phone. Then called up one of their text chains. "Favorite smell, new baseball glove. Favorite place. Wrigley Field. We didn't get to favorite sound but I'm guessing yours is either that perfect crack as you hit the ball just right or the roar of the crowd just after you reach home plate."

"Maybe." He shrugged. "You made some noises earlier that I could get particularly fond of."

"Forget the sex part."

"It's kind of hard to forget." He hit her with a grin.

She narrowed her eyes. "I think baseball would be hard for you to forget, too."

"It's really hard to forget waking up in the hospital with a concussion and a sliced-up head. Or being drugged. Or hurting people around you. Last year got messed up at the end." He looked away, arms locked around his knees.

Damn. She didn't want him to look like that. "But you've learned since then, right? You'll cope better next time. Know when to reach out."

"When not to keep secrets?" he said.

The soft words hit her like he'd delivered them with a bat. "Is that why you got so mad?"

"Part of it," he said. "I have to be honest about how I'm coping, about what I need. So I need the people around me to be honest, too."

"Okay," she said. She reached out, threaded her fingers through his. "No more hiding stuff." His skin was warm where his fingers gripped hers.

"Good."

It was enough just to sit like that for a minute. Just holding his hand. But then curiosity got the better of it. "What's the other part?"

"What other part?"

"You said it was part of why you were mad?"

"Ah."

"Well?"

Finn shook his head. "The other part is mine to worry about. After."

"After?"

He leaned forward. Kissed her softly, so softly she started to want him all over again. "After you leave."

"Call your sisters," Finn said before he hung up the next night.

Eva scowled at the screen of her iPad where his face had vanished from Skype. He had been nagging her to tell her sisters for the last two days. Which would be annoying if she hadn't known he was right and that she had to come clean.

Still, she'd been hoping for something a bit more fun over their call tonight than "call your sisters." Finn had seemed distracted.

If Greg was still hassling him then she was going to ignore his insistence that he could handle things himself and tell Greg where to shove his attitude. If that didn't work, she'd go to Don.

Of course, she had no way of knowing if Greg was hassling Finn or if something else was bothering him. The game tonight had been close and Finn had missed a play that had brought it even closer. In the end the Preachers had won by one lonely run. Still, a win was a win. So surely that wasn't it.

Men. So freaking complicated.

Maybe she'd ask Connor if he knew what was going on. He'd been hanging out with Finn, which was a very Connor thing to do. The big blond guy didn't say a lot— at least not to her—but his admittedly very nice face came with a soft side he didn't show often. He was often the guy who held things together when the team got itself messed up in some argument or another. Eva had no idea why he wasn't team captain. Maybe he didn't want it. He didn't seek the limelight. Pity. He'd probably be better at the job than Greg. He definitely would have handled himself differently in this particular situation. She'd never seen Connor bent out of shape over a girl.

Which was another pity. Someone needed to snap him up.

But Connor wasn't her problem. No, her problem was Finn and his uncanny ability to make her feel guilty.

That wasn't going to go away until she'd done as he suggested.

So she pulled a face at the screen and then dialed Lizzie, half expecting that she wouldn't answer the phone.

But soon enough her sister's face, topped by hair that was now streaked blond and bright purple, appeared on-screen.

"Nice hair," Eva said.

Lizzie nodded. "Figured I'd get it out of my system before med school. Don't think doctors get to have purple hair."

"Probably not," Eva agreed. "Pity, I kind of like it."

"Nothing stopping you going purple," Lizzie pointed out. "Or blue or something. You look good in blue."

Eva clutched at her long plait. The thought of chopping it as short as Lizzie and then torturing it with as much peroxide as Lizzie did to turn her dark brown hair blond was kind of horrifying. "Thanks, I'm good."

"Bor-ing," Lizzie said.

"I'm over thirty, I'm allowed to be boring," Eva said.

"Nope, you skipped your twenties, you still have wild and crazy to catch up on," Lizzie said, shaking her head hard enough to make the purple streaks bounce around dizzily. "The Preachers wouldn't sack you even if you shaved your head entirely. So go a little crazy."

"If I go a little crazy, I'll pick something other than hair mutilation, thanks." Eva said, smiling at Lizzie's enthusiasm. She'd picked the right sister. Lizzie was the most independent of the four of them. She'd probably celebrate Eva's announcement with a cartwheel or two. Not that that would be possible in her tiny dorm room.

Eva took a deep breath. "Actually, speaking of crazy—"

Lizzie grinned. "Let me guess, you got a tattoo?"

"No."

"A new car?"

"No, let me—"

"A boyfriend?" Lizzie looked so hopeful for a moment that Eva's heart squeezed with guilt. But she wasn't ready to explain Finn to Lizzie. Lizzie was a romantic at heart. She was still dating her high school sweetheart, having managed to hold that together through several years of long distance. She wouldn't understand Eva and Finn's agreement.

"Shut up and let me tell you," she said before Lizzie could make another wild suggestion.

Lizzie shrugged and took a swig from her Diet Dr Pepper. "The floor is yours, sis."

"I applied to photography school," Eva said.

The smile that bloomed over Lizzie's face was a huge relief. "You did? With what's-his-name? That famous dude you like."

"Isaac Haines. Yes."

"Wow. Go you. When do you find out?" She pushed her purple glasses up her nose. "Wait. Did you already find out?"

Eva grinned. "Yup. I'm coming to California."

"Oh. My God!" Lizzie leapt up from her bed and Eva was treated to a screen full of her suddenly shaking yoga-pants-clad booty as Lizzie boogied around the room. "That's awesome!" She plunked back down on the bed. "But Los Angeles, right? Not San Fran?"

"Yup. But that's driving distance at least. Better than the other side of the country."

"Yes," Lizzie said. "Have you told Kate and Audrey yet?"

"Kate's next. Audrey's on a trip, so I'll tell her when she gets back. So don't blow my secret, okay?"

"Cool." Lizzie tilted her head. "What are you going to do with the house?"

"Rent it out. I'll need the money. There's a bit left in the insurance fund thanks to you and Kate's uncanny ability to score scholarships, but that's only going to cover tuition and part of my rent, I think. I'm going to need some income. Probably a part-time job." If she could fit one in. Isaac's course was meant to be intense. He took some of his students on his jobs, and they got to assist in his studio—or assist the assistants, really—too. There wasn't going to be a lot of free time for other work.

"Makes sense," Lizzie said. "And before you ask, it's fine with me. I'm good for school now with the scholarship. Your turn." She wriggled on the bed again. "Oh my God. You're going to be here in California. When?"

"December. Depending on what everyone wants to do for Christmas, I'll either come out, find somewhere to live, come back here, and then move everything after the holidays. Or maybe we can convince Kate and Aud to do a California Christmas."

"Kate would be up for it. Not sure about Audrey. She'll do whatever the almighty Steve wants to do." Lizzie screwed up her face.

"Steve's not that bad," Eva said. "He's good to Aud."

"Steve is good to whoever is Team Steve." Lizzie didn't look any happier.

Eva wondered what Steve had done to tick Lizzie off. As far she knew, they'd only met twice. But that was something that Lizzie and Audrey were going to have to deal with. Eva didn't have to wrangle their relationship dramas anymore.

Thank God.

"We'll figure something out," Eva said. She hesitated. Lizzie was so excited, maybe it would be better to just spill all the beans now. Let the news she was moving to California draw attention away from Finn. Give her sisters something bigger than news of her love life to focus on. "There's one more thing."

"There is?" Lizzie sounded distracted. Probably already plotting all the things they could do together in California. Good.

"Yes. About what you said earlier. About a boyfriend."

"You have a boyfriend too?" Lizzie's squeal almost deafened Eva. So much for her being distracted by the move.

"Not a boyfriend," Eva said. "So don't get all excited. But I am kind of seeing someone."

"Who?"

"Finn Castro."

That earned another squeal. "Oh. My. God. He's gorgeous."

"Yes," Eva agreed. "But he's not here for long and I'm leaving anyway. So this is temporary. Do not get excited."

"Does Kate know? Or Audrey?"

"I'll tell Kate when I call her. And Audrey when she gets home from her trip. So no spilling the beans about this either, okay?"

"Okay," Lizzie sounded. "But I want all the details."

"There isn't that much to tell. Like I said, don't get excited. Now I gotta go and try and catch Kate. Everything good with you?"

"More than good now that I know you're moving here. Tell Katie kisses from me."

Sunday morning Eva decided to let Finn sleep in. The Preachers had played doubleheaders twice that week, and now that the season was settling into its rhythm she could see the weight of the schedule and the work starting to settle into him.

So she would let him sleep. Make breakfast and then wake him up.

She slipped into sweats and an old hoodie and snuck out of the bedroom, closing the door gently behind her. Then she opened up the blinds in the house—Finn slept like the dead, a skill she assumed was born of so much time spent on buses and on planes and in strange hotel rooms where sleeping at the drop of a hat could only be of benefit—so she didn't worry about waking him.

In the kitchen she put the radio on softly and then puttered about. Breakfast burritos maybe. Eggs and vegetables and fresh salsa and avocado on the side. Feeding an athlete was a skill she was learning. Finn ate like a horse but he also paid attention to what he ate. He wasn't fanatical—he was happy to eat burgers or pizza or junk every so often—but most of the time he leaned heavily on the protein and whole grains and fruit and vegetables. Sensible food.

She chopped peppers and onions, tomatoes and herbs, then grated cheese. Then turned her attention to the salsa. More herbs. More tomatoes. A chili or two— he liked spicy, just as she did.

She was rinsing her hands free of chili juice in the sink when the back door opened and Audrey walked in.

For a moment, Eva was too startled to react. All her sisters had keys to the house but in all the months that Audrey had been home, she'd only dropped by unannounced twice.

But then happiness at seeing her sister overtook surprise and she darted over to hug Audrey hard.

"Hey, what are you doing here?"

She stepped back, looked at Audrey. She looked . . . tired . . . Eva decided. Even though Audrey was dressed for visiting, makeup immaculate and the straight hair Eva envied gleaming from the razor-sharp bangs down to the tips . . . there were shadows under her eyes. "You want coffee?"

Audrey shook her head. "No. I'm good."

"You're up early." Audrey was the biggest night owl of the four of them. For her to be up and functional before nine a.m. on a Sunday was a minor miracle.

"I have a meeting with a client later," Audrey said. "She lives around here and wanted to meet at that café near the park so I thought I'd drop in first."

"Working on a Sunday? You must be really busy."

"Just a scheduling thing. Being out of town last week made a mess of my calendar."

"But your trip went well?" Audrey was working with a small tech company in Seattle on a rebranding project. They'd flown her up to Seattle to see their new office space and meet the team, and she'd tacked a few days onto the trip to see some of her Seattle friends.

"Yeah, it was good. Sucks that Steve had to fly out last night, though. We only had a few hours together."

"He'll be back before you know it. If you're so busy at work, the days will fly by."

"I guess."

"Hey, I thought I—" Finn's voice came from behind her.

"Whoa," Audrey said as Eva spun on her heel to see Finn standing, wearing just his boxer briefs and a T-shirt, in the doorway. Crap. In her surprise at seeing

Audrey she'd forgotten all about Finn. She turned back to Audrey, who was gaping at Finn with an expression that was 50 percent surprise and 50 percent good old-fashioned female appreciation for a hot guy. Judging by Audrey's expression, Kate and Lizzie had both kept to their word and not mentioned Finn.

"Um, hello," Finn said. "You're Audrey, right?"

Eva spun back to him. *Go get dressed*, she mouthed. He just grinned and stayed right where he was.

"Yes, I'm Audrey," Audrey said. "So you're apparently one-up on me because I have no idea who the hell you are."

"I'm Finn," he said. "I'm going to go get dressed." He vanished, and Eva turned back to Audrey.

"Okay, I know I've been away for a week, but dude, you have some explaining to do," Audrey said. "Why is Finn Castro in your house in his underwear?"

Eva blinked. "I thought you said you didn't know who he was."

"I'm not an idiot. That's not the sort of face you forget. And I pay attention to the Preachers. But he doesn't need to know that." Audrey pointed a finger at Eva. "Which brings me back to what he's doing here in his underwear."

"Would you believe that I rented out a room to him?"

"Not in a million years." Audrey grinned then frowned. "Wait. Is this a morning-after thing? Am I seriously cramping your style here? Or have you been holding out on me?"

"I was going to tell you today," Eva said. "I wanted to wait until you got back from your trip."

"I take it you already told Kate and Lizzie?"

"Only a few days ago."

"I thought you didn't date players?" Audrey said. "I mean, I can see why you might make an exception here, because that guy is hot like—"

"Hold that thought," Finn said walking back into the doorway, fully clothed and with his backpack hitched over his shoulder. Audrey had the grace to look embarrassed.

"Um, Finn, Audrey, Audrey, Finn." Eva said, somewhat awkwardly.

"Nice to meet you," Finn said, nodding at Audrey. He came over to Eva and dropped a kiss on her mouth. "I'm going to leave you two to catch up. You seem to have plenty to talk about. Call me later."

Before Eva could protest, he headed for the front door. She appreciated him giving her the chance to talk to Audrey in private—though at the same time some backup for this conversation would have been nice. But she'd already been through the twenty-questions-about-Finn process with both Kate and Lizzie—Lizzie having called her back the same night Eva had told her to demand more information and Kate just flat-out grilling her as soon as she'd 'fessed up—so at least she knew what to expect. As Finn's truck engine rumbled to life in the street outside, Eva moved back to the counter.

"How do you feel about breakfast?" she said, looking down at the pile of vegetables decorating her counter. There was no way she and Audrey would eat the same amount as she and Finn would've, but she'd done all the prep now, no point it going to waste. "Then you can interrogate me to your heart's content."

Audrey peered at the counter. "Breakfast burritos? Okay, I'm in. Move over, I'll finish the salsa while you do the burritos."

They cooked in silence for a few minutes, falling back into old routines.

Eva served up the burritos. "Are you sure you don't want coffee?"

"No. OJ maybe?"

"Coming right up." She poured coffee into her favorite giant mug and juice into a glass, and joined Audrey at the table. Her stomach rumbled as she took the first bite. Finn certainly worked up a girl's appetite.

When she looked up, Audrey was watching her, a curious expression on her face.

"What? I'm starving," Eva said.

"Late night?" Audrey asked with a smirk.

"Maybe. Eat your breakfast." She figured breaking the news to Audrey that she was leaving would be easier on a full stomach.

Audrey poked at the burrito with her fork then looked up again.

"So how long has baseball boy—"

"Finn," Eva interrupted.

"Finn." Audrey nodded, though she frowned slightly. "Okay. How long has *Finn* been around?"

"Not long. Since partway through spring training, I guess."

"That's nearly a month! You've been hooking up with one of the hottest guys in baseball for a month and I didn't know. Why didn't you tell me?" Audrey looked outraged.

"I've been busy. You've been busy. And actually—"

"I have some news," Audrey said at the same time as Eva finished her sentence with the same words.

Eva blinked. "Snap." Audrey didn't laugh, and Eva's stomach tightened. "You go first."

A nod. Audrey reached into the purse she'd hung over the back of her chair and pulled out a pregnancy test. Eva's breath left her in a rush.

"So this happened." Audrey put the white plastic stick on the table. The little window had two very clear pink lines. Eva knew exactly what that meant but she couldn't help asking.

"You're pregnant?" She watched Audrey, looking for a clue as to how her little sister might be feeling about the situation.

Audrey nodded. Then slowly, she grinned. "Isn't it amazing?"

Eva nodded automatically, brain whirling as she tried to catch up. "Were you guys trying? You didn't tell me." *Hey, Eva, I'm thinking about having a baby* seemed the sort of thing Audrey might have mentioned. Eva hiding her new boyfriend was a minor detail but a baby— even contemplating one—was pretty much the definition of huge news.

"No. We weren't trying. Guess they aren't lying about that whole birth-control-not-being-one-hundred-percent-effective thing." The grin grew wider.

"I guess." Eva tried to sound enthusiastic. Audrey was only twenty-four. Which was older than their mom had been when she'd had Eva, but it suddenly seemed way too young to even think about having a baby. "What does Steve think?"

"I haven't told him," Audrey said. "I only took the test

this morning. I went to the pharmacy, asking for something because my stomach was still upset. The woman asked if I could be pregnant. I didn't think so but better safe than sorry, right? So I bought a test. And surprise. I didn't want to tell him over the phone. But I had to tell someone so I came here."

"Huh," Eva managed. She knew she should be trying to act happier; Audrey's smile had faded a little. "I mean, that's great. That you came to tell me."

"I'm having a baby. It's amazing," Audrey said.

About a thousand things were whirling though Eva's brain. *Amazing* was one way of describing it. But it wasn't the only word that sprang to mind. She tried to focus. Audrey was happy about this. Eva needed to be, too. "Any idea how far along you are?"

"No. You know me. Wonky cycle. I've been so busy lately that I haven't really been keeping track. A couple of months maybe?"

"You only felt sick a few weeks ago."

"Not everyone gets sick straightaway. I'll have to make a doctor's appointment. Or an ob-gyn, I guess. I don't know, who do you see first?"

"You're asking the wrong gal about that one," Eva said. "But I can send you the details for who I see. Unless you've already hooked up since you got back."

"GP, yes. Ob-gyn, no. I was going to ask you about that."

"I'll send you the details." Eva's voice sounded flat, even though she was trying to summon some enthusiasm.

"Aren't you happy for me?" Audrey's eyes, so like her own, held a challenge.

"Yes, of course."

"You don't look happy."

"I'm just surprised," Eva said. "Give me a minute to catch my breath." She managed a smile. "After all, it's not every day I find out I'm going to be an aunt for the first time." An aunt. There was a thought. An aunt sounded good. All of the fun of a baby with the ability to hand the little darling back to the parents when things got messy or loud. She'd never raised a baby, but raising three teenagers had definitely squashed her maternal instinct down to a very small battered thing. She didn't know if she'd ever want kids of her own, but a niece or nephew was doable. Except . . . she wasn't going to be around for the first few years.

She stood, came around to Audrey, and leaned down to hug her. "Wow. An aunt." She pulled back. "Lizzie and Kate are going to go nuts."

Audrey smiled, looking distinctly relieved. "I want to wait to tell them. Steve should be the next to know. I just had to tell someone today."

"That's what I'm here for," Eva said. "Sisterly info dumping and venting twenty-four seven."

"Even with Hottie McBaseball in your bed?"

"Finn," Eva said firmly. "And yes, even then. Besides"—she grinned wickedly—"he's away a lot."

"That sucks. Even having Steve away one week a month is hard. Baseball schedules are way worse than that."

"It's not so bad with Triple-A, you know that."

A nod. "But I don't understand. What's made you change your mind on no jocks? I mean, I get it, he is hot—props on that—but there have been other hot guys on the team."

Not like Finn, there hadn't been. Or if there had, she'd been too swamped with responsibility to notice. Maybe that explained her recent craziness. Hormones reawakening after years of stress or something. But that wasn't the explanation to give her sister. "I don't know, we just kind of happened." She twisted her skull stud nervously.

"Oh no. That's lame. You're not telling me everything. You always play with your jewelry when you're hiding something."

Eva dropped her hand. "I do not."

"Yup, you do."

"Well, there goes my dream of becoming a professional poker player."

"And that was a change of subject. C'mon, sis. Spill the beans. You said you had news. Does that have something to do with this?"

Chapter Twelve

Damn. Confession time. She'd been nervous enough about telling her sisters before. Sure, Lizzie and Kate had, on the surface, seemed to take it well—but heck, Audrey had just announced she was going to have a baby. She might not be so impressed that Eva was leaving town right now. Still, Audrey had Steven. So she'd be fine. Eva had given her sisters the last decade. More than that. She rubbed her palms down her yoga pants. "Part of it does. I guess." She fiddled with her rapidly cooling burrito.

"Well, don't keep me in suspense," Audrey said. She reached for her glass, swigged juice, looking far more relaxed than she had when she first arrived. Maybe it was the relief of having shared her news. Maybe Eva would feel just as relaxed once she'd told Audrey hers.

"I applied for a photography course."

Audrey clapped her hands. "Oh my God! It's about time. And you got in?"

"Yes. It's two years. In Los Angeles."

Audrey's mouth dropped opened. "Los Angeles?

You're moving to California? Don't they have photography schools on the East Coast?"

"Not with Isaac Haines they don't."

"Isaac Haines?" Audrey looked blank for a moment. "Oh. Is he the guy who took all those shots you used to have on your bedroom wall? The dancers and stuff?"

Dancers and stuff? Well, Audrey had never really paid that much attention to photography until she'd become a designer. But did she really not know who Isaac was? The man was famous for his shoots of athletes, dancers, rock bands, and actors, both doing their thing and in portraits. Eva had practically papered her room in his work over the years. He gave a whole new meaning to the phrase *poetry in motion*. He'd even come to Saratoga a time or two during racing season to photograph the horses. Eva had practically stalked him. But apparently Audrey hadn't noticed. "Yes. That's him. He's a genius. He only takes ten students each year in his course."

"And you got in?" Audrey sounded shocked.

Eva had felt the same way when she'd gotten the acceptance letter. "Yes. It's the chance of a lifetime." Isaac apparently picked all the students by hand. Over the years, it hadn't always been people with lots of experience and other qualifications who'd made it, which was about the only reason that Eva had been brave enough to try in the first place.

"But I'm having a baby!" Audrey stopped, hands flying to her mouth. "Sorry. I mean, I always kind of figured when I moved back here that you'd be around, you know."

"I know. But I'm not even leaving until December.

So I'm here for the first part and we can go shopping for baby stuff together. Even when I go, it's not forever." She didn't know what might happen after she finished school. Plenty of Isaac's students had gone on to be very successful photographers. But time enough to worry about that after she finished. "And you have Steve."

Audrey chewed her lip for a moment. "I guess. It's just a surprise."

"Not as big as your surprise," Eva pointed out.

"I guess that's fair. But I don't understand what your leaving has to do with you deciding to sleep with Finn Castro. Isn't it bad timing, if you're moving away?"

Eva shrugged, ignoring the small piece of her heart that muttered *yes* in response to that particular question. "Finn's a great guy but he's younger than me. And he's got a career ahead of him. This is just a temporary thing."

"Temporary?"

"Until the end of the season."

"Isn't that a little . . . calculating? What happens if one of you falls in love or something?"

"We won't," Eva said. "Both of us know what this is. Finn wants to get back to the majors. And I want to go to school."

"Sounds lonely."

"Don't take this the wrong way but after living with the three of you for years, I can stand a bit of alone time. Don't worry about me, Aud. I know what I'm doing."

"I hope so." Audrey poked at her burrito. "This is cold. Can I zap it in the microwave?"

"I could make another one." She'd prepped for a

Finn-sized appetite. She and Audrey hadn't really made a dent in the pile of veggies.

"Microwave is good. I have to run soon anyway."

When Finn pulled into Eva's driveway, she was sitting on her front porch, rugged up in a sweater and looking thoughtful as she sipped coffee and rocked in an old-fashioned wooden porch swing.

"Sisterly bonding time over?" he asked when he reached her.

"Yes." Eva patted the seat of the swing beside her. He didn't wait for another invitation. It was sunny and warm and he couldn't think of a better place to be than sitting beside her.

"Did you tell her about your course?" he asked.

"Yes." She sounded flat, and she didn't look at him even as he eased an arm around her.

He was starting to worry. "Did she take it okay?"

Eva shrugged. "Not sure she was jumping for joy but it wasn't too bad."

"Then what's wrong?"

Her expression was torn. "I don't know if I should tell you."

"I can keep a secret," he said. "For starters, I don't really know anyone in this town to tell secrets to." He risked a smile, wondering if he could coax one out of her.

"Other than everyone on the Preachers," she said, but the side of her mouth lifted.

Just a little. Good. "Well, half of them aren't talking to me and I don't think the other half are all that interested in whatever's going on between you and your sisters. You already swore me to secrecy about school, so what's one more fact to add to that?"

"They're still giving you a hard time." Eva shook her head, lips pursed. "I'm going to kick Greg's butt."

"No, you're not. You're focusing on the wrong thing here. You were going to tell me something about Audrey? I'm assuming it is about Audrey?" Unless something else had happened this morning. He'd only been gone two hours. Long enough for him to work out and get back here. Not long enough for hell to break loose, surely?

"She's having a baby," Eva blurted out.

A kid? How old was Audrey? He tried to remember what Eva had told him. A few years younger than him, maybe? Lizzie was still in college, so she was the baby, and Kate was the second oldest. So twenty-three? Twenty-four? Young to be having a baby these days, perhaps, but it wasn't like she was a teenager. "Babies are good," he ventured. "If she wants one? Does she want one?"

"Seems that way."

"Okay." He nudged her with his shoulder. "Then the fact that you're going to be an auntie is good news, isn't it?"

"Yes. It's just a bit of a . . ."

"Shock? You didn't know she was trying?"

"I don't think she was trying. She's been with Steve less than a year. They're not engaged or anything."

"Well, not everyone believes in marriage."

"Do you?"

"I guess. Eventually. But we're talking about Audrey. Is the boyfriend—Steve, is that his name?—happy about the baby?"

"She hasn't told him yet. He's away on a business trip."

Maybe that was what she was worried about—how Steve was going to take it. "Hey," he said. "Are you going all mother hen on me here? Is Audrey okay?"

Eva smiled, the expression rueful. "Yes. She's really happy. And yes, I know I should be, too. But I can't help worrying."

"You're allowed to worry a bit. But you're also allowed to be happy. I mean, isn't this the point of raising kids, that they go off and have lives and raise their own and all that good stuff? I know she's your sister but under the circumstances, it's the same thing. This means you did good. If she's happy about it and feels like it works for her to do this now, then you did your job right."

"Have you been watching Dr. Phil during your workouts or something?" Eva said, smiling ruefully at him. "You're sounding too smart for a guy your age."

"If it helps, I can add *dude* to the end of all my sentences from now on."

"Thanks."

"No problem, dude. Now, speaking of age, Oliver called me while I was at the gym. He's throwing a birthday party for Amelia on Saturday night. It's not her actual birthday but it's the only day that works with the Saints' schedule for the next few weeks. I thought it would be fun seeing as I don't have another game until Monday and that's here. We could go up to the city Saturday, come back Sunday. What do you think?"

She looked startled. "You want me to come with you?"

"Why wouldn't I?"

"Are you sure?"

"Well, folks here know. I figure the news has spread to the Saints. And Amelia knows because I told Em—"

"You told your sister? You didn't tell me that."

"Didn't I? No big deal." He'd told Em because she'd kill him if she found out he was keeping it from her, but also because he figured it would give her something to talk to Amelia about. He wanted Amelia and Em back the way they had been before he'd messed up. So if talking about him was a way for them to have some quality girl talk, he was happy to be talked about.

"What did she say?"

"I believe it was something like 'Older woman, huh? Good one, little brother.' Then she started talking about her case." It hadn't been exactly that. But then, he hadn't made a big deal out of it. Eva was determined that they only had the season, so unless he could change her mind about that, letting his sister know how much he liked Eva was only going to make things harder at the end.

"Took it in her stride, did she?"

"I guess. It takes a lot to shake Em." Like him ending up in hospital after a fight, apparently. "So, do you want to come? It'll be cool. Oliver has a great apartment and Amelia always throws good parties."

Eva hesitated. "I don't know—"

"What are you worried about?"

"It just seems a little weird, I mean, we're not going to be together after the end of the season."

"They don't know that. Look, you probably know a lot of the people who are going to be there already, so that part isn't weird. And honestly, everyone would probably be more surprised if I turned up with you next—" He broke off that thought, realizing that telling her that his friends and family would be more surprised if he had a long-term relationship than if he brought a new girlfriend to a party wasn't really selling himself to her.

Eva burst out laughing. "You were going to say that they'd be more surprised if we lasted than if we break up, weren't you? Finn the bad boy, new girl in every town." She kept laughing. "I'm just your latest conquest."

He wasn't entirely sure why that was so funny.

She looked up at him and laughed harder. "And now you're mad about it. Did you think I hadn't heard about your reputation before you got here?"

He stared down at her. "So you used to follow my exploits in the newspapers, did you?" Not that there had been many exploits. To his surprise Eva blushed. "Wait. Did you?" Now it was his turn to laugh. "Ha! You did. Which means either you're a baseball gossip junkie or . . ."

"Shut up," she said. She glared at him.

"Oh no. This is too good. You had a crush on me before I got here."

"In your dreams." Her cheeks were rapidly turning red.

"I think that might be in *your* dreams." He grinned at her, stupidly pleased by the thought. "Did you have my poster on your bedroom wall?"

"No, because your head is too big to fit," she retorted, still blushing furiously.

Finn laughed. "Maybe. But how can you turn down

an invite to come to a fancy New York party with the man of your dreams?"

"Right now, I think it would be kind of easy," she muttered.

"Liar," he said and bent to kiss her. When they pulled apart and her eyes had gone soft and warm rather than annoyed, he said, "Come to Amelia's party with me, Eva Harlowe. Let me show you off. Or you can show me off." He grinned then held up his hands in surrender as her gaze sharpened.

"Does that mean you're dressing up?"

He nodded. "Did I mention it's black tie? I have this tuxedo . . ."

"That's not playing fair," she said. "Tuxedos give men an unfair advantage."

"Whatever it takes." He kissed her again. "So say yes. Then you can tell me what you'll be wearing so I can think about how much fun it will be to take it off you at the end of the night."

Saturday night, Eva stepped out of the helicopter and wondered how she'd tripped and fallen into somebody else's life. Someone way more glamorous than her. Someone who flew in helicopters with guys who looked very, very good in tuxedos.

Finn took her hand and led her away from the chopper, turning once to wave back at the pilot, a woman with short dark hair.

"Tell me again why the helicopter?" Eva asked, grabbing at her hair with her free hand.

"Fast," Finn said. "And Charles Air gives Saints' players a deal."

"How much of a deal?"

"Enough." He pulled her into the small terminal building.

"It's still a lot of money," Eva said.

"I can afford it. I haven't exactly been throwing money around since I moved to Saratoga. Stop worrying, let someone spoil you for once."

She had to smile at that even though part of her was busy trying to warn the rest of her that there was no point getting even a little bit used to being spoiled by Finn. Tonight was the other Eva's life. The fairy-tale version where everything in her life was perfect. Where her parents were alive somewhere and she didn't have a pregnant sister to worry about.

Thinking of Audrey made her stomach turn over. She'd spoken to her a few times during the week, to check whether she'd been to the doctor—yes, and she was definitely pregnant—and the ob-gyn—yes, and she was about eight weeks along—and then today to check in again. Audrey was still giddy with her news and Eva was torn between the creeping excitement at the thought of being an aunt and her old instincts to step in and take charge and make sure everything was okay.

But she pushed the feeling away. Fairy tales. That was all she had to worry about tonight. And not the kind that went horribly wrong at midnight. The kind that ended with a big fat *happily ever after*. Just for one weekend, she was going to smile and put on a gorgeous dress and dance with a tuxedo-clad prince.

It would be fun.

More than fun.

She tightened her hand around Finn's as they stood and waited for their luggage. "Are you really not going to tell me where we're staying?"

He nodded. "If I had my way, I'd blindfold you until we get there. But that might get us some odd looks. So you're just going to have to wait and see."

"You're enjoying this way too much."

"What's not to like? I have the weekend off for once, and I'm taking you to a party."

One of the terminal employees came up to them with a trolley loaded with their two small bags. And the coat bag that held her dress. She took that one. She'd paid a small fortune for its contents and she wasn't taking any chances. Oliver's shindig didn't start until eight and it was only just five. Hotel. Then change. Then they'd be on their way. Cinderella off to the ball. It was going to be great.

"Finn looks happy."

Eva almost swallowed her mouthful of martini the wrong way.

"Sorry, did I sneak up on you?" Amelia continued.

Eva blinked, caught her breath as the burn of vodka eased in her throat. "No, I wasn't paying attention." She smoothed her free hand down her dress nervously. She'd gone for a vaguely 1950s style. Fitted on top, swooping along her shoulders, and then a deep V-neck and back before the skirt widened to bell around her. It was fairly conservative if you ignored the fabric—red lace over nude silk layers that made it look like she was only wearing the lace from a distance.

She'd been worried it would be too much but given that half the other women were wearing full-length gowns and most of them wore jewelry that was possibly worth more than her house, she fit right in.

Amelia tipped up her own drink, and the sapphire-and-diamond bracelet at her wrist caught the light of the candles flickering around the room. The dark-blue lights glimmering off the stones matched her deep-blue dress. "The view is kind of awesome. I'm still not used to it." Oliver's apartment faced Central Park. Right now, the sweep of night-dark park sprinkled with rows of lights marking paths or roads looked pretty spectacular.

"As good as Hong Kong?" Eva asked.

Amelia, an economist, had apparently been working on a project for an investment bank in Hong Kong for the last six months. She was about to move back to New York.

"Hong Kong is amazing in a different way. I'll miss it. But Oliver has promised we'll go traveling when he retires. Or I'll get another overseas job then."

Eva raised eyebrows. "Is he thinking about that?"

"He says he is. I don't know. No one can make that decision for him."

"But his hand is holding up okay? Now that the season has started?"

"So far. He still has to have therapy and massages. He says it's almost as good as new." Amelia glanced back toward the room where Oliver was talking to Alex and Maggie Winters and Raina Coulter. "I'm not sure I entirely believe him." She turned back to Eva. "But we were talking about Finn. At least, I tried to start talking about Finn. You kind of changed the subject. Was that on purpose?"

Eva had been hoping Amelia wouldn't notice. But apparently you didn't get to be an economist at a fancy Wall Street bank by being slow on the uptake. "No."

"So is he?"

"Is Finn happy? You might be a better judge of that. You know him better than I do."

"He looks happy," Amelia said again. "More relaxed than I've seen him in a long time. I'm guessing that has more to do with you than Saratoga Springs."

Damn. Eva got the distinct impression that Amelia was probing to see whether Eva's intentions toward her de facto little brother were honorable. "He's playing well. I think he's coming to grips with everything that happened last year. He's finding his way to deal with it all." She gestured around the room. "All this. It's a lot."

Amelia nodded. "Yes, it is. But Finn's had more experience at it than you or me. He's always been good at fitting in wherever he finds himself. Ever since he was a kid."

"I can imagine. He knows how to turn on the charm."

Amelia nodded. "Yes. But he's not just that guy, you know. He's more than the charm. He goes out of his way for people he loves. All the way, in fact."

"I'm learning that. He certainly throws himself into things feetfirst."

"Mari—his mom—she used to say he was like a puppy. Either going flat-out after whatever he wanted or fast asleep. No middle ground."

"Maybe that's what he's found then," Eva said.

"Something more even." She shrugged, still not entirely easy with talking about him this way. "I don't know. I didn't know him before he came to the Preachers. I mean, I know what happened, why he came to us but I haven't seen any sign of that side of him." She eyed Amelia. "In fact, if I wasn't sleeping with him, I'd have said he was living like a monk."

Amelia almost choked on her drink as she burst into laughter. "He said you didn't beat around the bush."

"Well, I didn't think anyone here would believe we're just good friends. Not when he's dragging me to your birthday party out of the blue. But if that's what you wanted to know—whether he's staying away from the party side of life—then he is. Unless he's getting up to hijinks when they have away games. But I don't think so. Don would have told me by now. He probably would have told Alex and Lucas and Mal, too."

"I'm glad," Amelia said. She took a sip of her drink, relief clear in her big blue eyes. "I'm happy for him."

"He seems set on getting back to the Saints," Eva said.

"Do you think he's ready for that?"

"I'm not a baseball coach. I guess if he wants it enough, he'll do it. He'll figure out how to handle it. He knows he messed up last year."

"Has he talked to you about that?"

"A little. He's been very up front. Doesn't want any secrets. So I think he's trying to do things differently."

"His taste in women has improved," Amelia said with a smile.

"You mean I'm not his usual type?" Eva asked.

"No, thank God. Previously he's gone for sweet and

easy. Not what a guy like him needs. He needs someone who can see past the package and call him on his bullshit. Who isn't dazzled by his face."

"Not sure I can claim to be undazzled," Eva said. "It's hard not to be."

"I know. But I saw you two earlier. You made him laugh. And he's hardly left your side. That's good."

It would be good if she and Finn were a real thing. But, no. No thinking about reality tonight. That was for tomorrow.

"I'm happy to have him by my side. And other places." Eva grinned at Amelia. "But I'm guessing you don't want to hear about that."

"God, no. He's practically my brother. Go talk to Raina if you want to talk sex. She's good at that."

"Damn, and here I thought I was going to finally get the skinny on Oliver. He's been making hearts flutter whenever he visited the Preachers for years."

"Not your heart?" Amelia said. She didn't sound worried.

"No. I mean, he's gorgeous and very nice but no, Oliver never made my heart pound."

"And Finn does? Weird."

"No accounting for taste, I guess," Eva said. "Which has worked out well for both of us, in this case. So, shall we go back to our guys? Then we can have cake. There is cake, right? You're not on some weird New York no-fat no-sugar no-carbs diet?"

"Honey, have you not seen how many margaritas I've had tonight? There will be cake. Or Oliver will be sleeping alone."

"I knew I liked you," Eva said and followed Amelia back to the men.

"I could get used to this," Eva said as Finn poured her a glass of champagne. She looked down from the balcony where they stood as New York spread below her in a glittering wave of lights and shadows that made her fingers itch for a camera. Then she looked back at Finn. Gorgeous as the city was, it wasn't as riveting as Finn in a tuxedo.

"Stick with me, babe," he quipped, but his smile didn't quite meet his eyes.

She ignored the little pang of guilt. He should be with someone who would be happy to take what he was offering. But for now he was hers. So she'd take this night.

He tilted his own glass—the first drink she'd seen him have all night—and touched it gently to hers. "Nice party, yes?"

"Yes. Amelia looked like she had a great time."

"I saw the two of you talking. Did you like her?"

She had. And she'd liked seeing Oliver and Maggie and all the other people from the Saints she knew. It had been easier than she'd expected, as if that world was a skin she could slip into easily.

Not that she was sure she'd want to live there. Glittering glamorous parties with a few friends were the easy part of that world. The reality was hard work and separation and press and craziness. There was enough of that just around the Preachers to know that stepping up to the next level wasn't as easy as all the people

drinking and laughing and eating really good food in
Oliver's apartment tonight made it seem.

"I did. She's nice. She and Oliver seem good together.
It's nice seeing him settled down after all this time."

"He makes her happy, I'll give him that," Finn said.
"But enough about Oliver." He took her hand, drew her
back into the living room of the suite. Eva had kicked
off her heels—there was only so long a woman could
put up with four-inch heels no matter how sexy the shoes
were—and standing beside Finn in bare feet made her
acutely aware of just how tall he was.

He let go of her hand and moved over to the fancy
sound system sitting on one of the shelves; after a few
buttons were pressed, music spilled softly in the room.
Something slow and sultry. A woman's voice, low and
throbbing, singing about wanting the wrong man.

Eva knew exactly how she felt as Finn came back to
her and held out a hand.

"Dance with me?"

All this and he danced, too? Of course he did. He was
too graceful on his feet not to be a good dancer. No sane
woman would turn down the chance to dance with him.

She stepped close and he tucked his left hand at her
waist and pulled her into a classic slow dance. As they
moved slowly to the music and she moved with him, the
weight of his hand burning her skin through her dress,
she felt the world start to go away. The sensation was
familiar by now, the way everything faded to back-
ground noise when she was close to him.

"Did I mention I like your dress?"

She tipped her head back so she could see him. "You

may have said something about it." He'd told her she looked beautiful many times tonight.

"Good. Because it's doing a very good job. Sexy." His hand left her waist to skim along the end of the vee at the back, fingers sparking shivers as they hit skin.

"That's the idea," she said.

"I could barely concentrate all night. All those buttons. Very tempting." His fingers drifted down, came to rest on the tiny button at the top of a line of them that started where the vee ended halfway down her back and headed down.

"I'm thinking that's probably what the designer had in mind."

"Good. Maybe you should get all your clothes from them."

She smiled. "But then you'd never be able to concentrate. And I don't want to be accused of ruining your good form. No one wants to be the sports equivalent of Yoko Ono."

He laughed. "Okay, how about just after hours then?"

"That would require a bigger clothing budget than I have."

"I'd be more than happy to contribute."

"You know, a girl could take that the wrong way," she said, smiling at him. "It's not PC to offer clothes for sex."

He attempted to look contrite. "But if I bought them, I could rip them off you without worrying."

"Finn Castro, you are *not* ripping this dress." She smoothed a hand down her hip. "This dress is staying one hundred percent intact. Or you're a dead man."

"One hundred percent sexy. But that's my point. I didn't buy this one. So I can't ruin it." He pressed a kiss to her shoulder.

"You could buy some clothes I could rip off you." There. That seemed a good counteroffer to her. "Give me a Magic Mike moment. You've just proved you can dance."

"I think dancing and stripping are two different skills."

She thought of some of the dodgy male strip shows she'd gone to for bachelorette parties over the years and couldn't argue with that. Someone needed to invent the male equivalent of the kind of burlesque Raina and her girls did at Raina's club. Elegant. Fun. Sexy. Less waxed chests and awkward audience participation. More . . . seduction.

Of course, if you put Finn up on a stage, he'd just have to stand there and women would be throwing fifties and underwear at him.

Then she'd have to hurt them, so that probably wasn't a good idea.

"Obviously the only solution is a mutual no-ripping-clothes-off pact," she said.

"That's no fun."

"How about only ripping by prior agreement?"

His mouth quirked. "Tell me more."

"Some other time. Like I said, tear this dress and I'll have to cut you."

His laugh rolled across the room and set her skin alight all over again. God, she was far too fond of that sound.

"Message received. No ripping." He traced the vee

again. "I guess that means tonight I'll have to take it slow?"

Slow. That sounded good. Finn taking his time with her. Her taking her time with him. The thought made her sweat. Made her ache between her legs. "I can do slow."

"Good. Then turn around."

Nothing in her was even slightly interested in not complying with that request. She turned and waited, wanting him to touch her.

Wanting to just stand there suspended in the waiting, too. Frozen in this moment, where it was just the two of them. A perfect memory.

But then Finn's fingers stroked down her spine and she shivered again and decided that having him was more important.

He released the first button and then another before continuing down. Slowly. Pausing just long enough between each one to make her heart beat faster and the need for him to put his hands back on her skin build.

She still wasn't used to the way that he could light her up so easily. Wondered if it was the same for him, the hunger that rose up and drove all else aside.

He reached the last button and let his hands trail down the length of her spine again, stopping when they reached the lace at the waist of her underwear. It was red and lacy, like the dress. Only there was no lining on the underwear, just her skin.

Judging by the sound he made, he liked the image. She shrugged her shoulders so that the gown slipped down from them, baring even more of her skin.

"God," Finn muttered and then he pushed the dress down, carefully but with a definite sense of purpose.

When it fell down her body and pooled around her ankles, he bent and suddenly lifted her, cradling her against his body. She still loved the fact that he could pick her up so easily. She pulled his head down and kissed him as he walked toward the bedroom, kicking the door that separated it from the main room of the suite closed behind him as they passed through. The bed was gigantic, crazy big. Covered in a dark gray silky comforter that she'd wanted to roll around in earlier, but there'd been no time.

The only light in the room came from the opened curtains, which made the floor-to-ceiling windows a stark sheet of glittering light and dark city beyond. She knew that she should probably ask him to close them. There were other, taller buildings around the hotel, and who knew who might be watching. But as Finn laid her down and tugged her shoes off, she knew she didn't care. Knew that she'd lie here for him and do whatever he wanted as long as he kept touching her.

He pulled the lace from her body and pushed her legs open. Then stepped back, the light from the window turning him into a sculpted figure of shaded muscle and skin as he tugged off the rest of his clothes. She lay still, knowing he was looking at her, knowing he could see how much she wanted him. There was no hiding how turned on he was. His cock was hard and as she watched, he reached down, stroked it once, which made the throbbing between her legs intensify and she spread them wider, wanting to see him do it again.

Wanting to drive the heat that was pulling them closer to burn hotter. Brighter. More dangerously.

But instead, Finn dropped to his knees, pushed her

legs wider, and then spread her farther apart with his hands before he pressed his face between her legs and set to work driving her slowly crazy. Each stroke of his tongue or lap of his lips was deliberate, considered. Perfectly placed to tease her. Giving her just enough to turn her on more, push her further, but not enough for her to reach the edge. She dropped her head back, dug her hands into the silky comforter that slipped beneath her skin like his tongue was slipping over her clit and she fell into the sensation. Not thinking, just wanting and reaching the point where it was too much. Arching up into him until his hands clamped her thighs and held her still, positioning her so her could continue her slow torture and all she could do was take it.

When she felt herself begin to shudder, when she could feel the orgasm finally beginning to approach, he stopped, pulled back.

Then he thrust two fingers into her, just hard enough to push her over the edge while he watched her writhe.

She didn't have time to really catch her breath before he was gone again. Her chest was heaving, the pleasure still running through her, catching her up again with each pulse. But then he climbed back onto the bed, scooping her up with him so that they were stretched out face-to-face.

"More?" he asked.

She nodded and he smiled and rolled so that she was beneath him once more. He put a hand on her thigh, coaxing her leg up over his waist, and then pushed into her slowly.

The feeling almost made her come again. She expected him to be wild. Fast. But instead he moved slow.

Certain. Inexorable. Like something meant to be, his body in hers and his face above her. She didn't know how he could be so in control when she felt like she was dissolving into him. But he didn't falter, didn't change, just kept up the rhythm of it, each stroke seeming to hit her deeper, to push her wider and further back into the place where it was all just darkness and pleasure and Finn-Eva-Finn.

Kisses and hands and the slow sure movement of his body on hers as though he'd been born with the knowledge of how to undo her.

Until all she could do was give in completely to him and let him take her world apart in a shower of sensation so good she wasn't sure she was still even her.

An hour or so later she woke with her head on Finn's chest, hand splayed across the place where his tattoo began its dark curve across his torso, his arm curled around her. She blinked into the darkness, not entirely sure where she was. Her hand flexed and she felt the bump of the rougher flesh under the tattoo.

"Eva?" he said sleepily.

"I think so," she said and felt more than heard the low rumble of his laugh beneath her ear.

"My work here is done then."

"Conceited." She flexed her fingers slightly so the tips of her nails pressed into his skin. He made a happy noise.

"Satisfied," he corrected.

She eased back with the hand, instead, stroking the path of the tattoo. The first part of it, the odd curve of it across the upper part of his abs, hid a scar. But he'd never volunteered how he'd obtained it and she hadn't asked. But now, lying in the darkness, remembering Amelia saying something about how far he'd go for people he loved, her curiosity sparked.

"Can I ask you something?" she said.

"Move your hand about half a foot lower and you can ask me anything."

"Men are easy," she said, but that didn't stop her doing as he asked. Not that sliding her hand down to find his cock was exactly a hardship. She stroked it once, enjoying the feel of him hardening to her touch.

He made a muffled sound and arched his hips up but she didn't move her hand again. "Question, remember?"

"Ask away. Ask fast."

"How did you get the scar?"

"Scar?" he said, sounding confused.

"Under the tattoo?" She rubbed her thumb over the head of his cock.

"Oh. That."

"Yeah, that."

His hand came down over hers, wrapping her fingers around him under his grasp. "I donated part of my liver."

She jerked her hand in shock but with his hand around hers, the movement turned into another stroke that made him groan. He'd donated part of his liver? "When? Who to?"

"When I was eighteen. And to Amelia's mom. She needed it." He moved his hand again and his breath caught. "Do you really want to talk about this now?" His voice was hoarse. Hungry.

Part of her wanted to know the story. Part of her was confused. It seemed amazingly generous to do that for

someone you weren't related to. Amelia said he went all
the way for people he loved. Apparently she hadn't been
kidding. She wanted to know more. But part of her was
increasingly focused on what her hand and Finn's were
doing. At the feel of him, hard and hot beneath her hand
and the way she was going hot and needy again because
of it. So maybe explanations could wait. Right now she
needed the man, not his past. She rolled to her knees,
not letting go of him, swung a leg over his so she was
straddling him.

"Maybe not right this second," she said and bent to
kiss him.

It was near sunset when they got back to Eva's house on
Sunday. Finn had organized a late checkout and they'd
lazed in bed, eating room service and being silly until
the last minute. Nothing but Finn and Eva. No thinking
too hard about the way she didn't want to move too far
from him after the hours they'd spent entangled in
pleasure last night. The chopper flight back to Saratoga
Springs had been gorgeous in the sunshine and Eva was
trying to stay focused on the moment and ignore the
fact that her Cinderella weekend was almost over when
she followed Finn into the house.

But she'd barely made it into the hallway before
Audrey came running down the hall, nearly giving Eva
a heart attack in the process, and threw herself into Eva's
arms before bursting into tears.

Eva hugged her, patting her frantically. "Aud? What's
wrong? Is it the baby?"

That just earned her a sobbing head shake and Audrey

shuddering harder. For a crazy moment, Eva thought maybe something had happened to Kate or Lizzie—but someone would have called her if that had been the case. No, this had to be an Audrey-specific problem, so she shoved down the fear and focused on her sister.

There didn't seem like there was much to do but hang on and let her cry. Beside them, Finn was hovering, looking worried.

Go make tea, she mouthed at him and he retreated to the kitchen, pausing at the door to look back at her. She waved him on with a flip of her hand.

When Audrey's sobs started to ease a little, Eva tried to loosen the hug.

Audrey's arms clamped tighter around her.

Eva rubbed her back. "Aud, honey? Let's go into the living room. You have to tell me what's wrong. Come and sit down and you'll feel better." She spoke softly, falling automatically back into the tone she'd been using for years to talk her sisters off the ledge of various teenage dramas. Her mom voice.

More sobs followed her words but slowly the grip Audrey had on her eased and Eva was able to steer her, still crying, to the sofa. As she sat, Finn appeared with the box of Kleenex from the kitchen and a cool washcloth before he vanished again.

Eva tried to get Audrey to wipe her face down, difficult when she was still crying. Her sister's face was red and blotchy, mascara smeared, her breath hiccuping through the sobs. Eva passed Kleenex and rubbed Audrey's back again until the tears eased back a few notches, worry making her stomach knot as the minutes passed. Finn returned with tea in three mugs and took a seat across from them. It was impressive that he hadn't fled the way many guys would have when faced with a sobbing mess of a sister he hardly knew.

Audrey wiped at her eyes for the umpteenth time, then dropped the Kleenex on the rapidly growing pile on her lap.

Eva took a deep breath. "Do you want to tell me what's going on?" she asked carefully. She glanced at Finn. "Do you want Finn to go?"

"N-no," Audrey managed. She reached for one of the mugs, took a sip. Then another. It seemed to calm her a little. "He can stay."

"Okay." Eva waited. Let Audrey compose herself as she drank more tea. Then, "Can you tell us now?"

Audrey put down her mug, pressed her hands to her eyes. "Steve came home today." She stopped, swallowed, dropped her hands. The grief-stricken look in her eyes made Eva's chest ache.

"And?" Eva prompted.

"Well, he seemed happy when he got home. He said his trip had gone well. He wanted to go out for lunch but I'd made lunch so I could tell him about . . ."

"About the baby?"

"Yes. I thought he'd be thrilled. But he wasn't. And then we fought." Audrey bit her lip. Stopped for a minute. "God. He was so angry. Said I'd done it on purpose to try and get him to marry me. Told me I should get rid of it."

"What a dick," Finn said, voice grim. To Eva's relief, he stayed where he was, not adding any more commentary.

"Then what happened?" Eva said.

"Well, he was being so awful, I just had to leave. I came here—I forgot you were in New York—and then I just waited for you. I thought he might call me, come after me. But nothing. He doesn't want a baby," Audrey said. "He doesn't want *our* baby." She sounded like her world had just been ripped away from her, lost and confused and heartbroken.

Eva winced but hid the expression. She understood that feeling. Of having everything you thought was true about the world overturned in an instant. Audrey knew it, too. Now it was happening again. "It might just have been the surprise," Eva said, wishing she believed the words. Shock was one thing. Letting the woman you love flee your house crying and not coming after her was another. "Maybe he'll change his mind." She saw Finn lift one eyebrow at that, but she focused on Audrey.

"You didn't hear him, Evvy," Audrey said. Tears spilled out of her eyes again. "He was so angry. I thought he loved me. How can he say such awful things to me, if he loves me?"

"I don't know, sweetie." Eva hooked her arm around Audrey's shoulders again. "But don't give up just yet. He might come around." She had to hope for Audrey's sake that Steve wasn't the dick Finn had so rightly proclaimed him to be. Or try to hope. Right now her overwhelming emotion when it came to Steve was the urge to hit him with something heavy and hard. Like her car. Her fist clenched in her lap. How could that idiot treat her sister this way?

Finn cleared his throat and she looked his way. "More tea?" he asked.

Audrey shook her head. "No." She leaned against Eva,

looking exhausted. Now that the color from the crying fit was fading from her face, she was way too pale. That couldn't be good.

She squeezed Audrey's shoulders again. "Why don't you try and rest for a while? Take a nap?"

Audrey nodded slowly, expression dazed. "Maybe."

"Just for a little while. Then we can have dinner and talk some more. How does that sound?"

"Okay." Audrey's voice sounded distant. She shivered and wrapped her arms around herself.

Eva straightened. Definitely nap time. "Finn, there's a heat pack in the bathroom cabinet, under the sink, can you get that for me please?"

He nodded. "Sure." He rose and left the room. Eva turned back to Audrey. "Okay, c'mon, sweetie. Let's get you to bed. You'll feel better after a nap." She stood and tugged Audrey's hand. Audrey didn't resist, just stood, then didn't move, as though she couldn't figure out what she was supposed to do next. Eva felt the renewed urge to introduce Steve to a baseball bat the hard way. If only fantasy could be reality. But no. She had to focus on Audrey. Rein in the mama-bear instincts to focus on the wounded cub, not the bastard who'd hurt her. "It'll be okay," she said, putting her arm around Audrey again and urging her toward the hallway and the bedrooms beyond. "I'll figure something out."

After Audrey finally fell asleep, Eva found Finn back in the kitchen, drinking coffee at the kitchen table. She pulled out a chair, rubbed her neck a moment as she tried to relax.

"Want me to go over to their place and punch him?" Finn said.

"Thanks, but as appealing as that thought is, I don't think it would help."

"Then what? Alcohol? Food? Ice cream?" He reached over and pried her fingers away from her neck, replacing them with his own. She dropped her head forward, trying not to moan as his long fingers dug into all the muscles that had knotted up in small balls of concrete since they'd arrived home.

"That feels good."

"Good." He kept up the massage. "Kind of a mess, huh? Has Steve always been such a loser?"

She shrugged. "I don't really know him well enough to say. He's always been good to Audrey as far as I could tell. They seemed happy."

Finn made a disapproving noise. "Some people don't show their true colors straightaway. I mean, I can get him being surprised, if they weren't trying, but telling her to get rid of it is pretty fucking low."

"What would you do?"

His hands stilled. "I might not be happy if the mother wasn't someone I was serious about, but a kid is a kid. My kid. I'd want to be involved if she chose to have the baby. Not sure I believe in trying to force some sort of relationship if there isn't one but seems like you should be able to work something out so you can help out and be there and stuff. Hard but that's life. If you don't want a kid, keep your pants zipped, I guess. Or get the snip."

Did that mean he wanted kids? That was something she hadn't even thought about. Not that it was her problem if he did. Not if she was leaving. But right now, she needed to think about Audrey, not whether or not Finn wanted to be a dad one day. "Most guys your age wouldn't necessarily think that way."

He shrugged. "The world is full of dumb guys. You have to take responsibility."

"Would you have given me the same speech this time last year?" She studied him, wondering if he'd tell her the truth.

"Maybe not the keeping-it-zipped part, but the kid part, yeah. It's something you have to think about as a guy—maybe even more so if you're a guy that girls might have a reason to try and sleep with—don't get me wrong, I'm not saying everyone who wants to sleep with a baseball player is some gold digger out to trap him with a baby, but it has happened. You maybe never think it's actually going to happen but you think about it." His fingers moved on her neck again.

It would be nice if more guys thought about it. And came to the same conclusions as Finn. God. She really wanted to punch Steve. Anything to wipe the hurt from Audrey's eyes. It had been a long time since she'd felt this helpless. She'd seen her sisters through their parents' deaths and the inevitable dramas and heartbreaks of growing up and she'd always hated it when she couldn't fix things for them. But she'd gotten used to accepting she couldn't over time. Like any parent had to, she supposed. But now it was back. That feeling like the ground was shifting and that if she didn't work out how to make it stop everything would tumble over the edge into disaster. She knew it wasn't true. The therapist she'd seen off and on over the years had taught her to accept that it wasn't her job to make life perfect all the time. She knew it was true. But right now that fact sucked.

She needed to do something. But with Audrey asleep, it wasn't like she could go for a run, and wild sex with Finn seemed inappropriate. She rolled her shoulders irritably, felt Finn's fingers go still.

"Did I hit a sore spot?" he asked.

"I think Steve's the one who hit the sore spot." Her foot started to tap and she pushed her chair back. "I'm going to make dinner. Audrey will need to eat when she wakes up." What to cook, though? She didn't know if Audrey was still feeling queasy, as she had been during the week.

"Hey," Finn said. He put his arms around her. "Anything I can do?"

She leaned into his embrace, breathed him in. Then stepped back. "Actually, I hate to say it but do you mind if I kick you out? I think Audrey just needs some big-sister time."

He nodded. "No problem. I should get an early night anyway. But I'm here if you need anything. You know that, right?"

She did. Which was something else that was making her feel like things were shifting in a direction she wasn't ready for.

Chapter Thirteen

Monday morning Finn crawled into practice, feeling less than happy that morning had rolled around so quickly. He'd slept badly, worried about how Eva was doing with Audrey. He'd called her once after dinner just to check in but she'd seemed distracted, so he'd kept it short. Which had left him with nothing much to do. He'd watched a batch of game tapes for the teams they were facing the next week and then tried to call it an early night.

But his bed had felt way too empty compared with the previous night in the hotel, with Eva wrapped around him so close he hadn't been entirely sure where she started and he ended.

He actually hadn't spent many nights in his apartment since they'd started sleeping together. Nights on the road he was usually worn out from the game or looking forward to a game the next day and was used to making himself fall asleep in strange hotel rooms. But when he was in Saratoga Springs, he'd been hanging out at Eva's.

It had felt comfortable. Natural. Even though he knew

it was dumb. She seemed determined to cut him loose at the end of the season, but he still couldn't quite bring himself to stay detached.

He liked being with her too much.

Liked the sound of her voice, and the cutely serious expression she wore when she was studying her photographs or working, and the way her eyes looked more blue than gray sometimes when she laughed. Like the way she tasted and the way her skin slid under his hands. Liked how she felt under him and above him and—damn. He couldn't be thinking like this. She was dealing with an emergency—worried about her sister. His gut instinct was that if he made too many wrong moves right now, she might just decide it was easier to make that whole *It's over* moment happen sooner rather than later. It would take a crazy man to try to come between Eva and one of her sisters in trouble. And he wasn't dumb. So what he had to do was make sure he wasn't adding any extra drama in her life.

He really wished he could go and kick Steve's ass. But that would make her mad—maybe. It would definitely make the Preachers and the Saints mad if they found out. And a prick like Steve—the kind of guy who would pull the shit he'd pulled on Audrey when she'd told him—was just the type who would press charges or call the press or some other bullshit.

So no. No decking the loser boyfriend. Sadly. Audrey deserved better than him, that much was clear. Even if she was only half the woman Eva was, she had to be pretty awesome.

He turned the corner to Eva's office, wondering if she would even be at work today.

He'd brought her coffee. And a bagel. She'd probably made some big healthy breakfast for Audrey but she had a weakness for cinnamon raisin bagels—and carbs added endorphins or something, didn't they?

Mostly he just wanted to check she was okay.

When he reached her office, she was sitting behind her desk, scowling at her computer monitor.

"Morning, gorgeous," he said, which earned him a grin from Carly who was at the filing cabinets. The short blond grabbed a file quickly and then said good-bye as she practically scampered out the door.

Eva looked up as Carly passed her desk, her eyes distracted for a moment. Then she blinked, focusing on him. Then she smiled.

The smile made the tightness in his chest ease. Happy to see him. That was good.

He held up the coffee and the paper bag with the bagel. "I come bearing gifts."

"So I see. Gimme." She made grabby-hands motions at him and he passed the food and coffee over.

"Oooh, bagel." Her smile widened as she peeked into the bag. "You're evil but awesome. I need some extra fuel this morning."

He studied her face. She had on a bright-red blazer over a white shirt and gray skirt, and her eyes were highlighted by the usual dark liner. Her lipstick matched her jacket, but the makeup couldn't entirely distract from the fact that there were dark circles beneath her eyes. "Late night?"

"Audrey couldn't sleep. So we stayed up and talked."

"What does she want to do?"

"I think she's hoping Steve will come around." Eva

grimaced. "I don't know whether I want that or whether I think she'd be better off without him. Being a single mom is not an easy gig. She's going to stay with me for a few days. We'll see how things pan out."

"My offer to kick his ass stands," Finn said. "Or, you know, organize for some horrible fate to come his way."

"Let's see if he can grow a pair and try to fix things first," Eva said.

"What if he doesn't?"

She smiled, baring her teeth. "If he doesn't then you'll have to get in line behind me and probably Kate and Lizzie as well." Her tone was fierce.

Definitely no crossing her when it came to her sisters. "Has Audrey told them?"

"She hadn't even told them about the baby. I think she's going to wait a little longer on that front, too. Most people don't tell until the first trimester is done anyway. She's got four more weeks."

He wasn't sure if that rule worked for sisters. His parents both had big sprawling families, and no secrets seemed to get kept for long. "Might help to tell them. That way she knows she's got more people on her side."

"Her choice," Eva said. "She might change her mind in a few days."

He nodded, hoping his expression was reassuring. "Everything will work out. Call me if you need anything, okay?"

"You're not coming over tonight?"

"I wasn't sure you'd want me there."

"Come for dinner. You're off in the morning and I won't see you again until Wednesday."

"Okay." Dinner was good. Dinner wasn't *My sister*

needs me so run away now. So he'd go for dinner. See
what he could do to make things easier. And hope that
Steve the dick came to his senses before the team got
back on Wednesday night.

Wednesday morning as Finn was adding his duffel bag
to the pile of luggage waiting to be loaded back on the
bus, Don Mannings appeared at his side.

"Coach," Finn said, squinting in the early sunshine.
He studied Mannings for a moment. The guy didn't look
happy. Then again, his suntanned, well-lined faced
didn't often look pleased with the universe. "Something
up?" The Preachers had won their Tuesday game, and
Finn's performance had been solid. He couldn't think
of anything that would mean Mannings needed to haul
him over the coals.

"Walk with me," Mannings said, nodding his head
back away from the hotel lobby where most of the players and staff were milling around, drinking coffee and
talking shit as they waited for the bus to be ready.

Finn's gut tightened but he just nodded and walked
after Don as he headed down the hotel drive toward the
street. When they reached the street, well out of earshot
of anyone, Don stopped, frowning at the traffic crawling past.

"Going to take forever to get out of the city with this
traffic."

Finn nodded agreement, fighting the urge to ask what
the hell was going on.

Don watched the traffic for another minute or so then

rubbed a hand through his short gray hair. "I had a call from Dan Ellis earlier."

Finn froze. Dan Ellis was the Saints' head coach. There weren't many reasons for him to be calling Don. At least not that Don would want to tell Finn about. The only reason Finn would need to know would be if the Saints wanted him back. Either permanently or, more likely, temporarily. "Yeah?" Hopefully he didn't sound as painfully eager as he felt.

"He wanted to know if he could borrow you Friday." Don held up a hand. "Before you get too excited, it's strictly a Taxi Squad gig. Leeroy sprained his wrist doing some damned fool thing and they might need backup for Shields if it doesn't come good. You might not even play."

Finn nodded. He understood the convoluted rules of how the major-league teams could shuffle players back and forth between the main team and their Triple-A affiliate. He'd practically memorized them when he'd first played for the Cubs' Triple-A team. Being on the Taxi Squad was a one-day-only gig unless the Saints added him back to their main roster the following day. It was way too soon for that to happen.

"And we're playing Toledo on Friday. I was going to start you on first base again." Don looked annoyed.

"Well, it's not exactly an offer I can say no to," Finn said.

"Try not to sound so damned disappointed, Castro," Don said. But then he smiled a reluctant smile. "Don't worry. I understand. All of you want to get to the show. Hell, so did I in my day."

"Not everyone wants to be promoted," Finn said. "Connor's happy here. Some of the other guys."

"Connor's at the end of his run," Don said. "He's had his time with the big boys. Would've stayed there if he hadn't fucked up his shoulder. You're just getting started." He glanced back at the bus, frowned again. "But kid, if you don't think you're ready yet, tell me. I'll tell Ellis that you've got the flu or something. You're doing well here, so don't go if you think it's going to fuck with your head."

Finn hid the wince. He and Don had had some down-right blunt conversations about what had happened to Finn at the Saints and how he'd let the pressure twist him up. About how he was approaching things differently this time. As much as he wanted to get back to the majors, Don had a point. He needed to be ready for it—and to be honest, part of him found the prospect daunting. But he'd never walked away from shit that scared him and he wasn't going to start now. He nodded at Don. "Thanks but I'm good. It's just one day. Might be a good way to get a taste of it again."

"If that's what you want. Why don't you ask Eva to go up with you for the day? We can spare her. Probably owe her about three years' vacation time anyway. She hardly ever takes time off."

His chances of dragging Eva away from Audrey right now were probably close to zero. But he nodded at Don. "That would be great. I'll ask her tonight."

"Good." Don clapped him on the shoulder. "You go on back to the bus. I'll call Dan Ellis and we'll get on the road. Tell the guys, they'll be happy for you."

Finn managed to nod again. Some of his teammates,

like Connor, would be happy for him, he knew that. But when it came to the rest of the squad, particularly Greg, he had about as much a chance of the news going down well as he did convincing Eva to come with him to New York on Friday.

It was going to be an interesting ride back to Saratoga.

"Stop pretending you're not watching the clock," Audrey said at six on Wednesday evening. "You're making me tired."

Eva glanced over guiltily. With the team gone, she'd taken advantage of a chance to work from home so Audrey wouldn't be alone. But that meant she hadn't been there to see Finn when he got back. She thought she'd been hiding her impatience well. Apparently not, judging by the almost-amused expression on Audrey's face.

"Lover boy will be here soon," Audrey said. "You invited him for dinner, right?"

Eva nodded and tried not to look at the clock on her computer again. It wasn't really an invitation. It was her and Finn's routine now, to eat at her place the night he got home. Of course, that had usually been followed by them having some noisy and enthusiastic sex, but she couldn't see how that was going to happen tonight with Audrey sleeping down the hall in her old bedroom.

Audrey who was still quiet and teary and not eating enough. So far, Eva hadn't been able to convince her to contact Steve and see if things could be worked out. She kept saying Steve needed some time. They'd made one quick trip to Audrey's apartment on Tuesday morning to grab more clothes for her but that had just made

Audrey cry all over again, so Eva had thrown things into a bag in record time and brought Audrey back to the house as quickly as possible. Since then she'd been holding her tongue, not wanting to stress Audrey out any more than she already was.

The atmosphere in the house was strained and Eva was looking forward to seeing Finn just to see if having someone else there would make Audrey feel better for a while. Finn was good at putting people at ease. Maybe his skills would extend to her sister. She focused back on her laptop, trying not to notice the clock was telling her it was only about another fifteen minutes to Finn o'clock.

"What are we having for dinner?" Audrey asked.

Eva stopped her surreptitious clock watching. Audrey hadn't had much interest in food since Sunday. Eva had been coaxing her into eating, even resorting to "you have to eat for the baby" at one point. "I was going to do some steaks. Baked potatoes." Baked potatoes were one of Audrey's favorites. "Are you hungry? I can make you a snack."

Audrey stretched a little and shook her head. Her hair was caught up into a messy bun and Eva didn't think she'd actually washed it for a few days, but she'd actually made it out of her pajamas and into yoga pants when Eva had told her Finn would be coming out for dinner. That was an improvement. "I can wait. Lover boy isn't going to be long, is he?"

"Finn," Eva corrected. "No. He said he'd be done at Hennessee around six. Then he'll probably go to his place and ditch his stuff then come here."

"Is he staying over?" Audrey wriggled her eyebrows

theatrically. It was juvenile but it was at least a sign that she might be emerging from her understandably sad mood.

"Maybe," Eva said. "That's what lover boys do, after all." Except when their style was cramped by visiting sisters.

"Thank God I have earplugs," Audrey said.

"You do?" Maybe Finn's style didn't have to be cramped after all.

"Yup. I keep them in my bag for when I travel. I can never sleep well in hotels."

Before the conversation could travel any farther down the path of whether or not Audrey would be able to hear her and Finn—which wasn't a conversation she really wanted to have—the doorbell rang.

Eva sprang up, unable to keep the smile from her face. "That'll be him."

"He doesn't have a key?" Audrey asked.

"No." She headed for the door before she had to explain that one, she and Finn had only been seeing each other for six weeks or so; and two, she wasn't planning on giving him a key when they weren't going to be together after the season ended.

That thought made her stomach knot suddenly and she shoved it away. There was no deviating from the plan. She was enjoying Finn now, and then she had a whole new life to start.

She pasted a smile on her face and threw open the door.

Then felt her mood snap to happy at the sight of Finn. "You're early," she said then laughed. "Sorry, that sounded wrong. I'm *glad* you're early." She rose up on her toes to kiss him. He pulled her against him and turned it into the kind of kiss she had been planning on delaying until later.

"I'm glad I'm early, too," he said when he finally let go of her.

"Good. Come in. I'll get started on dinner."

Apparently what Audrey had needed to distract her from her problems was dumb baseball stories. Eva watched her sister smiling and couldn't help wanting to kiss Finn for cheering Audrey up. She'd actually eaten two-thirds of her meal as Finn had told tall tales about exploits of players he'd known. At least, Eva hoped some of them were tall tales. She knew things could get a little crazy in the major leagues, but she really hoped the thing about the goat wasn't true. Still, she wasn't going to interrupt Finn and ask about it when he was working his magic on Aud.

By the time Audrey pushed her plate away and leaned back in her chair, sipping at her club soda while trying not to laugh at Finn, Eva was ready to do anything the man wanted.

"So," Audrey said when she finally stopped laughing. "I'm planning on an early night. What are you two up to?"

"Not much—" Eva started at the same time that Finn said, "Actually, I—" They both stopped.

Eva frowned at him over the table. "I was thinking of staying in. Do some quality Netflix time. An early night sounds good to me too." An early night with him.

Finn grinned at her, clearly knowing exactly what she

was thinking about. "That sounds good but some of the guys are going down to Jose's."

"You want to go?" Eva blinked at him. Finn hadn't been that interested in hanging out with the guys since they'd gone public. She and Jenna and him had spent a bit of time with Connor and a few other players but that was mostly dinners. Not bars. "Is it someone's birthday?" She couldn't think of anyone on the team who had a birthday in May but she'd been distracted this week so maybe she'd missed it. She stood, gathering plates while she thought about it.

"Not a birthday." Finn shrugged. "But I have some news."

"News?" Eva sat back down with a thump. "What kind of news?" There was only one thing she could think of that was likely.

"Saints want me on Friday," he said, clearly delighted.

She tried to find a smile, fighting the feeling that she'd just had the wind knocked out of her. This was good for Finn. And she didn't want him long-term so if he ended up going back to the Saints earlier than expected, then she was just going to have to suck it up. She forced the smile wider.

Finn shook his head at her. "Don't worry, it's just a one-day thing. Nothing permanent."

"Still, it's a good thing, right?" Audrey said. "They must think you're playing well down here to call you back up."

Eva's face felt weirdly frozen. Audrey was right. It was a good thing and she should be happy for Finn. But all she could think was *Not yet.* Stupid.

Finn shrugged one shoulder and then lifted the plates

that Eva had been gathering. "Maybe. But Connor decided we should celebrate. Any excuse for that man." He was downplaying. Eva could tell he was excited. That he wanted to go and celebrate. As he should. It was a good sign that the Saints weren't dooming him to play for the Preachers forever. That he might be slowly redeeming himself. She should be happy for him.

"Well, you two should go. Have fun," Audrey said. She was smiling but Eva didn't entirely believe the expression.

"Are you sure?" Eva asked. "I can stay here with you."

Audrey waved her away. "Like I said. I'm going to bed. No one ever tells you that being pregnant is exhausting." She rose, one hand fluttering down to her stomach in a gesture that was becoming familiar to Eva. It gave her a pang of worry every time she saw Audrey do it. "If you stay here all you're going to hear is me snoring."

Finn grinned at her. "We won't be late. Training in the morning." He turned back to Eva. "So what do you say?"

Not yet, was what she thought. But she ignored the tiny chill in her stomach. "Just give me a few minutes to change."

Chapter Fourteen

Jose's hadn't changed much. She had been here a few times over the years on the rare occasions she'd accepted invitations to hang with the players and the coaching staff. It was an old-school bar, a sprawling space with a couple of pool tables at one end, a bunch of tables up at the other, and a tiny open space that sometimes did duty as a dance floor in between. The decor leaned heavily to man cave with sports posters and beer ads and even a couple of Preachers jerseys hanging on the walls. Three TVs over the bar showed sports most of the time—at least on the nights she'd been here—though the volume was turned down to allow the music coming from the jukebox to dominate. It served plenty of beer on tap and did great Buffalo wings and chili fries. People who came here tended to be laid-back compared with some of the hipper bars and clubs that the younger crowd—and the racing scenesters—frequented. All of which made it one of the places the Preachers' guys liked to drink. No one tried to hassle them—or only rarely—and they could let their hair down.

When she and Finn walked through the door, everyone else seemed to have arrived. Connor waved at them from across the room where he'd commandeered one of the long tables near the pool tables. Eva scanned the room as she and Finn made their way over to him. Most of the team was here. Even Greg was sitting at a smaller table with Pietro and a few of his friends. Hopefully that was a sign that tensions between him and Finn had eased, and she sent him a smile as she walked past. He nodded at her but then turned his attention back to the guys he was with.

"It's the man of the hour," Connor said as they reached his table. "And his far prettier companion." He leaned across the table and kissed Eva's cheek. "Ready to dump this infant and fall madly in love with me?"

She laughed at him. "I have more sense than to ride that roller coaster." Connor was funny, a talented player, and one of the good guys, but when it came to women, he was Teflon. Women flocked to his blond, blue-eyed, chiseled-chin, all-American-boy looks and tended to fall at his feet. Where, being Connor, he picked them up, slept with them if he was so inclined, made them feel like goddesses for a few weeks, then managed to slide them out of his life again. None of the girls who'd ever worked for the Preachers had had any more success with him than the women he met elsewhere.

"I'm wounded," he said and handed her a beer. "You'll have to drink with me to help me get over the pain. You too, Castro." He passed Finn another beer.

"Or we can drink to you going up to the Big Apple." He raised his glass and toasted Finn.

"Don't get too excited. You haven't gotten rid of me yet," Finn said. He held a chair out for Eva and then took the seat next to hers. He swigged a mouthful of beer but then put it back on the table. Eva would be surprised if he drank much more of it. He'd drunk some champagne at Amelia's party—a glass or two—but he hadn't seemed inclined to drink much at all since she'd known him.

Connor's expression turned more serious. "It's a step. Celebrate the little things, that's my motto. Right, Eva?"

She nodded. That was one lesson she'd learned. Take time to enjoy the moment and the small victories. Because life could change in a second. She tasted her own beer. It was cold and yeasty and not too bitter. She'd never been much of a beer drinker—getting drunk on horrible cheap baseball-park beer as a sixteen-year-old had ensured that she'd never developed a taste for it—but she could switch to wine or soda after this one. "Right."

Finn shook his head, "You two are like the optimists' club."

"You're telling me you're not an optimist?" Connor said.

"I like to think I'm more a realist these days."

Connor snorted. "I've never met a professional ball-player—at least one starting out like you—who wasn't a wild optimist. You all think you're going to be Hall of Fame zillionaires."

"Are you saying I'm not a contender?" Finn said, with a grin. Eva watched him. He was relaxed with Connor.

That was another good sign that things were good with the team, right?

"Who knows?" Connor said. He considered Finn, face mock-serious. "Maybe you've got some talent."

Finn rolled his eyes. "You're great for my ego."

"Not my job to blow smoke up your ass. Talent isn't all it takes."

"Dude, what happened to celebrating small victories? You're going all serious on us."

"You started it. Okay." Connor drained his beer, put his hands flat on the table. "Who wants another? One more drink then Eva and I are going to whip your butt at pool."

"I'm good," Eva said and smiled at Finn. "Ready to lose?"

"Don't tell me you're a pool shark on top of all your other talents?"

"I've played some," she said. Her dad had taught all four of them to play nine-ball. It had been one of his passions besides baseball. His dad had played, too. Her aunt and uncle had a table in the basement of their house, so they'd played a bit even after he'd died. Though she was probably rusty. She couldn't remember the last time she'd played pool.

"I'm going to lose all my money, aren't I?" Finn said.

"Unless you want to bet your clothes."

His eyes went dark for a moment and she smiled demurely at him. Then he lifted an eyebrow and leaned closer so she could feel his breath on her neck. She resisted the shiver that threatened at the sensation.

"I'm more than happy to give my clothes to you, Eva. All you have to do is ask." He pressed a kiss against her neck so that this time she did shiver but then pulled back and grinned at her. "Though maybe not with Connor and the guys as an audience, so you're just going to have to wait."

"Fine by me." It wasn't. She really wanted to go home and shag him senseless but tonight was about him so she was going to have to practice patience. "I'm perfectly content staying here and winning all your money."

"That's the spirit," Connor said. He put a fresh beer on the table in front of his chair and a soda in front of Finn. "So. Out of the chairs, people. There's pool to play."

For the next hour or so, they played pool and ate wings and then played more pool. It was easy and relaxing and for a while Eva forgot about Audrey. When she remembered, she looked at her watch, feeling guilty. It was past nine. "We should go," she said to Finn.

He nodded at her. "Sure. We'll just finish this game." He and Connor were playing Pietro and Michael, the Preachers' catcher. She nodded at him. Finn, as it turned out, was a not-so-bad pool player himself.

Her parents would have liked him. The thought gave her a familiar stab of pain and she grabbed her bag. "Just going to the ladies' room."

In the bathroom, she leaned against the wall, eyes closed, willing the sudden sadness away. It still surprised her at times, how fiercely grief could flash back. After all these years it still hurt. Though the moments tended to be shorter now, and she knew how to ride them out. Still, moments like these—when she had something she wanted to share with them—were hard.

Of course, if her parents were alive, she probably

would never have met Finn. She probably wouldn't have been living in Saratoga Springs, for a start. So it was dumb to be upset that they couldn't meet him, right? She shook her head at her reflection, grabbed some paper towels to dab at the tears threatening in her eyes. Particularly dumb if she was determined to go through with the only-until-the-end-of-the-season plan. She was just being emotional because she was worried about Audrey. Audrey who was still at home alone, so Eva needed to get her act together and get home to her sister.

She washed her hands, smoothed back her hair, and reapplied her lipstick. Armor back in place, she went to find Finn.

But when she walked back across the room toward the pool tables, Finn was standing, cue in one hand, face grim as he listened to Greg—who was standing about three feet away—say something Eva couldn't quite hear.

Her stomach sank. Crap. This was the last thing they needed. She closed the distance between her and them, getting there just in time to hear Greg say, "You're not so special, Castro. You might fool the ladies but you don't fool me."

"Sorry you feel that way," Finn said. It was obvious he wasn't sorry at all. "I'm not looking for trouble here, Cutler. In fact I was just leaving."

"Yeah, you might not look for trouble, but it seems to find you, doesn't it? Never your fault. Guys like you just slide on by and leave problems in their wake. I don't want you here, messing up my team. Getting yourself into places you shouldn't."

That was her, she assumed. Her temper spiked. Fucking Greg. She'd never encouraged him. Why couldn't he just grow up and get over it? She took a step forward but Connor's hand clamped over her wrist.

"Don't," he said softly. "This has been brewing for a while. Better to let them get it out of their systems."

"How? By having a bar fight? That'll go down well with management." Not to mention with the Saints. She kept her eyes on Greg, red-faced and mean-eyed. Finn might have stuck to just one beer, but it was clear that Greg hadn't.

"It won't get that far," Connor said.

"How do you know?" she said.

At the sound of her voice, Finn's head turned. "Eva," he said, sounding surprised, as though he'd forgotten she was there. He took a step toward her and Greg put a hand on his chest, shoved him back.

Finn's attention snapped back to Greg. "Cutler," he said and pushed Greg's hand away. "Get over it. You didn't get the girl."

For a moment Greg just stared at him. Then he turned an even darker shade of red.

"Oh shit," Connor said just as Greg pulled his arm back and took a swing at Finn.

"That looks like a fight to me," Eva muttered, horrified, as Connor surged forward while Finn dodged Greg's punch. Connor got between the two of them before Finn could respond in kind, thrusting his body into the trouble zone and pushing Finn back, Greg tried to reach for Finn around Connor and Connor shoved him away with his other hand.

"Little help here," Connor snapped at Pietro, who was watching. Pietro shrugged but stepped forward and grabbed a handful of Greg's shirt, pulling him backward away from Connor.

Greg twisted, getting free of Pietro's grip, and for a horrible second or two Eva thought he was going to go after Finn again, but he just stayed where he was, breathing hard and glaring at Connor and Finn.

Which somehow made her even more mad at all of them. She stepped forward herself.

"Are you done?" she said in her best icy *Do not mess with me* voice. "Because you're all behaving like three-year-olds. Idiot three-year-olds who are trying to get themselves suspended from the team for a few weeks. What the hell are you thinking? Coach will have your asses if he hears about this."

"No one's going to tell him," Greg said.

She spun on her heel to face him. "Maybe I will. Did you think of that, Greg Cutler? Up until now I've kept quiet about this. About you morons and your excess testosterone and your harassing Finn. I figured grown men would figure it out eventually. But maybe I was wrong about that. Because three-year-olds often need an adult to step in. So are you an adult or a three-year-old? An adult—a man—would know that I am not a toy that someone else isn't letting him play with. I'm not someone to throw tantrums over. I'm a damned person and I make my own damned choices. And I am not impressed with this shit, Greg. Not one little bit." She glanced over her shoulder at Finn, wanting to make sure that he got the message as well. He held up his hands and nodded. She turned back to Greg. "So are we done here?"

Greg just stared at her a long moment. Then he shook his head, shoulders sagging. "Sorry. I was out of line."

She should tell him that he owed Finn the apology. But that might be pushing it. Greg was backing down now, but she'd just stomped on some male egos fairly hard. Better to leave it for the moment, then make sure it was sorted out for good later. Put Connor on the job. He was senior enough on the team to lean on Greg. She nodded at Greg. "Okay. Good. Now I suggest you go home. Sleep it off." She glared around the circle of men. "You all have practice in the morning, so that goes for all of you."

She turned away from them, started walking through the bar, where, she realized she had become the center of attention. Carlo, the barman, tipped his chin at her when she caught his eye, and she felt her knees wobble slightly. What the hell had she just done? Yelled at practically the entire team in a bar. What had she been thinking? She was almost at the door when Finn caught up to her, stepping in front of her to open the door. Which was both polite and annoying in her current mood. As she stepped through it, he whispered, "That was very cool, Eva Harlowe." She ignored him until he added, "And very hot." Then she held out her hand as he shut the door behind him and let him take her home.

Friday morning Eva met Jenna to go running before work. Finn had taken a flight to New York late Thursday, and she hadn't slept well without him. So she figured she might as well haul her butt out of bed and do something useful with her time.

Jenna, who was an annoying morning person, met her at their usual spot, looking far too awake in black running gear and bright-pink running shoes.

"Whoa," she said, peering at Eva over the tops of her sunglasses. "Somebody didn't get enough sleep last night."

Eva looked down at her old Preachers T-shirt and black running tights. "It's too early in the morning to pick on my fashion choices."

"I wasn't criticizing your fashion choices, I was criticizing the dark circles under your eyes," Jenna said. She cocked her head. "Finn been keeping you up all night? Though if he has, you should be more glowy than you are. Is he doing it wrong? Need me to offer him some advice?"

Eva grinned. "I'm sure you have mad skills but Finn doesn't need any help in that department. Thanks."

"Then why the dark circles?"

"I just had a bad night, okay? It happens."

"That's when you're supposed to wake up that person lying next to you in bed and get them to either talk it out with you or distract you if you know what I mean. Finn doesn't need beauty sleep. He's pretty enough. Wake that man up."

"That man is in New York," Eva admitted. She hadn't mentioned Finn's trip to Jenna, she realized.

"New York?" Jenna frowned. "Crap, did they recall him?"

"Just for the day," Eva said. "But he left last night."

"Phew," Jenna said. "He's not allowed to leave. He's too nice to look at."

Eva didn't think that was why Jenna wanted her and

Finn to end in rainbows and unicorns and a big fat engagement ring. Wasn't going to happen. "Just a day," she repeated, though there was a thread of worry in her gut. Finn wasn't the only guy at the Preachers on optional assignment. There were a few others who'd played first base at times as well. The Saints could've picked any of them but they'd picked Finn, despite the fact he had been sent to the Preachers to sort himself out. So either they were desperate or they were impressed enough by what they'd seen of his form at the Preachers so far to start reconsidering their stance.

"You didn't want to go with him, see him play up there?" Jenna asked.

She shook her head. "I didn't want to leave Audrey." Finn had asked her several times to come with him. Even offered to talk to Oliver and get her a press pass so she could spend some time taking pictures of the game. She'd wanted to say yes. But Audrey was still way too quiet and sad. Finn had said he was okay with her staying but she had her doubts. Damned if she did and damned if she didn't.

"She's still staying with you?" Jenna was the only other person that Eva had told about Audrey's pregnancy. Audrey had said it was okay. "Crap. So dickface hasn't come to his senses?"

"Not yet."

"Double crap."

That was about her assessment of the situation. If Steve hadn't had a change of heart by now, she doubted he ever would. Not that she'd shared that opinion with Audrey. "Okay, enough about my exciting life. We're meant to be running. So move your butt." She took off and soon enough Jenna caught up and settled into place beside her as they crossed the street to hit the park, where they usually ran their circuit.

They went at an easy pace, the early-morning sunshine warm enough to make the experience pleasant.

"Any news from Lana?" Eva asked when they finished their first loop and stopped for a brief stretch-and-water break.

Jenna nodded. "We FaceTimed the other day. She's still coming home in August. So that's good." She looked pleased.

"Not long now," Eva said.

"Says the girl getting laid regularly," Jenna said. "Six months is a loooonnnggg time. Their Internet is too spotty for decent Internet sex. My vibrator is going to get RSI."

"Ew," Eva said. "Overshare."

"You asked," Jenna said. "I miss her. I miss sex with her. There's only so far meditation and exercise and battery-operated devices can get you."

"I know," Eva said. "It is a long time." Jenna and Lana seemed to be coping okay long distance. They were solid despite any bumps. But that was because the two of them worked at it.

"On the plus side," Jenna said, "I've gotten some very steamy love letters. I think Lana missed her calling. She should take up writing romance or something." She fanned herself and swigged more water.

"I think we need to run some more," Eva said. "Get you some extra endorphins."

"Running endorphins just aren't the same," Jenna said.

Eva could only agree. Exercise had lifted her mood a bit but not the same way that Finn would have. Which was a thought that only made her feel more depressed. She'd have to get used to coping without Finn again in a few months. So she might as well start practicing now. "Let's run," she said and took off.

Finn stepped back into the locker room at the end of the game and tried to reduce the ridiculous grin on his face. He'd only played the final innings, when Dan Ellis had decided Oliver's hand had had enough for the day, but damn, it had felt good. He'd forgotten—or hadn't let himself think about—the rush of playing before such a big crowd. The Saints were on a winning streak at the moment and the fans had turned out in droves, filling Deacon Field to maximum capacity. He'd played well. Gotten two outs, which had stopped the Yankees from catching up to the Saints' score. All in all it had been a damned good day. If only Eva had been there with him, it would've been perfect.

He went to the locker he'd been assigned—not his old one—and grabbed his towel. Oliver was sitting on one of the benches, already showered and changed, his hand soaking in a bucket of ice and water.

"Good game," Oliver said.

"How's the hand?" Finn asked. He hated ice therapy. It worked but it wasn't fun.

Oliver grimaced. "Okay. Right now I can't feel anything but cold."

"They gave you a workout tonight." The Yankees'

batters seemed to have been under the mistaken impression that Oliver's hand was a weak point in the Saints' fielding and had slugged balls in his direction. Until he'd caught two of them in a row, sending the batters slinking back to the dugout.

"They tried." Oliver grinned. "We showed them. Call me shallow but I always enjoy beating the Yankees the most."

"That seems to be a theme around here."

"Yeah, well, play for the Saints long enough and you'll get tired of the *New York's third rail of baseball* tone of being the smallest team in town."

He could see how that would get old. Maybe he'd get the chance to find out. "Did you ever want to play for another team?"

"Nah. Saints are my home," Oliver said. He lifted his hand out of the bucket, flexed and straightened it slowly a couple of times, then lowered it back in with a grimace. "Some guys like to keep moving, some guys don't get a choice. I had a choice but I liked where I was, so I stayed."

"You could have made more money playing for another team."

"I make plenty." Oliver said, frowning slightly. "You got a move on your mind?"

"I'm hardly in the position to choose. I'm going to have to go wherever I'm sent for now." If the Saints didn't call him back, they could trade him. Whether any other team would want to take him on was another question.

"True. But keep playing like you have been for the Preachers and you'll be back here soon enough. If we keep building the way we have over the last few years, then a few years here and you'll have more control over where you go. If you want to go."

The problem with that theory was that he didn't have a few years. If he was ever going to want to make a move, it would be to California with Eva. But that wasn't going to happen because one, he wasn't even back at the Saints yet, and two, Eva would probably dump him if he suggested it. He shrugged and nodded toward the showers. "I'm going to clean up."

"You around tomorrow?" Oliver asked, voice a shade too casual.

Technically the Saints had until three p.m. tomorrow to tell him if they were keeping him on longer, but Dan Ellis had already told him that wasn't happening this time. If he'd known, he would've organized a flight back to Saratoga for tonight but he hadn't, so he'd made plans with Amelia. "I'm heading back tomorrow. Amelia wanted to have breakfast, I didn't really get much of a chance to talk to her at her party. So I'll do that and then head home to Saratoga."

"Ah. Sorry. But I'm glad you're seeing her. She misses you. And Em."

Oliver knew exactly what it meant that he was going home to Saratoga. Though Finn wasn't sure he knew exactly when he'd started thinking of Saratoga as home. Or maybe not Saratoga itself but being with Eva. "Well, at least I'm in the same state, unlike Em."

"Yup. I think Amelia would like to move Chicago to New York so Em is closer."

Did that mean they were getting along better? "That sounds good. Except for the part where it means my parents are closer, too. I love them but I don't want my mom dropping by to check on me every other day, know what I mean?"

"I do," Oliver said. "Luckily my mother is distracted by grandkids. Maybe you should work on that."

"I think for now, I'll leave that part up to Em. She's the oldest, she should have to produce rugrats first." The thought of babies made him think of Eva and Audrey. He should call, see how things were doing with Audrey. But it was late. Maybe better to let Eva get some sleep. She'd texted him to wish him good luck earlier. He was going to have to content himself with that for now. "Look after that hand," he said to Oliver and headed for the showers.

Chapter Fifteen

"Eva."

Someone was shaking her shoulder. Why was someone shaking her shoulder? She'd only just gotten to sleep about two seconds ago. At least it felt that way.

"Eva! Wake up."

The voice was louder. Audrey's voice. Audrey's voice sounded scared.

Her eyes flew open. "What?" she asked, blinking against the unexpected light. Audrey had turned on the lamp on her nightstand.

"I think I'm bleeding."

Now Eva was fully awake. Throwing back the covers to swing her legs out of bed before she knew what she was doing. "You think? What does that mean?" Pulse pounding, Eva stared at Audrey, who was pale but standing there so she couldn't be bleeding a lot, surely?

Audrey bit her lip. "I am. Not a lot, but I am."

Shit. Eva didn't know much about pregnancy other than what she learned from watching TV shows. But bleeding never seemed to be a good sign on those. "Are you in any pain?" She looked at her phone. Two a.m. Not a good time for a medical emergency.

"No. But can we go to the emergency room? I don't want to wait until my ob-gyn is open in the morning."

"Of course." Eva said. There would be no waiting. Not when something might be happening to her future niece or nephew. "I'll get dressed." Audrey was wearing sweats and a hoodie over one of the big T-shirts she slept in, her feet shoved into Uggs. That was apparently as dressed as she was going to get.

Eva patted the bed beside her. "You should sit down. And don't freak out."

"Too late," Audrey said but she sat, face pale, breathing in and out at a pace that suggested she was trying to calm herself without much success.

Eva found the jeans she'd been wearing earlier, tugged them on, and then found a bra, a sweatshirt, and shoes. Then her purse with her keys.

"Okay, let's go." She was about to suggest that Audrey should pack some stuff in case she had to stay at the hospital. But staying at the hospital implied that there was something to worry about, and right now keeping her calm was the important thing. She could always come back and grab some stuff for Audrey if she needed to. Audrey was still sitting on the bed.

"C'mon, Aud," she repeated.

Audrey's hands dug into Eva's quilt. "I can't. What if I go to the hospital and they tell me I'm miscarrying?"

Eva took a deep breath. "Okay. You're freaking out. That's okay. But whatever is happening, it's better that you have doctors and nurses to deal with it. So let's make that happen. Then whatever else comes next, you'll be taken care of. And I'll be right there. I won't leave you. But you have to come with me now." She reached down and eased Audrey's hands free from the quilt, keeping hold of them. "Just hang on to me, take a deep breath, and stand up. I've got you, you know that."

"I know," Audrey said, and stood.

"So how's Eva?" Amelia asked at eight the next morning as they studied the menu at the café she'd chosen.

Finn had been expecting the question. Just not quite so early in the conversation. They'd barely sat down at the table. "Can we at least order coffee before you start interrogating me?"

"Nope," Amelia said. "Caffeine will make you wily. I want the truth."

"Caffeine won't make me wily, it will make me coherent. It's way too early on a Saturday morning for no coffee."

"You're the one with the flight back to Saratoga. Blame your travel schedule."

"Regardless of whose fault it is, the fact remains, it's early and I need caffeine. I refuse to answer questions without it. Coffee is a basic human right."

"God, so cranky. I'd forgotten you were like this in the morning. Does Eva know or have you been on your best behavior for her?"

"That's a sneaky way of asking a question. Not going to work." He smiled thankfully at the waiter who'd just come over to their table. "Coffee, black, please. Biggest mug you have." He waited while Amelia ordered green tea and the waiter left.

"Green tea?"

"I got the taste for it in Hong Kong," Amelia said. "It's better for you."

"It tastes like grass," Finn said.

"Coffee tastes gross at first, too."

The waiter arrived back with Finn's coffee and a fancy clear teapot thing full of green leaves for Amelia. He took their food order and disappeared again. Finn inhaled coffee-scented steam gratefully, then took a gulp. It was strong and hot, just the way he liked it. His brain started to sputter to life.

"Good," Amelia said. "Now you have coffee. So back to the important stuff. How's Eva?"

"She's good," he said, True but evasive. The perfect answer for prying sisters.

"I like her," Amelia announced.

"Yes, you told me that at the party."

"Do you like her?" Amelia lifted an eyebrow, face innocent, as though she were asking about the weather rather than Finn's heart.

"I brought her to your birthday party. Do you think I'd bring a girl to a family party if I didn't like her?" He drank more coffee, hoping it would kick-start his brain into working well enough to figure out a way to end this conversation.

"True. But do you like her or *like* her?"

Finn sighed. There was really only one way to cut off this line of questioning. Tell the truth. Which was probably the kindest thing to do anyway. Amelia had obviously liked Eva but there was no point in letting her get too invested in the idea. "Look, I like her a lot. But when it comes to me and Eva, there's something you should know."

Amelia look alarmed. Then she frowned. "What did you do?"

"What makes you think I did anything?"

"Because Eva seems sensible to me. You, on the other hand . . ." She let the sentence trail off and stuck her tongue out at him.

"Eva is sensible." Too sensible. "And nice. But she's also moving to California at the end of the season—do not tell anyone that, no one at the Preachers knows anything about it."

"California," Amelia said blankly. "What's in California that isn't in New York?"

"School. She wants to be a photographer and there's a very exclusive course in Los Angeles she got into."

"There are photography courses in New York," Amelia said, still frowning.

"Yes. But not with Isaac Haines."

"Isaac Haines? Isn't he the one who did those photos of the Cubs for their stadium the year you were there? Those were great."

"Yes. That's him. He's a big deal in sports photography. Or athletic photography. I don't know what the hell you call it but he doesn't take many students at a time and Eva got into his class. So she's going to California."

"Well, long distance sucks but it's doable," Amelia said. "I mean, Ollie came back here before my assignment in Hong Kong was over. We made it."

"I know," Finn said. "But Eva was very clear from the start that isn't what she wants."

"I don't understand."

"She and I are just for the season."

"That's stupid," Amelia said, looking annoyed. "She likes you, I could tell."

"I know," Finn said, spreading his hands. "But if it's what she wants, I can't exactly force her to keep seeing me."

The waiter interrupted his point by returning with their meals. Finn stayed silent until the guy left again.

"You have to show her you're serious. Are you serious?" Amelia said. "Or is this six-month-long booty call fine by you?"

"No," he said. "It's not. And I am serious about her. Which makes me an idiot." He scowled down at his omelet. The conversation had killed his appetite.

"You have to change her mind. Tell her how you feel."

If only it were that simple. "If I do that, I think she'll dump me right now," Finn admitted.

"Why?"

"I don't know. She's set on doing this her way. You're a woman. You figure out the logic. I can't."

"It sounds to me like she's being careful. Protecting herself. So you just have to show her that you're trustworthy. So she lets you in. Then she won't want to let you go." Amelia smiled. "Simple." She waved her fork in the air, looking satisfied, as though she'd solved all his problems.

The trouble was that putting Amelia's theory into practice wasn't going to be quite as simple as she thought.

* * *

Eva pulled her front door open on Saturday only to jump about two feet in the air when she found Finn standing on the porch, hand raised to knock.

"God, you scared me," she said.

"Sorry," he said. "Bad timing. Were you going out? I thought we were going to have lunch today?"

She'd completely forgotten about lunch. Or Finn. "I have to go pick Audrey up from the hospital."

"Hospital? What's wrong?"

"She had a bit of a scare last night." She didn't think Finn needed the full gory gynecological details. She wasn't sure she was ready for the full gory gynecological details herself. Watching Audrey get poked and prodded by the doctors and nurses last night hadn't been fun. Holding her hand, waiting for the results hadn't been much fun, either. "But she's okay. They just wanted to keep her in for observation."

"The baby is okay?"

The concern in his voice made her relax a little. *He's here now. It's okay.* The thought rose unbidden in her head and she froze. No. No getting used to leaning on Finn. He wasn't going to be around forever. She made herself relax. He wasn't going to be around forever but she could still let him help her now. She nodded at him. "Seems to be. They're not sure what happened but everything is okay for now."

"Good. That's good, right?"

"Yes," she said firmly. She'd had a moment or two last night when she'd thought it might be easier all around if there was no baby. But then the doctor had put the ultrasound thing on and they'd heard the heartbeat, fast and steady. That was the moment when the abstract of

Audrey's pregnant had become a reality. As long as this baby was what Audrey wanted, then she would support her. "It's good."

Finn stretched out an arm and pulled her toward him. "Come here."

His chest was broad and warm against her cheek as he hugged her. The urge to just let him take care of everything was overwhelming for a moment. But she couldn't get used to that. She hugged him back and then eased away. "Thanks, I needed that."

"You look tired," he said. "I'll drive you to the hospital."

It took a while to get Audrey settled once they got back from the hospital. She looked more tired than Eva felt, which was saying something. But after some grilled cheese and juice and a shower, Eva managed to convince her to go back to bed. The doctor had said Audrey needed to rest for a few days, just to be cautious. When she came back into the kitchen, Finn had cleared the table and taken care of the dishes.

"You get extra brownie points for that," she said.

"For what? Basic hygiene?" He shook his head at her. "My mom would kick my butt if I left you with the dishes. I was raised to do my share. Of everything. Em and I both had to share all the chores. None of this boy-stuff and girl-stuff nonsense. She didn't want me growing up like her brothers did. None of them even knew how to use a washing machine when they left home. Or make toast from the way she tells it."

"I think I like your mom," Eva said.

"She'd like you," he said and offered a lopsided smile before he put the dish towel hanging over his shoulder back on its hook by the oven. "They'll probably come see me play sometime soon. You might meet her then."

"Long way to come from Chicago." She was stalling. The thought of meeting Finn's parents was kind of scary. Also kind of pointless. No point meeting them and liking them. No point them deciding they liked her.

She couldn't remember the last time she'd met a man's parents. Frankly, the few guys she'd dated more than twice, she knew from school or around Saratoga and she'd already known their parents, too. Not that that made it any less awkward. High school dating was one thing, but meeting parents that you used to call Mr. and Mrs. Smith in high school and having them insist you were too old for that now and you should call them Lucy and Sean—all the while knowing they knew you were sleeping with their son—was another level of weird.

Which was why she'd kept things simple. Until Finn. Finn who drove her to hospitals and made grilled cheese sandwiches for her sister and did dishes and kissed like a god. Finn, who it was getting harder to imagine life without.

"You're thinking very loudly over there," Finn said softly. "Penny for your thoughts."

"They're hardly worth that," she said. "I think I'm just tired."

"Well, Audrey's sleeping. We could sleep, too," he offered. "Or you could. I can hang out here. You don't need to entertain me."

"That sounds very tempting—" The front door banged open and she realized there was something she'd forgotten to tell Finn. "Um, hold that thought." She fled the kitchen, heading for the front door before Lizzie and Kate started yelling her name to see where she was like they usually did when they arrived home. She didn't need them waking up Audrey.

"Eva!" They squealed in unison when she appeared and the next minute she was wrapped in a double sister hug that was exactly what the doctor ordered. When Lizzie started squeeing a little too loudly she was forced to abandon the hug and order her to be quiet.

"Audrey's asleep," she said and hated the way both Lizzie's and Kate's expressions turned worried in an instant. She'd called them both from the hospital last night because Audrey had asked her to, and Kate had promised to get them both on planes. Eva hadn't been certain Kate would be able to get Lizzie here, but apparently the woman was a miracle worker. It wouldn't surprise her if she'd shoehorned some sort of private plane deal from one of her friends. She'd made some odd friends during her accounting career, some very odd, very rich friends. She'd even dated an actor for a while, which had only added to the circle of people Kate knew who lived lifestyles that seemed to come straight from the pages of the tabloids. But for now the how didn't matter. What mattered was that they were both here in Saratoga and all four of them were together.

"How is she?" Kate said.

"Okay," Eva said. "Freaked out, I think. She was freaked out before this."

"I can't believe she's having a baby," Lizzie said.

"I can't believe Steve is being such an asshole," Kate muttered, expression turning fierce.

"Oh, I can believe that part," Lizzie said.

Kate tipped her head. "You never did like him. Why?"

Lizzie shrugged. "I don't know. Bad vibe. He's the kind of guy who'd try to grab his girlfriend's sisters' asses at family holidays, you know?"

"Did he do that to you?" Eva demanded.

"Not yet. But then again, I made sure he never got the chance. I do not like the dude." Her expression suddenly brightened, eyes widening as she looked past Eva's shoulder. "On the other hand, hel-lo. That guy I like."

Eva turned and saw Finn standing in the doorway to the living room. Oh God. Her sisters and Finn. She'd been trying to avoid this happening. It would've been bad enough explaining to Audrey when Finn and her called it quits. It was going to be three times as bad with all of them.

"That's Finn," she said.

"Duh," Lizzie said and waved at Finn. "Hey, Finn. I'm Lizzie." She elbowed Kate, who was also staring at Finn with an appreciative look on her face. "This is Kate."

Finn apparently took this as an invitation and came to join them in the hallway. "Hi." He looked at Eva and raised his eyebrows. "I take it you forgot to tell me something."

"Um, yeah. Lizzie and Kate are here for the weekend. They came to see Audrey."

He shrugged. "Okay. Good. Hi," he said, facing her

sisters. "Do you guys have bags or something? Did you come in a cab?"

"Yeah," Lizzie said. "Our bags are on the porch."

"I'll get them," he said and walked out the door before Eva could stop him.

"He's not a bellboy, Lizzie," she said. "You can carry your own damned bags."

"Hey, he offered," Lizzie said. "Damn. He's even better than in his photographs. Go, sis."

Kate nodded agreement. "Seconded. That man is—" The front door opened again and she cut off her sentence as Finn appeared wheeling two carry-on bags with another backpack hitched over one shoulder. The backpack would be Lizzie's. Kate was a ninja when it came to packing light.

"I haven't had a chance to make up your rooms yet," Eva said as Lizzie and Kate relieved Finn of their bags.

"We know where everything is," Kate pointed out. "And you always made us make our own beds. We'll be fine. You must have been up all night. You go sit down and let Finn here make you a coffee or something."

"I would kill for coffee," Lizzie chimed in. "Plane coffee sucks and there wasn't time to get the real stuff before I left for the airport at crazy o'clock this morning."

"Coffee, I can do," Finn said solemnly. He hooked his arm around Eva's shoulder. "You heard your sisters. You go sit down. I got this."

At midnight, Eva gave up trying to sleep and reached for her phone. Finn had gone home after he'd provided enough Chinese takeout to feed a small army, insisting she needed time with her sisters. It had been great hanging out with all of them, but now she was alone in bed again with nothing but her thoughts to drive her crazy. She needed a distraction.

She dialed Finn's number before she could talk herself out of it. To her relief, he answered straightaway. Not asleep then.

"Can't even last a few hours without me, huh?" he said. She smiled just because it was him. She wasn't, however, dumb enough to confess that he was right.

"Actually I'm just calling to see if you were being sensible and resting up before tomorrow."

"Is lunch with your sisters going to be that tiring?"

"You have no idea." Lizzie and Kate had been too distracted with fussing over Audrey to spend too much time giving Finn the third degree this afternoon, but by tomorrow their curiosity was bound to start getting the better of them.

"I can handle it. I like them."

"They're better in small doses."

"Liar. You love having them all there."

Damn, he really did know what she was thinking. "I miss my sisters. That's not unusual."

"No. I even miss mine from time to time."

"From time to time? You mean on the odd days when you're not Skyping or texting with your whole family." One thing Finn definitely couldn't be accused of was being distant from his family. Hell, he'd given Amelia's mom part of his liver and she wasn't a blood relative. Eva still needed to get the full story about that out of him. But tonight she was too tired to grill him about his life story.

He laughed and she heard the distinctive creak of a mattress. "Are you in bed?"

"It's after midnight. Where did you think I'd be?"

Finn in bed. An image that wasn't likely to help her sleep. "You answered the phone so fast, I figured you were probably up watching ESPN or something."

"I am. I'm just doing it in bed."

"Watching TV in bed is a terrible habit."

"Well, I'd rather be doing other things but my girlfriend ditched me for her sisters."

"You ditched yourself," she protested. "I said you could stay."

He laughed. "A wise man once told me to never stand in the way of female bonding. Audrey needs all of you. I'm not part of that."

"She likes you."

"That's good. But I'm not her sister."

And he never would be part of her family. Not if she let him go. Tonight the thought made her eyes prickle. She rubbed them with her free hand. No crying. No changing her mind. Finn had to go at the end of the season. One of them should leave. Because she was starting to have a horrible feeling in the pit of her stomach that she was going to have stay here with Audrey if Steve didn't come to his senses.

"Eva?" he said softly. "Everything okay over there?"

"Yes," she lied. "I'm just tired. It's late." Which was true. She felt as though she'd gone twenty rounds with a prizefighter, every inch of her tired and achy.

"I can come over."

"You have practice in the morning."

"You have work. Never stopped us before. If you need me, all you have to do is ask."

Oh she wanted to. But she couldn't. She could do this herself. She had to do this herself. It was how she'd been doing things all along. Lonely sometimes. But safer. "No. I'm okay. I should let you go."

"Tell me a secret, then I'll hang up." Finn said, which was how their phone calls usually ended.

She didn't want him to hang up. "Who says I have any secrets?"

"Everyone has secrets."

"Tell me one of yours." Finn's secrets were likely to be more fun than hers.

"I asked first."

"You show me yours and I'll show you mine."

His sudden intake of breath was loud in her ear. "You sure I can't convince you to take this call to Face-Time?"

"Certain," she said. Talking to him lying in the dark was intimate enough. She wasn't sure she wanted to see his face as well. Or whatever else he might show her. "Tell me a secret, Finn."

"I'm allergic to gummy bears."

"That's a fact, not a secret."

"Nobody knows."

"Well, apart from me now knowing how to murder you if I ever get the desire, I'm still saying it doesn't count. Tell me a proper secret."

"You'll be the death of me, Harlowe." He sighed.

"You started this."

"Okay. I'm scared I'm never going to be good enough

to get back to the Saints. That yesterday was it." His voice sounded raw.

Her breath caught in her chest. "Finn. Don't be crazy." She didn't know what to say. Didn't know how she felt about knowing he still wanted to leave. Even if she was determined to see that he did. "You're too good to stay here."

"Good isn't always enough," he said. "Sometimes things just don't work out. Your turn."

"I kind of had a crush on you before you got here." She felt her face practically glowing in the dark from the heat of embarrassment.

"I knew it!" He sounded smug.

She groaned. "I don't want to talk about it. It's too embarrassing."

"It's not embarrassing. Trust me, if I'd seen a picture of you before I'd come here, I'd have had a crush on you, too."

"Now you're just trying to make me feel better."

"Is it working?"

"Maybe? Can I tell you another secret?"

"Always."

"I'm glad I decided to call you."

"Me too. Now go to sleep. Either that or let me talk dirty to you."

"Good night, Finn," she said sternly, ignoring how much she wanted him to do that. By herself. She had him for a little while but not forever.

"Eva Harlowe, you're no fun."

Chapter Sixteen

On Wednesday after morning practice, Finn was having a much-needed coffee break when his phone rang.

"Castro," he said, answering without looking at the screen. It wasn't Eva's ringtone or his parents or Em's.

"Finn. Dan Ellis."

He almost dropped the coffee as the words registered in his brain. Why was the Saints' coach calling him? "Dan," he said cautiously. "It's good to hear from you."

"How's life in Saratoga Springs?"

"Good." Which wasn't exactly the truth. Eva had been very quiet the last two days since her sisters had left. Too quiet. He'd tried to get her to talk to him but she'd refused, saying nothing was wrong. He didn't believe her. Which made him nervous. They'd spent half the night making love but even that hadn't eased the worry riding him. She'd been almost . . . too enthusiastic. He was all for wild sex, but something had been off.

"Good. Look, I won't keep you in suspense. We have a doubleheader Saturday in Minnesota. I want you to come along. Give Oliver some backup if he needs it. You in?"

"Of course." There wasn't much else he could say even though he didn't really want to leave Eva right now. The Preachers had a home game Thursday and then Saturday was the Bisons, which was just a day trip.

"Great. One of the gals will call you later with the travel details. We're flying Friday afternoon."

"That's fine."

Dan talked a bit longer, saying he'd send Finn some tape of the Twins' latest games, but he eventually hung up. Finn's coffee had gone cold and he tossed it toward the trash can harder than he should have, as a flash of anger heated his gut.

He narrowly avoided hitting Connor, who opened the door to the locker room just as the coffee arced into the trash can beside it.

"Something wrong?" Connor asked.

"Coffee's cold," Finn said.

"Besides that?"

"No."

"You sure about that?"

"I'm fine, Connor. Go worry about someone else for once."

Connor folded his arms, closed the door, leaned against it. "Who put a bug up your butt?"

Finn felt his bad mood ratchet up a notch. "No one. All's good in my world. In fact, I'm going to Minnesota this weekend."

"The Saints called you up again? For the double-header?" Connor grinned. "That makes sense with Oliver's hand."

"Yes."

"And the reason you're not happy about it is . . ."

"I am happy about it."

"Yeah. I can tell from that smile that isn't on your face. Something else wrong?"

"No." He wasn't discussing Eva with Connor. Not today. He didn't even know if there was something to discuss.

"Okay," Connor said after a beat. "You don't want to talk. But don't let whatever it is mess this up for you."

"It's just going to be like last time. I'll be back here on Sunday."

"If you say so," Connor said. He moved away from the door. "You should go tell Eva."

It was the only smart thing he'd said in the whole conversation.

Eva watched Finn climb up through the stands to where she was sitting in the front row of the top tier of seats and felt her stomach tighten. This was her favorite place to sit and have lunch in nice weather, with a view of the field below her. An empty ballpark was weirdly soothing. But the look on Finn's face wasn't. He was annoyed about something. Or worried, maybe. The set of his mouth and shoulders was stiff but she couldn't see his eyes behind his sunglasses, which made it hard to tell what he was feeling. She put the salad she'd been eating down next to her phone and water bottle and waited for him to reach her.

"Hello," she said when he came up the last of the stairs and sat beside her. He wasn't even breathing hard.

Annoying. She was fit, but climbing up the stands was a bit of a workout.

"Hey," he said. "Am I interrupting?"

"Just me and my exciting salad here," she said. "Enjoying the sunshine."

Finn shifted on the seat, staring down at the field. "It's a nice day."

Hmmm, they were talking about the weather. She didn't think that was a good sign. She picked up her salad. Took another bite, chewed. Swallowed. Finn still hadn't said anything. "So did you just feel like some exercise?" she prompted.

"Maybe I wanted to see you," he said.

"That would be nice but if that was the reason, I'd hope you'd look happier to have found me."

He shook his head, mouth quirking. "Everyone thinks I'm in a bad mood today."

"That's because you look cranky," she said with a smile, trying to keep the mood light.

"Maybe I have resting bitch face," he said.

"No. You, my friend, have resting gorgeous face and you know it. Wanna tell me what's up?" She stabbed more salad onto her fork.

He sighed. "I'm going to Minnesota this weekend."

She froze. "The Saints called you up again? Already?"

"Don't freak out."

"I'm not." She was. She knew what it meant if a team started calling up one of their Triple-A players repeatedly. She took a breath, tried to think.

"You have resting freaked-out face."

That made her smile though it didn't entirely ease the

feeling twisting her stomach into knots. Pride warring with denial and sadness and . . . hell, she didn't even know what else she was feeling. "No, I don't. It's a good thing, right? Really good."

He nodded. "I guess."

She tried to sound happy. "You want to go back to the Saints. This is a sign you're getting what you want."

His foot was tapping restlessly on the concrete. "Maybe the Saints isn't all I want."

Her heart turned over. But she couldn't have this conversation with him. She had to be able to let him go. "Don't."

"Don't what?"

"Don't start. We have a deal, remember?"

"I remember. But—"

She leaned over and kissed him to shut him up. Kissed him desperately as though she could wipe away all the confusion she felt with the sensation. It helped for a few seconds but then he pulled away.

"Eva—"

Her phone shrilled into life. The "Sisters Are Doin' It for Themselves" ringtone that she'd set for Audrey. Her stomach clenched and she snatched it up. "Aud? Are you okay?" Audrey's checkup with her ob-gyn on Monday had been all clear, though her doctor wanted her to come in for weekly scans for now.

"There are boxes," Audrey said. She sounded like she was crying.

That didn't make any sense. "Boxes? What boxes?"

"Steve sent all my stuff over. Oh Eva, he really isn't going to change his mind."

"I'll be right there," Eva said. "Fifteen minutes." She

hung up, pressed her hand to the back of her neck where the muscles had suddenly turned to rock.

"What is it?" Finn asked.

"That bastard Steve has apparently just sent all Audrey's stuff back to her. I have to go home."

"I'll come with you."

"No—you have practice."

"I'm coming. Don't argue."

When they reached her house, Audrey was sitting on the front steps, boxes piled behind her. There was a small moving van pulled up at the curb, with a couple of guys unloading still more boxes.

Eva bolted from the car as soon as Finn cut the engine, desperate to get to her sister. "Aud."

Audrey burst into tears and Eva threw her arms around her, murmuring soothing things. She watched over Audrey's shoulders as Finn walked over to one of the men unloading the truck and said something she couldn't quite hear. The guy pulled out one of those electronic delivery gizmos, pointed at something on the screen, and shrugged.

Finn said something else and the guy held up his hands, pointing at the screen again.

"Audrey," she said, noticing the sobs had died down a little. "What happened?"

Audrey lifted her head. She looked shattered. "They came to the door. Said there was a delivery for me from Steve. I thought maybe it was flowers or something so I signed and then this truck came and they started unloading the boxes. I tried to call Steve but I just got his voice mail."

Eva bit back the names she was calling Steve in her head. *Deal with the facts first, then deal with Steve.* "He hasn't contacted you at all?"

"No." Audrey sniffed. "Oh God, Eva. What am I going to do?"

Finn was headed in their direction. Eva tightened her arms around Audrey. "We'll figure something out."

Finn stopped at the bottom step. "The guy said it's definitely from Steve. Wouldn't say anything else. Christ. I'm sorry, Audrey."

Audrey's answer to this was to start crying even harder.

The movers came up with two more boxes. "These are the last." The older of the two looked at Audrey with sympathy. "Where do you want them?"

"Just leave them on the path," Finn said, expression fierce. "I'll take them into the house."

The guys nodded, then turned to go.

Eva stared at the boxes a second. "Wait," she called after them. "Isn't there any furniture?"

The older guy turned back. "One of the boxes was marked computer gear but no, nothing bigger than that."

Eva turned back to Audrey. "Audrey, didn't the two of you buy all your stuff together when you moved here?"

Audrey nodded. "A lot of it. We both had bits and pieces but we bought the kitchen table and our living room stuff and the bed together. The TV, too."

"So he thinks he's just keeping all that?" Eva said. "Oh hell no."

She looked at Finn, who was clenching his jaw.

"I think I might go have a word with Steve," he said.

"Good idea," Eva said. "I'll come with you."

"No," Audrey said.

Eva looked at her in surprise. "Sweetie, he can't just treat you like this. Not to mention try to rip you off."

"I know." Audrey's voice was suddenly firmer. "But I need to talk to him, not you two. I deserve the explanation."

"You're not going by yourself," Finn said. "A guy who will do this might do anything."

"I'll go with her," Eva said. Her head was throbbing. God. What a mess.

"I'm coming, too," Finn said, shaking his head. "I'm not leaving you two alone with this douchebag."

"We can't all go," Audrey objected.

"Yes, we can." Eva said. "But first, we need to deal with these boxes. See if there's anything else of yours that he's conveniently forgotten to send."

It took about an hour to carry all the boxes into the house and for Audrey to go through them and confirm that the only stuff missing was her furniture. The big desktop computer she used for her design work was there, along with a pile of portable hard drives that she seemed very happy to see. But she was still determined that she was going to be the one to talk to Steve.

The drive to her apartment was a largely silent one.

Finn's truck felt crowded with three of them squished into it. Eva's thigh was pressed against his and she could feel the tension in the long muscle. Hers probably felt just as tight. She really wanted to hurt Steve right now. She wouldn't, but she wanted to. Badly. No one treated one of her sisters this way.

Audrey wanted to go up to the apartment herself but Finn shook his head.

"No, we'll all go up. You can talk to him if you want. Eva and I will stay in the hall or something. But I want him to know we're here. Make sure he doesn't get any ideas about trying to intimidate you."

"He might not even be home."

"We'll deal with that, if that's what happens. You have a key, right?"

"Yes. Unless he's changed the lock." Audrey looked stricken all over again and Eva squeezed her hand.

"You can do this," Eva said. "But you don't have to. Finn and I can go in and you can stay here."

Audrey shook her head and opened the door. Eva and Finn followed her up to the apartment, where she knocked on the door.

Soon enough Steve opened it, then immediately tried to shut it again when he saw Audrey. Finn thrust out his arm and pushed the door back. Steve didn't have the muscle to withstand Finn's. He fell back a step but then moved forward again, trying to block the door with his body.

"What are you doing here?" he said to Audrey.

"I wanted to see you," Audrey said. "To talk to you."

Steve's face went carefully blank. "There's nothing

to talk about." "She's having your kid," Finn growled. "You can at least man up enough to talk to her."

Steve glared at Finn but obviously wasn't willing to challenge him. He stepped back, jerked his chin at Audrey. "Come in. Say what you have to say."

Audrey stepped forward. Eva went to follow her but she shook her head and waved her back.

"Okay," Eva said. "But remember we're right here." She glared at Steve, hoping he'd get the message that Finn wasn't the one he really should be worried about. Right now she felt like she could tear the idiot's head off without much effort.

Audrey disappeared into the apartment.

Eva heard the murmur of voices, wondered if she should really be listening in but then gave up pretending she wasn't going to.

"What are you doing here?" Steve said hotly.

"I want an explanation," Audrey said. Her voice was steady and Eva curled her fingers into fists, wondering how much that calm was costing her sister.

"I thought you should have your stuff." Steven sounded like he thought what he'd done was perfectly reasonable.

"So you just sent it to me? What the hell, Steve? Who does that?" Audrey sounded less calm now. Finn's hand closed around Eva's wrist as she stepped forward without thinking. He shook his head and mouthed, *Let her do this.* Eva scowled at him but stayed where she was.

"Look, Audrey, I'm sorry. But I don't want a kid," Steve said.

"Well, that's nice but the fact is I'm pregnant. And don't even think of telling me to get rid of it again. Not if you're particularly attached to your balls. I'm keeping this baby."

"That's your choice, not mine. I don't want this. I might have to pay you child support or something but that's it. I'm not going to be part of the kid's life." ·

"I don't understand," Audrey said, and Eva heard the edge of tears in her voice again. "I thought we had something here. I thought you loved me."

"I care about you. But I never told you I wanted kids. And I don't. Definitely not now. So I'm sorry, but no, it's me or the kid."

Bastard. Eva moved again, filled with rage. and Finn's grip tightened. She shook her head at him, tugging at her arm. He let go but blocked her path.

"She has to do it," he said softly. "She needs to decide."

He was right. She hated it, but he was right.

"That's not a choice," Audrey said. "I'm having this baby. Your loss. So I want a check for my half of the rent and the deposit. Plus the table and the bookcases. You can keep the bed. I'll find a lawyer, find out about child support."

"So it's all about the money then?" Steve said.

The sound of a slap was perfectly clear. Then Audrey reappeared in the doorway, looking furious. Steve followed on her heels, one side of his face red.

"Come back—"

Finn stepped into his path as Audrey reached Eva. "I don't think so."

"She fucking slapped me." Steve's voice was outraged. Like he'd expected Audrey to be perfectly happy about what he'd done.

"If you ask me you got off lightly," Finn said, voice deadly calm. "Now back off. I'm a lot bigger than Audrey. And a lot less polite."

"What fucking business is it of yours? Who the hell are you, anyway? You screwing Eva? Hope you're careful with condoms. She's probably as big a slut as her sister—"

Finn stepped closer, not quite touching Steve. "Watch your mouth," he snarled. "You say one more word about Eva or any of her sisters, or if you cause any trouble for Audrey, and you'll regret it."

"You and—"

"Do not push me." Finn said. "Audrey, Eva. Go get in the car. Steve and I will be done in a minute."

Steve's eyes flicked to Eva's. Frankly he looked scared, and for a moment she almost felt sorry for him. But that was his problem. "Good-bye, Steve," she said and led Audrey back down to the car.

When they got back to the house, Audrey dissolved into tears again. Eva took her down to her room, made her splash water on her face, passed Kleenex while she sobbed and sobbed.

She really wished she could send Finn back to actually beat the crap out of Steve. Finn had come back to the car looking furious and with a check in hand for five thousand dollars but she hadn't seen any marks on his hands. So she didn't think he'd done anything other than intimidate Steve into writing the check, as much as he might have liked to.

"What am I going to do?" Audrey wailed, reaching

for another Kleenex. Her face was a complete red blotchy mess.

"We'll figure it out," Eva said, automatically. "It'll be okay."

"I can't do this by myself," Audrey said. "I can't, Eva. I don't know anything about being a mom."

"You'll learn—" Eva began but Audrey started crying again, deep gulping sobs that made Eva feel like each one was stabbing into her. God. She couldn't stand seeing Audrey like this. Broken and in pieces. She'd worked so hard to help her sisters recover after their parents had died. To help them put their lives back together so they could be happy.

How dare Steve take that away from Audrey? From Eva? All that work and love and effort and it still wasn't enough to keep Audrey safe from pain.

"You won't leave me, will you? You'll stay? I can do this if you're here," Audrey said, and Eva's heart broke, too. She hugged Audrey, rubbing her back like she'd done when she was a devastated eleven-year-old.

"I won't leave you," she said and knew it was the truth.

And with that her world had changed again.

When Audrey fell asleep, over an hour later, Eva came out of her room to discover that Finn had stacked all the boxes neatly against the wall in the hallway. He was sitting on the sofa, watching something on his laptop.

"I thought you would have gone back to Hennessee," she said from the doorway.

"I wanted to know that you're okay."

She nodded. It was a lie but she couldn't face the truth. Not yet. "You can go. I'm going to call, tell them I'm not coming back. It's nearly four anyway."

"Which means I've missed practice. I don't have to go." His eyes looked very green as he studied her face. He looked as though he was going to say something but then he closed his mouth again.

"What is it?" she asked.

"It can wait." He put the laptop aside.

Oh God. Now what? "Just tell me."

"We didn't really finish talking about Minnesota."

Minnesota? What was in Minnesota? The Preachers didn't have a game there—then she remembered. "The Saints called you up again."

"Yes."

Twice in a week. Or close enough. She knew what that meant. She'd seen enough guys come and go not to know it was a good sign for Finn's chances of being re-called.

So he'd be going back to New York. But she was staying here. Her stomach twisted suddenly, tears rising in her eyes.

"Hey," Finn said. "I can say no. If you don't want to be here alone with Audrey."

She didn't even know how to begin to respond to that. Her brain seemed to have melted. She'd told Audrey she'd stay. Now it looked like Finn was going. Which meant she was the one left behind. God.

"I—" Her phone buzzed into life in her pocket. She pulled it out, thinking it would be someone at Hennessee checking up on her but instead the screen said ISAAC HAINES.

Damn. Her deposit was due by the end of this week. She'd already written the check. But hadn't posted it. They were probably checking up on her, seeing if she was going to accept the office.

"I have to take this," she said to Finn and then walked into the kitchen before pressing the button to take the call. "Eva Harlowe."

"Ms. Harlowe, this is Isaac Haines." The voice on the other end of the line was deep and rumbly, just the way it sounded in the interviews and YouTube talks she'd heard him give.

She hadn't dreamed he'd call her himself. "Hello," she managed to say.

"I was just calling to check up on your acceptance. You're the last student on the list," Isaac said. "I hope you'll be joining us next year. I loved your portfolio. You have great potential."

Do not cry.

Her phone was biting into her hand she was gripping it so tightly. Isaac Haines was talking to her. Praising her work. And she was going to have to open her mouth and kill her dreams. "Thank you. That means a lot to me."

"Ms. Harlowe, is that a yes?"

"I'm very sorry, but I can't," she said, exerting every inch of self-control she possessed to say the words without crying. "My circumstances have—there's a family—I mean, I'm sorry but I just can't move to California at the moment."

"Are you sure?" Isaac says. "We have a waiting list of my next choices. I can hold your place a few more days if you need to think about it. I meant what I said,

Ms. Harlowe, I think you're very talented. I think I could teach you a lot."

"I'm sure," she said, wishing she could just disappear. "I'm sorry to have wasted your time. But I can't."

"Well, I'm disappointed," Isaac said. "Maybe you can apply again next round."

"Maybe," she agreed. "Thank you." She ended the call.

"What the hell was that?" Finn said from behind her.

Chapter Seventeen

"Were you listening in on my call?" Eva demanded.

Finn stared at her. Seriously? She was going to bust his balls for overhearing a phone call? "I was in the next room, Eva, it's not like you were out of earshot. Tell me you didn't just do what I think you did."

Her mouth went flat. "It's my life."

"You just turned down Isaac Haines? You're not going to California?" He didn't understand what she was doing.

"Yes."

"Are you going to tell me why?"

"Because my sister needs me. I'm not letting her go through this alone."

"Audrey isn't a child, Eva. She'll manage."

Eva's cheeks went hot. "I don't want my sister to have to 'manage.' Not if I can help her."

"By throwing away your dreams? That's crazy."

"Why is it crazy to want to help my sister? Didn't you tell me you gave part of your liver to Amelia's mom? She isn't even related to you!"

She had a point. But not a good point. The two situations were completely different. "Not the same thing. That was a few months of my life. Not throwing away my shot at a whole new career. Amelia's mother was dying. Audrey's just having a baby."

"Just having a baby. Only a man would say that!" She glared at him. "Have you forgotten that the father of that baby just dumped her? That he's not going to be there for her?"

"No. I hadn't forgotten. I agree, the situation sucks, but explain to me why you're the one who has to suffer because of it?"

"Staying with my sister isn't suffering. She needs my help. It's what families do."

"It's what you do," he said.

"What's that supposed to mean?"

"You give up what you want. Photography school, the life you were planning. You let them go. Hell, you're so scared of having something that you can't even have a relationship without a built-in expiration date." He saw her flinch, knew he should feel guilty about pushing her at a time when she was so stressed, but he needed her to get what he was saying. To hear the truth. Maybe that would be enough to get through to her and make her see that what she was doing was ridiculous.

"I'm not scared—"

"Oh really? Then why did you just jump on the first opportunity to bail on going to school?"

"Because my sister needs me," she yelled.

"That's an excuse, not a reason."

"It's my life, Finn. Not yours."

"Because you won't let me be part of it. You're too

scared to do that." He threw up his hands, saw her jaw clench. Wondered what the hell he could say that would get through to her.

"I'm not scared. I told you how I wanted things to be between us. It's not my fault if you didn't believe me."

"Can't you see how crazy that sounds? Who does that? Okay, maybe it seemed reasonable at the beginning, but you and I are more than a fling, Eva. You know that. You know we work. Are you seriously telling me you're still going to be perfectly fine walking away at the end of the season? It's not going to hurt you at all to let me go?"

Her chin lifted. "Yes. In fact, I'll tell you something else. I don't think we should wait until the end of the season. It's obvious that the Saints are going to recall you. So there's no point hanging on to this. I think we should call it quits now."

Suddenly he had a lot more sympathy for Steve the dick because she might as well have just slugged him. "Excuse me?"

Her eyes were dark, unreadable, no sign of doubt on her face. "You heard me."

"You're breaking up with me?"

"Yes."

"Because you're staying here? That doesn't even make sense. If I go back to the Saints I'm only a forty-minute flight away. It's not like you'll be living in California."

"You'll go back to New York, you'll be busy. You won't have time for this. And I won't, either. It'll all be too hard. So why drag things out? Ending it now is the best thing to do." She sounded like she believed what she was saying. Like it was all perfectly logical instead of the stupidest thing he'd heard in his life.

"Eva, this is *me*. I know you. You might think I'm too young and too whatever the hell story it is you've made up in your head but I know you. This isn't what you want."

"It is. I'm sorry, Finn."

He took a step forward and she moved back, until she bumped into a chair. God. Did she think he'd hurt her? He froze, appalled at the thought. They stared at each other. She looked like she wanted to be anywhere but here with him and the sick sharp pain of it hit him all over again. He couldn't think. Couldn't figure out what to say to her.

"Tell me a secret."

She winced. "Finn, don't."

"Tell me a secret," he repeated. "No, tell me the truth. Tell me you don't care about me."

She stayed silent, looking away. Fingers digging into the upholstery of the chair she stood beside.

"Then I'll tell you something. I love you."

Her head snapped up. "What?"

"You heard me. I love you."

She held up a hand. "Don't. Don't say that to me. We're ending. You're leaving."

"I'm not leaving, you won't let me stay." He heard his voice go rough, fought to stay calm.

Her eyes blazed. "Because I'm not going to be the one left again. I'm not going to let Audrey be the one left behind and I'm not going to be left, either." Her voice was shaking. "I can't. Not again. Not now. Everyone gets to leave and I'm just left here. With all these missing pieces in my life, pretending it's all okay. I'm not doing that again."

"But I don't have to be a missing piece. I don't want to be that." He didn't know how to get through to her. Not this pale distant woman who was nothing like the Eva he knew. "Eva, I told you I love you."

"That wasn't our deal."

"Deals change."

"No. Please, if you want to be the good guy, be that guy who makes the big grand gesture, then just do the right thing and let me go. That's what I need."

"Life doesn't work like that. I said I love you. Tell me you don't feel the same way."

She flinched like he'd slapped her. But then she shook her head. "I'm sorry. Good-bye, Finn, please go."

"You ready for this, Castro?" Oliver said as they stood waiting to take the field on Saturday afternoon.

"I'm fine, old man," Finn said. He smiled at Oliver, to show he was joking, then focused back on the end of the tunnel ahead of them, trying to remember all the statistics and strategies Dan Ellis had been cramming into his head for hours.

"Forget about all the theory," Oliver said. "Focus on the game. Just us and bats and the ball. That's all. Simple."

"Yeah," Finn said. "Simple." Baseball. He knew how to do baseball. Apparently he was crap at relationships but he could do this. Even when every inch of him wanted to be back in Saratoga trying to talk some sense into Eva. Eva, who had refused to speak to him since

Wednesday. Hadn't even come to work. Which made her message about where they stood easy enough to understand. She was done with him. She didn't want him. At least, not enough to actually take the step to get over her own damned fears and come get him.

He understood how that felt, the fear part. He'd spent a good part of the previous season trying to drown out his own fears with the whirl of parties and booze and women who circled the players.

It hadn't worked. He'd had to do it the hard way.

And maybe Eva was going to have to do it the hard way as well, but he couldn't help her with that part. The whole thing was killing him, but he had to get on with his own damned life in the meantime.

Which left him with baseball. With playing the best damned game he could every time he set foot on the grass and just see what happened.

It seemed as good a plan as any.

"Let's do it," he said and followed Oliver out into the spotlight.

Nearly three hours later, he followed Oliver back into the locker room with the first of the two games locked away with a Saints win. He had to admit it felt damned good. Now they just had to turn around in a few hours and do it again. He grabbed a bottle of water and chugged it without stopping. It was a blazing-hot day—Minnesota wasn't the hottest state in the country but it was doing a damned good imitation of it—and the inside of his favorite glove currently resembled a very sweaty swamp. But he had others.

Oliver flopped onto the bench near the locker he was using and stuck his hand into the bucket of ice waiting for him. He'd traded off innings at first base with Finn but he'd done the final one. Leeroy was in the outfield, his wrist still recovering from the sprain he'd had the previous week. He probably would have been put on the disabled list but four of the team had come down with stomach flu during the week and the Saints needed as many experienced players on deck as they could get. So they were babying Leeroy to make sure he could do his best at bat.

"You know," Oliver said, "sometimes I fantasize about playing a nice winter sport. Hockey or something." He tipped a bottle of water in his hand over his head. "Either that or we need air-conditioned stadiums."

"You're too pretty for hockey," Finn said. "You'd look weird with no teeth."

"I'd rock a gold grill," Oliver said. "And I'm too old to be pretty. Unlike you." He snagged another bottle of water and started chugging it.

"I'm not the one bitching about the weather." Finn drank, too.

"Just making conversation," Oliver said. "If you want, I can talk about Saratoga Springs."

Fuck no. Finn shot Oliver a look. "I take it Amelia told you about me and Eva."

"Yup. I'll also point out I've been very restrained not bringing it up. You fucking up with Eva Harlowe. Christ, kid."

"You're bringing it up now," Finn gritted out. "I don't want to talk about it."

"You need a distraction."

"I need to focus," Finn said. He picked up his towel. "I'm going to shower. Have fun with your ice bucket."

He actually saw the moment when Leeroy broke his wrist. He'd seen the batter swing, seen the ball rocket out back over Connor's head and soar toward the outfield. He'd swung to follow the arc of the ball, ready to catch it if by some miracle one of the other guys stopped it and sent it his way. He saw Leeroy barreling toward it, then watched as he leapt up then came down awkwardly, ankle buckling. Saw him throw out his arm to catch himself as he fell and saw the wrist give way. Saw the way Leeroy's face went blank for a moment then twisted with pain before he cradled his arm to his chest, his mouth opening in a groan Finn heard over the horrified roar of the crowd. He'd watched with the rest of the team as Leeroy was carried away, trying not to think about what the hell it might mean for him. Then he'd had to focus back on the game.

He hadn't expected several hours later to be sitting in a borrowed conference room in the Twins' admin building, facing Dan Ellis along with Alex Winters, Lucas Angelo, and Malachi Coulter, the three men who owned the Saints.

He hadn't really missed alcohol all year. He'd stayed away from it mostly because he knew he needed to learn to manage his stress in other ways, but it wasn't as though it had been hard. He hadn't longed for a drink, which kind of proved his theory that he wasn't an alcoholic. But he really could have used a shot of something right now.

Something to calm the tangle of hope and fear in his gut. But no. No taking the easy way. He could do this on his own.

He'd had time to shower and change back into his street clothes before Dan had swung by the locker room to tell him that Alex and the other two wanted to talk to him.

Oliver, still icing his hand, had raised his eyebrows as they'd walked out past him, but Dan hadn't said anything more so Finn had just kept walking behind him.

And now he was here. Facing the men who held his career in their hands for the second time in less than a year.

"Finn," Alex said, leaning back in his chair. In dark jeans, white shirt, and navy jacket, he looked his usual blond billionaire self. "That was a good game. Games."

"Thanks," Finn said. "Dan has the team playing well."

"That was a compliment for you, not Dan," Lucas said. His suit was the same navy as Alex's jacket, tailored to within an inch of its life. Whoever Lucas's tailor was, he made a fortune off the always immaculate Dr. Angelo. And probably another fortune from men who wanted to have Lucas's style.

"Not sure I deserve it."

"You just came down, played a doubleheader with a team you haven't had much to do with in six months, and fit right back in," Mal said. He pushed back his too-long hair. "Take the compliment."

Finn nodded. Mal folded his arms. Unlike the other two, he had on a well-worn Saints bomber jacket, black jeans, and biker boots. Of course, he'd probably been down in the bowels of the stadium telling the Twins' security team how to do their job for half the games. Hard to keep a suit clean if you were checking out crawl spaces and lighting towers.

"You could put the boy out of his misery," Dan said.

Alex grinned. "But this way is more fun."

"Sadist," Mal muttered.

"Finn, you've probably figured out that Leeroy broke his wrist in that fall," Lucas said. "It's a nasty break. He's out for the rest of the season."

Finn tensed. "That's too bad." He managed not to sound happy about it. Hell, he wasn't happy about it. Or at least, not happy that Leeroy was hurt. He liked Leeroy.

"That leaves us short a backup first baseman," Alex continued. "So we were wondering how you were doing with everything?"

"You mean you're wondering if I've learned my lesson and stopped being an idiot with his head up his butt?" Finn asked.

"Something like that," Mal said with a nod of acknowledgment.

"I hope so. I've been a lot . . . happier . . . this year. Got my head on straight. You were right to send me to the Preachers. I needed some time to figure things out. But I think I have now."

"So you think you're ready to come back to New York?" Lucas asked. "Back to everything that goes with playing for us?"

"Yes, sir," Finn said. "I am." A few days earlier, he would have had to stop and think about it. But that was when Eva was still talking to him. Not after he'd told her he loved her and she had ditched him.

Alex tilted his head. "Nothing keeping you in Saratoga?"

Crap. Apparently they knew about Eva. Or at least, they knew that they'd been dating. He had no idea if they knew that that was over. But it was over. At least as far as Eva was concerned. So he had to make this decision without factoring her in. He straightened his shoulders. "No. I'm good to go."

Alex and Lucas exchanged a look and then Alex shrugged, leaned forward, and extended his hand. "In that case, welcome home."

"I hope I'm not interrupting," Don Mannings said when Eva opened the front door on Sunday afternoon.

She blinked in surprise. Don was not someone she expected to find on her doorstep on the weekend. He and Helen had dropped by from time to time when the girls were still here but since Lizzie had left home, they'd changed the routine to inviting Eva to dinner every few months. She and Helen sometimes had lunch or coffee, but usually that was planned.

"Don. Hi," she said, trying to sound pleased rather than surprised. "No, you're not interrupting. Come on in."

He followed her into the house then stopped as he spotted Audrey curled up on the sofa watching some brainless reality show. "Hey, kiddo. What are you doing here?"

Eva hadn't had a chance to explain the Audrey situation to anyone at the Preachers yet. She'd called in sick Thursday and Friday after breaking up with Finn, not wanting to risk seeing him. She wondered if Don was checking up on her because of that.

"Audrey's staying with me," Eva said.

"My ratfink ex-boyfriend knocked me up and then dumped me," Audrey said, lifting her chin.

Don looked startled. "Um—"

"It's fine," Audrey continued. "I'm fine."

His expression changed to unconvinced; he looked at Eva with a what-the-hell expression, but she shook her head. There wasn't much Don and Helen could do to fix this particular screwed-up scenario.

"Okay. You let Helen know if there's anything we can do," he said to Audrey. "Anything at all."

Audrey nodded, chin still tilted up as if she was expecting a lecture and was ready to defend herself. "Thanks."

"Coffee?" Eva said brightly. "Or beer. I think I have beer in the fridge." Which Audrey couldn't drink and she couldn't bring herself to tip down the drain because Finn had brought it around one night before he'd figured out that she didn't really like beer. It had been sitting in her fridge for weeks.

"Coffee's good," Don said. "Early start in the morning."

The Preachers were off to Ohio this week. Which Eva was grateful for. A couple of away games meant that if she timed things right on Monday she could probably avoid seeing Finn for a few more days. By then she'd have managed to find her game face again. Be able to face him.

She put fresh coffee in the coffeemaker, switched it on, and then rummaged in the pantry for some cookies. By the time she'd put them on a plate and Don had settled into a seat at the kitchen table, the silence was getting awkward.

"So," he said eventually. "How are you feeling?"

"Good," she said, willing herself not to blush. "Just a bug."

He nodded, shifted in his chair. "I thought it would be best if you heard it from me," he said. "Leeroy Jones managed to break his wrist during the second game the Saints played against the Twins last night."

It took her a moment to figure out why he was telling her. Then it hit her. "The Saints are recalling Finn?"

"Yes. Dan Ellis called me today. I'm sorry. I know you and he were . . . close."

She bit her lip. Finn was leaving. God. It hurt to think about. She'd always known he would. She'd told him he had to. But she hadn't known it was going to feel so bad to let him go. Which made her a world-class idiot. Who wasn't going to cry in front of Don. She took a breath, wrestled her calm back into place with an effort. "It's okay. We were just casual. I always knew he'd go back."

Don rubbed a hand through his hair. "Well, I don't know. The times I saw him looking at you, he didn't look all that casual to me."

It hadn't felt all that casual, either. She knew she'd done the right thing but the right thing was goddamned painful. She and Audrey were probably keeping Kleenex afloat at this point. Though she was trying her best to hide from Audrey just how upset she was about Finn. Audrey had enough on her plate. Eva had made her own choice and she wasn't going to let Audrey feel any guilt about it. "We both knew the score."

"New York isn't that far away," Don said. "You could make it work."

She shook her head. "You know what it's like. All that travel. It's hard even for couples who are married."

"Hard isn't impossible. Helen and I figured it out."

"When you played for the Saints, MLB wasn't quite the circus it is now," Eva pointed out. No social media. No blogs. No paparazzi. She was sure there'd still been plenty of women who'd been happy to sleep with ball-players back then, but it hadn't been such a pressure cooker.

"No. But that doesn't mean it can't be done. If you met someone who wasn't quite so . . . casual."

Eva tried not to flinch. She couldn't even think about someone who could follow Finn Castro. "Right now, I'm focusing on Audrey. She needs me."

Don frowned then shook his head. "Okay. But you know if you need anything, you only have to ask, right?"

She leaned over and patted his hand. "Yes. Thank you. Now. I promised you coffee. Milk, three sugars, right?"

"Yup." Don glanced back at the living room and Audrey. "No chance of her getting back together with the father?"

"Right now I'd say the chances of that are about the same as the Cubs winning five World Series in a row over the next five years," Eva said. "Frankly, I think she's better off without him. He's kind of showed his true colors since Audrey found out. And they're not good colors." She wished she felt the same way about Finn. That she was better off without him. Her brain believed it but the rest of her didn't. And he was really going to be gone now. Not just out of her bed but out of her life altogether. Back in New York, playing the game he was born to play. Just like she thought she'd wanted.

Chapter Eighteen

"You know, if you keep checking the baseball scores on your phone, I'm going to confiscate the damned thing," Jenna said at their Friday-night dinner three weeks later.

Eva jerked her head up guiltily. "I was just checking my email."

"You were checking the scores for that team that the guy you claim not to care about plays for. For the tenth time. The game only started half an hour ago."

"I don't care about him," Eva said. She shoved her phone into her purse, removing the temptation. "It's just that the Saints are still on their streak. In case you haven't noticed, I was a Saints fan well before—well, well before many things. If they keep playing like this they're going to make the divisional championship again."

"They lost the divisional championship last year," Jenna pointed out.

"They're playing better this year." She pointed her

fork at Jenna then stabbed a chili fry. "No doubters allowed."

"Well, at least you are paying attention to something," Jenna said. "That's better than moping."

Eva chewed her fry angrily then stabbed another. "I do not mope."

"Oh please," Jenna said. "You are the Queen of Mope Town. No, wait, that might be Audrey. You are the Crown Princess of Mope Town."

"Am not." She totally was. But she wasn't going to admit that much to Jenna. She didn't want to admit that much to herself.

"If you're not moping, why is this the first time I've been able to drag you out of the house in three weeks?"

"I've been busy." She had been. If feeling wretched while trying to put on a happy face for your pregnant sister and the world counted as an activity. Honestly, she was starting to feel jealous of the fact that Audrey was allowed to be openly miserable. Audrey, at least, had a baby to look forward to. Whereas Eva had . . . just more of the same. Saratoga. The Preachers. Looking after everyone. Every time she thought about it too hard, it was hard to breathe. She put down her fork, pushed away the half-eaten plate of fries, appetite vanishing. "I'm full. Get these away from me."

Jenna shook her head. "Good grief, you can't even finish your food. Tell me again about how you're not missing Finn at all?" She glanced at her watch and pushed her own plate away. "Okay. If you're only going to pretend to eat, we're going back to your place. You can pretend to watch a movie with me and Audrey. I'll make popcorn. And cocktails. Audrey can have virgin ones and I'll put the extra booze in yours. Maybe alcohol will cure your moping."

"Eva!" Lizzie threw open the front door as Eva and Jenna walked up the front steps.

"Lizzie?" Eva said, wondering if she was having some sort of bad chili-induced hallucination. "What are you doing here?" She turned to Jenna. "What's going on?"

"Come inside," Lizzie said. She pushed a strand of her short blond hair off her face then grabbed Eva's arm.

"What's going on?" Eva repeated as she followed Lizzie into the living room.

Jenna gave her a little shove toward the sofa. Where Kate was sitting with Audrey. Kate looked kind of annoyed. Audrey looked teary and vaguely stubborn.

"This is an intervention," Jenna said. "An Eva-is-being-a-selfless-idiot intervention." She directed a distinctly unimpressed look at Audrey. "It may be an Audrey-is-being-a-selfish-idiot intervention as well."

"I don't understand," Eva said, looking among the four women, who were all watching her. Lizzie looked determined, Audrey upset, and Kate and Jenna both looked plain old cranky.

"Quite frankly, neither do we," Kate said. She looked sideways at Audrey and then back to Eva. "When Jenna called me and told me you'd given up your place in that photography course and dumped Finn, I thought she was playing some sort of weird prank."

Eva folded her arms. "It's my life."

"No," Kate said. "It's apparently Audrey's life."

"Hey," Audrey protested.

Kate looked at her. "No. You're letting Eva step in because you're in a tough spot. And I can give you a pass on asking initially because you're hormonal and heartbroken but I'm not giving you a pass on holding her to her promise."

Audrey turned pale. "I don't want to have a baby by myself."

"No one wants that. But you won't be by yourself," Kate said. "Eva's not leaving until December and then I'll be down as much as I can."

"I'm not leaving at all," Eva said. "I turned down my spot. The deadline was weeks ago."

"Hush," Lizzie said. "Kate's exercising her inner Virgo and organizing the world."

Eva opened her mouth to say something else but Lizzie put her hand over it. "Let Kate do her thing."

"Eva, you were planning on renting this place out while you were in school, to help cover your expenses, right?" Kate asked.

"Yes. But now I don't need to because I'm not leaving." Eva folded her arms over her chest, narrowing her eyes at Kate.

Kate ignored her, and Eva was starting to wonder if she really was hallucinating. "So I'm going to help Audrey find a good lawyer and she'll have child support plus whatever she makes from her business. She works from home so that makes things easier initially. I'm willing to help her out with rent for the first year." She looked at Audrey. "You can pay me back eventually."

"You're such an accountant," Audrey muttered.

"None of which is relevant because I'M NOT GOING," Eva said, voice rising to nearly a shout.

"Yes, you are," Lizzie said. "Kate spoke to that Haines dude. Your deposit is all paid and everything."

Eva gaped at her. How had Kate managed that? Isaac Haines had a waiting list a mile long. Her spot should have been filled weeks ago.

Jenna smirked. "See. Taken care of."

"No." Eva said. "This is ridiculous. I'm not going to let you do this."

Kate shook her head at her. "No. It's not ridiculous. You worked for so many years to make sure we were all okay, Eva. So now it's our turn to do something to make sure you get what you want. You did a great job stepping in when Mom and Dad died but you're done now. You can go back to just being one of the four sisters and let us help you like you helped us."

"But Audrey—" Eva started.

Kate held up a hand. "No. Audrey will figure this out. How to be a mom. After all, she had the perfect example."

"You mean Mom?"

Kate shook her head. "No, dummy, I mean you. We all grew up knowing what it means to step up to the plate. And how to do it brilliantly. Because we had you. But you did that job. And it's Audrey's turn now."

Eva saw Audrey's eyes widen and felt the wind go out of her argument as she watched Jenna and Lizzie nodding in vigorous agreement with Kate. "I—"

"Shut up and say yes," Lizzie said. "Then you get to be in California with me. Sunshine and your baby sister. What more could you want?"

"I think the answer to that question is Finn Castro," Jenna said.

Eva's head snapped back to her. Oh no, they were not going to talk about Finn. "No, it's not."

Jenna flopped down into the nearest armchair. "Crap. You're miserable without him. Don't even try to deny it."

"I'll get over it."

"You shouldn't have to get over it." Lizzie said. "He made you really happy. I hadn't seen you that happy in forever."

"Seconded," Kate said.

"Even I can't argue with that one," Audrey muttered. "Finn was really a good guy. He's not a Steve."

"Thank God," Lizzie muttered. She shut up when Audrey glared at her.

"Finn and I were never going to work," Eva pointed out. "He was always going to leave and go back to the majors. I was right about that. And I was going to California."

"Only for a couple of years. He's a baseball player. He must travel to California at least once a month during the season. Plus he must have approximately eleventy billion frequent-flier miles and a pretty damned good salary so he can afford to fly to see you or fly you to see him in between," Jenna said, smiling evilly.

"Plus, you're going to study with a guy who's a famous sports photographer. So surely some of your assignments are going to involve photographing sports," Lizzie said. "You could pick baseball for your assignments. It's the perfect excuse to go see Finn play."

They were all so pleased with themselves, it was

infuriating. But they were forgetting one big issue. "It's a moot point. We broke up."

"People get back together," Jenna said. "People have fights about stupid stuff and say stupid things and then stop being stupid and make up all the time."

"I think what you need to ask yourself," Audrey said suddenly, "is what you would do if none of this stuff was in the way. In a perfect world, would you pick Finn to be with? If the answer is yes, then you figure out how to make it work in the real world."

Eva gaped at her. Audrey, who'd begged her not to go, was now arguing that she should? What the hell did that mean? And what the hell was she meant to do about it?

"So how's life in the fast lane?" Connor asked Finn a few days later. "You tired of the good life yet?"

"Tired, yes. Over it, no." Finn said, juggling the phone into place so he could hold it tucked between his ear and his neck while he packed his gear bag. "I'd forgotten just how crazy the schedule is."

"Yeah but now you're doing it all in extra-cushy planes and buses with people to carry your bags and fulfill your every whim."

If only. The only whim he had these days was the unrelenting wish that Eva would materialize in his hotel room one night and tell him she loved him. Whims were stupid. "Trust me, there's not that much whim filling."

"Dude, you're doing it wrong. I got plenty of whims filled when I was in the majors."

"Just keeping my head in the game," Finn said with

a laugh designed to convince Connor that he was going to be doing some of that kind of whim filling any day now. When the truth was he had zero desire to touch any woman who wasn't Eva.

"So when are you coming back to Saratoga?" Connor asked.

"Actually, I have Thursday and Friday off this week, so I'm going to come down and pack up my apartment. Want to swing by and help me shove stuff in boxes? I offer beer and pizza as payment."

"Sure," Connor said easily. "I think we get back Thursday morning so I'll come around once Coach lets us go. You gonna haul your stuff back up to Manhattan yourself?"

"I've got moving guys coming. I've found another place in New York for now. My other apartment is still sublet. I'm not sure I'm going to keep my truck. Not really practical in the city." He needed something smaller for commuting to Staten Island. The truck would be hell to park in Manhattan. "Know anyone who's in the market?"

"I'll ask around."

"Thanks."

"Anything else you want to know?" Connor asked. "You know. How people are?"

Finn's jaw tightened. "Is 'people' code for Eva?" Finn had told Connor the whole story after Eva had dumped him. He'd had to tell someone other than Amelia and Oliver. Someone less complicated. To his credit, Connor had been sympathetic and hadn't called Finn an idiot for agreeing to something so stupid in the first place.

"Possibly," Connor admitted. "I thought you said she'd turned down that photography thing."

What? "She did. That's what she told me." Had she changed her mind? Was she leaving after all? A stupid surge of hope rushed through him. He shoved it away. Eva moving to California was just as out of reach as Eva in Saratoga if she wanted nothing to do with him. More out of reach, in fact. He had an excuse to drop in at a Preachers game occasionally, after all. But none for crashing a photography school on the other side of the country.

"Well, Carly told me that Eva announced she's leaving at the end of the year. I haven't asked her myself but Carly said she was going to California."

Finn sat down on the locker room bench. Fuck. She was leaving. And she hadn't changed her mind.

"You still there?" Connor said.

"Yes."

"Are you going to call her?"

"And say what? This just seems to put us back where we started. She's leaving. No long distance."

"Yeah, that was before you two broke up. I'll tell you one thing, I don't think I've seen her smile since you left. That girl misses you. So think about it. Maybe you can see her when you come down?"

He squelched another surge of hope. Connor might think Eva missed Finn, but Connor was the eternal glass-half-full or maybe even all-the-way-full guy. Eva was probably just stressed about Audrey. "She made it clear that she didn't want to see me."

"Doesn't seem to me like that's working out so well

for either of you. You haven't been Mr. Sunshine lately, either. So maybe you should do something about it."

Eva saw Connor's BMW pull up outside Finn's apartment building and watched as Finn climbed out and went inside. Connor was still in the car, as he'd promised. She waited a minute, wiping suddenly sweaty palms on her skirt, and then got out of the car she'd borrowed so Finn wouldn't spot hers. She walked over to Connor's car and knocked on the window. It slid down and Connor nodded at her.

"Thanks for doing this," she said.

He shrugged. "You two talk to each other and I'll consider myself repaid."

"He doesn't know?"

"I didn't tell him anything," Connor said. "I didn't want him backing out at the last minute."

"He's mad at me, huh?" Her stomach twisted, the nerves that had been making her feel sick all day doubling.

"You did dump his ass," Connor said with a shrug. "Mad is a reasonable reaction."

She nodded. "What does he think you're doing?"

"I got my agent to fake-call me. Told him it was about an endorsement so I had to take it. You go on up. I'll hang out here for a while. Maybe take a nap." He slid his seat back, leaned back, and closed his eyes.

"You can sleep here on the street?"

Blue eyes opened and he smiled at her. "Eva, after fifteen years in pro baseball I can sleep just about anywhere. Go on. I'm fine down here. Not in any hurry to start packing boxes anyway." He closed his eyes again.

Obviously he wasn't going to give her any reason to keep stalling. Eva turned, stared up at Finn's apartment building for a long moment. Then she took a breath, wiped her hands again, and headed for the door. She knew Finn's entry code. Hopefully the apartment hadn't changed it in the weeks he'd been gone. Because she didn't really have a Plan B for getting into his building if that didn't work. She didn't want to risk calling up to him to let her in. What if he refused? It didn't bear thinking about.

The door buzzed open when she entered the code and she headed up to Finn's apartment, heart pounding heavily. It had been racing all day while she'd been waiting for Connor to text her to say Finn's plane had landed and they were on the way back to his apartment. How he'd managed that without Finn noticing was another unanswered question. Maybe when Connor retired from baseball, he could turn his hand to being a superspy.

The thought of Connor in a tuxedo sipping a martini and seducing beautiful women didn't actually seem that far-fetched and it made her smile, which at least eased some of the nerves currently stomping her stomach into a puddle of what felt like pure acid.

When she reached Finn's dark-gray door, she hesitated, fear holding her back from taking the final step and knocking. Then she imagined sitting through another sisterly intervention when they heard she'd screwed this up and chickened out. Anything had to be better than that.

She banged on the door, trying to sound like she was Connor.

"Okay, hold your horses," Finn yelled from inside. "That took you long enough—" His words cut off as he opened the door and saw her.

Finn.

The words she'd prepared vanished from her brain and she just stared at him. He looked good. Even in an old band T-shirt and jeans so old they were more white than blue. And, oh God, she'd forgotten how good he smelled. She gulped in a breath both to try to feel less like she was going to puke and to get more of that damned delicious smell.

"Eva," he said, voice wary.

Say something. She tried to make her brain work. It had stuttered to a halt at the sight of him. "Hi." Her tongue felt weird in her mouth. She fought the urge to squirm even as her cheeks began to heat.

"What are you doing here?"

"I wanted to see you. Connor told me you were in town."

"Of course he did. Couldn't let it go," Finn said. He shook his head, looking unsurprised at this news. He stepped back from the door. "Do you want to come in?"

"Thanks." God. Could this conversation be any more awkward? She felt like she had in those early days when she was trying to not let him see that she liked him. Horribly self-conscious and fairly certain she was going to fail spectacularly at maintaining any scrap of dignity.

The apartment smelled dusty and warm, the way buildings did when they'd been closed up too long. The room was warm, too. Hot really. She could hear the air-conditioning clattering above her, but it hadn't made much impact yet.

She looked around to distract herself from the heat. She hadn't spent much time at Finn's place. Her house was way more comfortable so they'd spent most of their time there. Now the apartment looked even more barren than usual. A stack of flattened moving boxes waiting to be filled was leaning up against the wall in the hallway, several Sharpies and rolls of packing tape on the carpet next to them. Finn's duffel was dumped near the door.

He was really leaving.

Seeing the moving stuff made that crystal-clear. Her throat tightened and she took another deep breath. She wasn't going to get emotional. Not yet.

Finn was really leaving and if she didn't do something then this might well be the last time she ever saw him again, other than on some sort of screen.

"What can I do for you, Eva?" he said. "I don't have a lot of time to get this place packed up."

"I know. I mean, Connor told me." She winced mentally at the words. "You've been playing well. At the Saints."

His carefully neutral expression didn't alter. "It's working out okay," he said. "Anything new with you?"

"I, um, changed my mind about school. I'm going."

"To California."

"Yes."

"Well, congratulations." He didn't sound like he meant it. He sounded close to mad. Which, as Connor had pointed out, she could hardly blame him for.

"What changed your mind?" His gaze sharpened. "Is everything okay with Audrey? She didn't—"

"Audrey's fine. The baby's fine." Everyone was fine. Except her. She was going to have a nervous breakdown if she couldn't figure out how to say what she'd come here to say.

His smile flashed briefly before his face went back to that disconcerting flat unreadable expression. "I'm glad. So what then?"

"My sisters. They kind of read me the riot act. Said it was time for me to stop trying to fix everything."

He nodded. "I see."

"They're right," she said. "I mean. I guess I got used to having to be there for them all the time. To being the one who has to step in and take charge and fix everything. It's a hard habit to break."

"Love tends to be that way," he agreed and she thought her heart might stop. But she plowed on. There was no easy way to say what she'd come to say, no way to make it less awkward and terrifying, so she was just going to talk and hope she might make sense.

"So Kate is helping Audrey out with things for a while to help her get her business ready for when she has to ease back when the baby comes and she's going to find Audrey a lawyer and make sure everything is— oh God, I'm babbling. I'm sorry." She took a breath. It didn't help much. "Short version. Audrey is taken care of, so I can go to school after all."

"I see. Well, that's good. That you worked that out. That you're going to California." He tugged at his T-shirt with one hand. The other one flexed at his side as if he didn't quite know what to do with it.

"Yes," she agreed. It was now-or-never time. "But there's still one problem."

He went suddenly very still. "Oh?"

She nodded, wondering if he could hear how hard her heart was pounding. "That thing you said before. About love being a hard habit to break. That's my problem. Because I really miss you, Finn. I can't kick you."

He blinked, eyes looking so very green when they focused back on her. "Am I missing something or did you just tell me you love me in a very ass-backward way?"

Not exactly the reaction she'd been hoping for. She'd been hoping perhaps for cheers and being carried off to his bedroom. That might have been overly optimistic. But she had to finish what she'd started. "Yes."

"Say it."

"Say what?"

"Say, *I love you, Finn Castro.*" His eyes were brilliant now. All his attention focused like a laser on her. She knew that color. The color of Finn Castro looking at something he wanted. And right now he was looking straight at her.

"I love you, Finn Castro." Her voice shook, cracking on his surname.

"Say, *I was an idiot for breaking up with you, Finn.*" He was smiling at her now—a real delighted smile— and the misery that had been making her bones and skin and heart hurt for weeks vanished as if someone had flicked a switch.

"I was an idiot for breaking up with you, Finn."

"Say—"

"Shut up," she said. "I need you to kiss me now."

"Say it again," he said, voice hungry.

"I love you, Finn Castro. I want it to work out between us. I know it's going to be hard for a while. Long distance. But we can make it work, can't we?"

He nodded. "I'd rather have you some of the time than none of the time."

"You would?"

"Yeah. Like I told you, a very long time ago when you were determined not to listen to me, I love you, Eva Harlowe."

"Then kiss me already," she demanded, finally, finally closing the gap between them so she could touch him again. So the world was back how it should be. "Never stop kissing me."

"Now, that's a deal I can live with," he said and pulled her back into his arms where she belonged.

Epilogue

Eva wasn't sure she'd ever been anywhere quite as loud as the owners' box at Deacon Field right after the Saints won the World Series. The noise from inside and outside was deafening. Cheers and applause and the music blaring through the PA system.

She found herself hugging Amelia without quite knowing how she'd gotten her arms around the other woman. Both of them jumping up and down and yelling, "They won," as they hugged.

As the noise started to die down, Eva looked around the room, at all the ecstatic faces.

Alex and Lucas and Mal were standing side by side, looking somewhat stunned.

"It's amazing," Amelia said, following Eva's gaze. "The Saints were nearly dead in the water and now, what, six years later and they've won the World Series? I can't imagine what those three must be feeling."

"Pretty damned good," Eva said, bouncing in place some more. Finn. She wanted to get to Finn. To kiss him and tell him how proud she was of him. The camera she'd been using to shoot pictures of the game earlier thumped her hip and she pulled the strap over her head and ditched it near her chair. This was one moment she didn't want to live through her lens.

"That might be the understatement of the year," Amelia said. "God, how long until we can see the guys?" She looked toward the door, the same longing and impatience Eva felt clear on her face.

"I'd imagine it might be a while yet. There's the trophy presentation and then there'll be press and all that stuff." She tried to sound interested. She couldn't care less about the presentation or the press, she just wanted Finn. Of course, he deserved his moment of glory and a chance to enjoy all the hoopla that went with it, so she was going to try to be patient.

Amelia pouted. "Well, that sucks. We're the people they should be with."

"Let them enjoy the moment. We get to celebrate with them later." Eva smiled at her and snagged two glasses of champagne off a passing waiter. "Here." She'd been too nervous to drink anything alcoholic earlier. The series had been hard-fought and the game today had been close. "We can start the celebrating now. Let them catch up later."

"I'll drink to that," Amelia said.

As she'd predicted, it was almost two hours before she finally got to see Finn. He wore a smile a mile wide and his sweaty and stained uniform. He'd lost his cap somewhere along the line. He'd been wearing it for the trophy presentation but now his dark hair was sticking up in spikes from a mixture of sweat and the champagne they'd probably been spraying around the locker room.

But as he caught sight of her and his smile grew even brighter, she thought he'd never looked so good to her.

Finn pushed his way through the crowd of people in the function room, picked her up, and twirled her around. "We did it."

"I think you did it," she said. "I didn't have much to do with it."

"You did more than you know." He put her down, bent down, and kissed her. As always she felt her pulse bump into crazy overdrive, responding to the feel of his mouth on hers.

"Get a room," someone nearby yelled and they pulled apart.

"World Fucking Series," Finn said. A grin that was half stunned spread across his face. "Amazing."

"Absolutely," she agreed.

Finn nodded, then bent and kissed her hard again before he pulled back. "I spoke to Tom earlier."

"Tom, your agent?" Eva asked, trying to catch her breath. How long until they could get away from all these people?

"Yes."

"Did he want to congratulate you?" She wasn't entirely sure why they were talking about Tom tonight of all nights. She was aware that winning the World Series would open up more opportunities for Finn—endorsements and stuff like that—but surely tomorrow was soon enough to start talking business?

"That was part of it." He drew her a little way away from the crowds. "But not all of it."

She shook her head. "Don't you want to come celebrate? We can talk about boring business stuff in the morning."

His smile widened. "This is non-boring business stuff."

"Tonight all business stuff is boring." She wanted to celebrate with him. First here with the Saints. Then all by themselves.

"Even if I tell you I have an offer from the Angels?"

This conversation was getting weird. "The Saints' dance squad? You changing careers on me?"

Finn laughed. "No. The Los Angeles Angels. The baseball team. That's based in, you know, Los Angeles. Where you are moving in about a month's time."

She felt her mouth drop open. Was he kidding? "You're moving to Los Angeles? How?"

"Being on a winning World Series team changes things." He looked so happy she had to believe he wasn't playing some sort of trick on her.

"But will the Saints let you go?"

"I think I can talk them around."

She looked up at him, stunned. She really hadn't thought about what would happen if the Saints won. Until today it had been hard enough to wrap her mind around the idea that the Saints had actually made it to the World Series after a tough divisional championship series against the Blue Jays. That they might win. It had been three–all against the Nationals in the World Series going into this game. Everything had been down to tonight, which hadn't left much room for thinking about anything else.

"But do you want to go? Leave the Saints?" Why would he want to leave the Saints? She knew he'd loved playing for them, was grateful they'd given him another chance. He'd worked like a dog all season to prove just how grateful. He and Oliver had become good friends. And Amelia lived in New York. Eva had always figured that if Finn went to another team, he'd want to go back home to Chicago.

Finn nodded. For a moment the light glinted off the faint silver line that was all that was left of his scar. "I like it here. And I'll always be grateful to them. Hell, maybe I'll even want to come back when you're done with school, but I didn't grow up a Saints fan like Ollie. This team isn't my life. You know he once said to me that sometimes it takes a while to find which team is your home."

Eva smiled at him, feeling so happy she wasn't sure where to even begin. They weren't going to be apart. No long distance to manage—well, no more than they'd had this season with the normal level of travel involved in the majors. Finn was coming with her. "And you think the Angels might be that for you?"

He shook his head. "No. I think home is where you are, Eva Harlowe."

Which left her with nothing to do but kiss him again.